# A DEGREE OF DEATH

## Bryan Lawson

"Whatever space and time mean, place and occasion mean more. For space in the image of man is place and time in the image of man is occasion."

- Cynthia's favourite quotation (from the Dutch architect Aldo van Eyck, 1918-1999)

About A DEGREE OF DEATH Bryan Lawson

A member of the Singapore Parliament is found murdered on a footbridge in Chester. A DEGREE OF DEATH is a crime novel about the past sneaking up on the present and making a real mess of things. It is September 2005. Murky oriental history is entangled with events at Deva University in Chester, a brand new institution doing its best to invent tradition. But do these new ivory towers hide more worldly pursuits, and what really goes on behind the genteel façades in the historic city of Chester?

DCI Carlton Drake is widely recognised for being as clever as he is tall and clumsy. He resumes duties after a sabbatical, taken for personal reasons, to investigate this diplomatically sensitive case. By contrast his high-flying young assistant Grace Hepple is stylish but inexperienced. Together they uncover an intriguing mystery.

The investigation takes Drake to Singapore where he discovers that the past is never far from the surface in this modern metropolis. Chinese societies, illegal ivory trading, academic jealousy and raw ambition jostle together to create a confusing and dangerous cocktail.

About BRYAN LAWSON

Bryan Lawson is an architect and psychologist and has studied the relationship of people to place and published over 300 books and articles. For many years he was Head of School and Dean of the Faculty of Architectural Studies at Sheffield University. His first book "How Designers Think" has been in continuous print since 1980 and sold over 100,000 copies.

He has now seen the light and turned to crime.

Details of all books by Bryan Lawson together with news of forthcoming publications and a blog can be found at: -
www.bryanlawson.org

3rd edition 2018
© Bryan Lawson 2018

# Prologue

There it was again. Zhao Meng briefly caught sight of the hooded figure over the sea of heads before he was pushed down three steps into the vast hall. The file of men ahead formed a silent snake that shuffled forward intermittently. He recognised two faces from his neighbourhood but they deliberately avoided his gaze. A hum of activity from the front did nothing to relieve the depressing hush. Darkness was falling for the second time since he had been brought here so it must be 23rd February. The soldiers marshalling them wore nametags and blank expressions. Zhao Meng passed the time trying to commit to memory their names and faces.

The queue edged forward again and then there it was, right before him. The figure loomed, static as a memorial sculpture save for the occasional nod or shake of its head. The shroud was a silk of deep crimson but Zhao Meng doubted the colour would bring its usual good fortune. A fist in the small of his back shoved him forward a pace. He stumbled past the apparition, unable to take his eyes off it. Of the face inside the hood there was no sign yet Zhao Meng felt its stare. Two fingers drummed impatiently on the desk in front of him, their owner looking enquiringly at the crimson figure alongside. The head nodded. The nod shivered its way down through the folds of the cloak and fell out into the empty air above the shoes. The shoes! They were familiar, tantalisingly so. Zhao Meng felt a strong grip on his right forearm now stamped with a purple triangle.

He was marched through the door to the left of the desk and out across a courtyard to an open truck. The huddle of men already onboard left little room for Zhao Meng. The rear flap slammed behind him cutting into his shoulder. The engine spluttered grudgingly into life and dragged its dismal load out into the darkness.

The truck lurched and slewed its way through the night; on they went each clutching at his neighbour to stay upright. Zhao Meng watched the stars; they were headed north. The axle below him periodically grumbled unheeded complaints about the driving, the road or both.

Without warning the driver braked violently. Before Zhao Meng had regained his feet he was pulled down roughly onto sandy ground. A new moon shimmered in the ripples of a gentle sea; maybe this was Punggol. Zhao Meng's arms were tied together behind his back and strapped to two complete strangers. He could not see their faces.

They were pushed down the slope of the beach; perhaps it was Changi. Onward and downward they staggered, half a pace late in their stumbles. Water splashed on his face as they stamped around in the shallows. Quickly it was up to his waist. He was tugged off balance as all three struggled instinctively but pointlessly against the ropes binding their arms.

A loud crack pierced the night sky. The man to his left slumped tightening the ropes. They lurched sideways. A second crack. A ghastly scream deafened Zhao Meng's right ear. The bundle of men toppled into the sea and rolled into deeper water. He struggled against all the dead weight around him to get his head above the water. He never heard the third shot.

# 1 - Paper

Normally the fourteen-hour flight was long enough to sleep off the worst effects of jetlag but this time his mind was still trying to catch up. Clutching a freshly poured whisky he sank into the armchair by the tall bay window, its leather cushions enveloping his elderly frame. The hills on the distant Welsh borders were flooded with that gentle northern sunlight he had come to love. Jimmy Cheung savoured his visits to England even after so many years.

The day had gone better than he expected. It was three years since he first met Hamish McFadden from the Deva University of Chester. Jimmy had always seen it as his special responsibility to advance trade between Singapore and the United Kingdom; Hamish's unit was an ideal partner. The invitation to become a 'Distinguished Visiting Professor' flattered Jimmy, as it was meant to. Being a founding member of a young country he was a sucker for the traditions and ritual of 'old' Europe.

When, two years previously his son, Sheng Tian, took a post at Deva University, Jimmy was almost prepared to believe that lectures might be in Latin. Now it appeared that even Singapore, a mere whippersnapper in the nation business, was older than this University. Deva's charter was awarded in 1999 but the prospectus preferred to focus on its origins in a college founded in 1965. There had been some reference to Jimmy's visiting post being part of the celebrations for a significant anniversary on September 12th. How extraordinary! The date leapt off the page as he stared at it, his mind lurching back through the decades. This was surely not the time to think about those years!

The sky darkened. At last, Jimmy thought, dusk was falling but it was only a flock of rooks swooping down to roost in the tallest ash tree bordering the lawns below. A drooping lower branch swayed violently hinting at an impending storm. His aging eyes did not see the stocky figure staring unblinkingly up at his window from deep in the shadows and bushes.

Jimmy flicked through the university documents, all exquisitely designed to conceal the youth of the institution. The red, black and gold coat of arms with its Latin motto headed the descriptions of elaborate ceremonies and pictures of the robes worn by the dignitaries of the body academic. The Vice-chancellor's invitation, printed on handmade paper, oozed tradition; it even smelt British! Jimmy had sent his curriculum vitae to the Registrar, only to get another offer by return. The University, reluctant to admit that one of its distinguished professors had absolutely no degrees at all from any university, was offering him an honorary doctorate. So today he had been given the degree with all the pomp that Deva could manufacture.

The single malt began its journey down Jimmy's neck, lingering just long enough to point out that it had hung around for more than fifteen years waiting for precisely this moment. Even the whisky was older than the university! One more glass would be enough. He called the university driver and asked him to wait a little longer.

It was when he returned the telephone handset to its cradle that it suddenly hit him. A crease of horror folded across his face drawing a line of sweat behind it. He tugged the room swipe card from his shirt pocket looking for reassurance but found only the university crest. The telephone dial was stubbornly unequivocal; there was no avoiding it. He was in room 4! How could his daughter let this happen? Was Janet's expensive Western education prepared to argue with over a billion Chinese? Was 'four' not still a homonym for 'death', and the unluckiest of numbers? Her normal attention to detail was slipping.

Jimmy sought calmness from the whisky, slumped back in his chair and returned to the fading view below him. Chester was all black and white. The buildings were black and white, the iron fences around the fields matched neatly and even the cows had caught the fashion. It was most definitely not Chinese and yet the scene was reassuringly calligraphic. The sun had looked over the horizon a couple of times and seemingly thought better of it. You could never tell when it would go dark here. In Singapore this whole business was over and done with in half an hour and you could get on and enjoy the balmy evening. The diurnal certainties of the tropics structured life so conveniently. Breakfast at seven with the rising sun; dinner at seven with the setting sun.

It had been a surprise to see his sister Emily at the ceremony. As children they had fought as brothers and sisters often do. He had seen little of her since she moved to London. Even at lunch they began to quarrel but now their disputes were about politics rather than children's games and sweets.

There was one final piece of business for the day, and then he could retire to the genuine tradition of his hotel suite in the centre of Chester. He looked again at the date. Images that he had kept suppressed for years were suddenly released from their cerebral jail. They crashed around in his head and slithered down his spine. Jimmy instinctively smoothed the hairs on the back of his neck and sipped his whisky.

The River Dee knew roughly where it was going without being quite sure how to get there. Its halting progress through Chester fascinated onlookers as it tripped over itself, splashing against the stepped embankment of the Groves on one bank and tumbling over the weir towards the other. Katie Lamb inhaled the calm evening air but Denson was always warning her that important events have a habit of happening when you least expect them. She scanned around. A family was feeding the swans on the river by the bandstand. Two tour guides, impatient to get home to their families, were herding the last day-trippers onto coaches. A crowd of delinquent black-headed gulls played their special version of dare, floating towards the weir, taking off at the last possible moment then swooping around only to bob down again past the pleasure steamers moored for the night on their buoys in the centre of the river.

She scanned around preparing herself for the questions she knew Denson would fire at her. She could see three people up on the suspension bridge; an old chap was leaning over the rail in the centre and a couple of schoolgirls at the far end were nudging each other and giggling. She climbed the steps to the side of the bridge leading up into the park. The benches were empty save for a discarded copy of the local newspaper that Katie tossed into a litterbin.

It was just as the paper rattled its way down the metal cage that the scream rocketed up into the evening air. Stuttering at first, and then quickly reaching a crescendo, it bounced off the water scattering the gulls and encircling Katie. She froze, her feet refusing to move, her head twisting this way then that, her eyes wide open demanding a clue. Her brain searched for an appropriate response and reminded her that she was on duty; her first solo patrol.

She turned and broke into a run, retracing her steps around a bend in the path. The two schoolgirls hurtled towards her off the bridge. One was screaming hysterically. The other, some way behind, was affecting an attitude of impatience. The first girl charged headlong into Katie clutching wildly at the skirt of her uniform.

'He's dead, he's dead,' she choked between sobs.

'Calm down now,' said Katie patting her head as the poor thing clung to her leg, burying her face and trembling with fear. 'Who is dead?'

'The old fella on the bridge,' sniffed the second girl between chews on her gum.

It was nearly ten in the evening when the wooden deck of the bridge shook reluctantly to the bumptious tread of Detective Inspector Martin Henshaw, jaywalking into his first solo murder. He had worked on countless cases as Chief Inspector Drake's sergeant at the Met but now this was his own show and, in his opinion, it was long overdue. He was determined to make an entrance and had left his arrival until all the preliminary scene-of-crime procedures had been completed. Arriving behind the blue canvas screens he was met by the combined stares of Dr. Cooper and the body. The former conveyed a lack of conviction about Henshaw's authority and the latter a mixture of sadness, and terrible surprise.

The pathologist returned to muttering at his Dictaphone 'Oriental male, approximately seventy years.' The victim was slumped against the iron trellis balustrade. His understated elegance suggested prosperity in the life so recently and abruptly terminated. His black slip-on shoes were polished like a guardsman's boots, his trousers neatly pressed and his fine white cotton shirt had a buttoned up mandarin collar. He looked ready for a smart evening out. The roughly circular tear in his shirt and the surrounding blood illustrated an alternative story narrated by Dr. Cooper. 'Looks like the bullet has passed straight through the heart...probably killed him more or less instantly...surprisingly little external bleeding.'

Around the victim's neck was a compact stainless steel digital camera. Neither of his cuffs were done up yet both his sleeves were rolled down. His trouser pockets were still stitched up as if straight from a bespoke tailor. Only the left hip pocket had been unpicked and it contained a small stitched leather case protecting an exquisite ivory cylinder with Chinese writing embossed on one end. His shirt pocket contained a swipe card that appeared to be a key of some kind, perhaps from a hotel room. There was nothing else to identify him.

Henshaw issued instructions to send photographs of the cylinder down to his mate at the Met who would get their oriental specialist to look at it. Only then did Henshaw catch a glimpse of the rippling river Dee below. They were high up and dead centre of the span. This was a strangely public place to commit a murder. Why choose to shoot someone here?

The pathologist stood back grunting with satisfaction at the completion of his duties. Henshaw nodded and watched the scene-of-crime officers preparing to remove the body. As they moved the pathologist's floodlight, something glinted on the deck of the bridge. Henshaw kneeled down to examine a silver cufflink. It was a solid bar design with a domed face, white and printed with a red Chinese character. It must have been lying under the victim's body. Of the other link there was no sign so Henshaw gave instructions for the whole length of the bridge and paths at either end to be fingertip searched.

As he walked back to his car Henshaw thought he had handled things pretty well. The pathologist would now do a more thorough lab investigation of the body and any items found on the bridge. He would keep the bridge sealed off. Yes, he was doing all the right things so far. But what to do next? He clearly needed to establish the identity of the victim and hopefully that would lead to some ideas about motive. As it was, there was very little to go on.

His route took him along a path through the park back to Newgate Street where his car was parked. His phone rang; it was Jeff Bootham, his old school friend who was a reporter on the local paper.

'Blimey Jeff, you're quick off the mark.'

'Don't get many murders round here; got to make the most of it when we do.'

'How do you know it's a murder?'

'Come on Martin, don't bullshit an old friend.'

'Actually you might be able to help. The victim has no identity but looks Chinese. We need anyone who knows him to come forward as soon as possible. You could…'

Pssssssssss. Henshaw looked at his phone and tapped it angrily. Surely there must be a good signal this close to the centre of town. The phone not only refused to confirm or deny this, it refused to confirm anything. Damn, the battery must have run out!

Crack. The sound came from deep in the rhododendron bushes lining the footpath; it sounded like a twig breaking. The path skirted the ruins of a church and someone could be following him through there. Henshaw told himself that he was imagining things, quickened his pace, and headed for his car, phone-charger and bed.

'Tall' is a word not often used about Detective Chief Inspector Carlton Drake; it's not so much inaccurate as inadequate, hopelessly so. Cynthia could recite a list of imaginative descriptions preferred by friends. There were mountains, animals obviously including giraffes, and an assortment of landmark buildings. It was these architectural examples that Cynthia was most fond of since they also acknowledged her own profession.

His mother, with uncanny prescience, often told the young Drake that 'if he carried on growing he would soon be tall enough to be a policeman.' When cross with him she would add 'looming' to the list of crimes that he had unknowingly committed. It must have been then that he developed the stoop that others now recognised as characteristic. He had only become aware of this on overhearing Henshaw talking on the phone. 'I can recognise Drake walking down a street a hundred yards away,' he laughed. 'He sort of picks his way along and looks like he's apologising to the pavement for treading on it.'

Whoever had designed this aircraft showed no appreciation of the length of Drake's legs. The woman sat in front shuffled irritably to indicate her unhappiness about the position of his knees but Drake was oblivious to her discomfort. He was sure that the same lake had just passed underneath for the third time. The Peak District landscape was becoming infuriatingly familiar. Why had he agreed to travel in this cramped tin can? The whole point of his 'retirement' was to have more time for the things he wanted to do. No correction. That was what he had said. It seemed the sort of reason you were expected to come up with. In reality he could no longer live with the awful feeling in the pit of his stomach that he was letting people down. He had caught a look in the eyes of colleagues that he was not expected to see let alone understand. If they had been shouting it out loud, he could not have got the message more clearly. They were compensating for him, covering for his lack of direction, understanding his inability to give leadership.

The aircraft flaps whirred with renewed enthusiasm for landing and Drake felt his eyes moisten as he reflected on the real reason for his 'retirement.'

Then there had been the phone call. 'I need a favour from you Carlton' the voice had begun. It belonged to Fergus Marshall, Commander in charge of Special Operations Branch at the Met. They had been college mates and Fergus was the only member of the service to use Drake's first name.

'You remember giving D S Henshaw a reference for that Inspector post in Chester?'

'Of course; a tricky one,' Drake grunted. 'The lad is bright but impetuous; he would make a false start in a marathon. It's probably a bit early for him.'

'He's in at the deep end with a politically sensitive murder,' groaned Fergus.

'He has to learn from his own mistakes.'

'Ordinarily I would agree but the Foreign Office wants a senior figure involved. It's exactly what we formed the Unit for.'

Fergus had persuaded Drake to stay in the force by describing the 'Diplomatic Unit' as a 'retirement home.' Suddenly it sounded rather different.

'Fergus, diplomats and murder investigations usually make unhappy bedfellows.'

'Exactly. You managed us through that problem with the Saudi Embassy so you will be able to shut the FO up. The victim was here to get an honorary degree from the local university.'

'What university? I didn't know Chester has a university!'

'Well apparently it does. Sorry Carlton but this really is urgent. You can be back home in a few days.'

Drake was sure Henshaw could manage the case and he could quickly hand it over to him. A voice in the deeper recesses of his brain tried unsuccessfully to remind him that he had never handed a case over to anyone before. So here he was flying circles over the Peak District.

Henshaw shambled towards the terminal building in a sleep-deprived daze. Yesterday had been a long and frustrating day. Facts about the case seemed few and far between and to cap it all he been had woken this morning by a call from the Chief Constable no less.

'Henshaw, do you know who this man is?'

'Yes, Chief; I've interviewed his daughter. Looks Chinese but apparently he is some Singaporean visiting the University to get an honorary degree. His name was James Cheung, known as Jimmy and….'

'Henshaw, I know his name! The point is that he's a member of parliament in the middle of some diplomatic discussions with the Foreign Office for goodness sake!'

'What!' Henshaw had exclaimed. 'Nobody told me that.'

'Well they have now! Special Branch are sending up a diplomatic advisor. You'd better get going to Manchester airport to collect him off the early shuttle from Heathrow.'

Before Henshaw gathered his thoughts, the phone went dead, leaving him full of questions and doubts. What sort of person would this "advisor" be? How would they work together? It was the last thing he needed on his first murder. It felt like he was playing some game with the crowd watching his every move before he had even read the rules. He made a quick call to his driver, threw on some clothes and grabbed his case file.

Now Henshaw's mind was further numbed by the combined scream of four jet engines striving to delay the return to earth of their Jumbo until at least the start of the runway. A woman in front of him dropped her suitcase, covered her ears and cowered with little evident faith in the pilot. Henshaw dodged around her and pushed open a door.

'Manchester Airport,' said the signs on the door and they ought to know. Henshaw was not convinced. He remembered his childhood collection of cards showing pictures and technical details of aircraft and airports. Surely this place had been called Ringway?

Minibuses and taxis were competing aggressively for a spot within spitting distance of the doors. Paradoxically once out of their vehicles the drivers, all male, chatted amicably as they stood shoulder to shoulder in prominent positions waiting for their clients. They held signs proclaiming Bolton, Blackburn, Oldham, Liverpool, Sheffield and of course Chester. Few passengers seemed to want to go to Manchester, so Ringway could easily have been named after any number of northern cities. Henshaw guessed that Chester Airport would not sound very zippy when looked at from the other side of the Atlantic, Sydney or for that matter Singapore. So Manchester it was.

This meandering train of trivia was interrupted by Henshaw's driver thrusting a phone under his nose. There was a text message. Henshaw scrolled through four times but it refused to change; 'Chief Inspector Carlton Drake of the Diplomatic Unit is on the Heathrow shuttle.' Emotions jostled each other in his mind. Good, Drake would know what to do next but would the man never leave him alone? What the hell was this Diplomatic Unit thing and what was Drake doing in it anyway. Surely he had taken early retirement?

The arrivals board flipped to show a delay on the Heathrow shuttle. Perhaps a shot of caffeine would get him thinking straight. He sat reviewing the case over a cappuccino in a cup large enough to hold a pint of beer. Henshaw tried to get his mind to rehearse the case so far. He must be ready for Drake's questions.

Control had logged a call from the manager of the Grosvenor Hotel, reporting a missing guest, a Mr. Jimmy Cheung. The victim's daughter, who was also staying at the hotel, had given identification but she couldn't offer any suggestions about possible enemies or motives. Apparently her father had led a blameless life and was here to advise the local university. He liked walking through the park and watching the boats and birds from the bridge. The schoolgirls who had found the body were frightened and incoherent so Henshaw had backed off from that interview for now. An apparently harmless old man had been killed for no obvious reason in a very public place and yet no one had seen it happen.

Henshaw found his mind repeatedly turning to the victim's cufflinks. Why had they come off? There were no signs of a scuffle and the victim's shirt cuffs appeared totally undamaged, not even stretched. Had he taken them off before the attack, intending to roll up his sleeves? Surely the early autumn evening had not been warm enough for that? And what was the significance of the mysterious ivory cylinder in its little case? Was it valuable? Precious even? At least he should hear back soon from the Met's expert on that.

Henshaw turned to look again at the arrivals board and knocked over his half-consumed coffee. The cup swam in a pool of pale brown liquid spilling over the saucer and threatening the Chester Evening Leader. Just missing the flood, the newspaper article trumpeted its message.

**MURDER ON THE SUSPENSION BRIDGE**

Yesterday evening as the sun was going down the peace of our city was shattered by screams heard by people walking and sitting along the Groves. They came from two teenage schoolgirls crossing Queen's Park Bridge on their way home as they stumbled across a dead body. Police are remaining tight-lipped today about the name of the victim but witnesses have told us that he looked Chinese. Police have asked anyone who was in the Groves or near the bridge yesterday evening to contact Detective Inspector Henshaw on....

The crowds emerging into the arrivals hall were mostly in denial about the end of their holiday; lads in shorts and teenage girls in unfeasibly cropped tops showed off their tans, trying not to shiver in the autumn morning. Excited children ran miniature trolley cases over the feet of parents. Fathers with faces far too pink for their health, scanned for signs of their bus or taxi. Among these was visible first the head and then the incongruously suited body of Drake plodding towards Henshaw, carrying that huge Gladstone bag. The sight was a shock. What was left of Drake's hair was now entirely white and his face drawn and sad; he was surrounded by people and yet lonely.

'Ah Henshaw. Good to see you, well done on this Chester job. Scene-of-crime first.'

That was more like the Drake he knew, no outward emotion and straight to core business. Henshaw had worried about whether he should express sympathy when they met or was it best left unspoken? Drake had solved the problem for him.

The unmarked police car sat in its privileged but understated way on double yellow lines in front of the terminal building. Drake somehow managed to fold his ungainly frame into the Jaguar, leaving Henshaw to drop his battered bag in the boot. Damn! If he'd known it was Drake they would have come in a Range Rover.

'I am sorry, sir' he started, 'we didn't have time to get hold of a larger car this morning.'

There was no answer. Drake had picked up the newspaper and was reading the murder report. He waved his hand in a familiar dismissive gesture and Henshaw passed him the case file.

They circled the grey concrete mass of the multi-storey car park and drove off the airport site passing the long-haul terminal and the new up-market hotel, both eloquent testimony of the thriving travel sector. Soon they were on the motorway to Chester with the Jaguar doing its best to respect the silence as they swept through the countryside. The sun beamed through the rear window confirming their westerly direction.

'I'm sorry about all this Henshaw. It wasn't my idea to be looking over your shoulder.'

Henshaw couldn't remember ever hearing Drake apologise but Drake was already issuing instructions; the man had taken over already.

'I need to see where Jimmy Cheung had been staying.'

‘Deva University had given him an apartment but he had booked a suite at the Grosvenor Hotel. His daughter is waiting there.’

‘We’ll see her next. Any idea why the murder was in such a public place?’

‘It’s puzzling,’ admitted Henshaw. ‘It feels like the location was carefully chosen but I can’t think why.’

# 2 - Cotton

Drake filled his lungs with air freshened by a sudden shower and began the lengthy process of exiting the car. Henshaw ducked under the blue and white tape across the entrance to the bridge. He exchanged a nod with the uniformed constable on guard duty and pulled the tape up for Drake to follow. A commotion from behind signalled trouble. Drake, already halfway through stepping over the obstacle, straddled the tape like a failed high jumper. A group of curious schoolboys cheered ironically as the constable moved them back with an ostentatious show of authority. Henshaw wondered when things would start going right.

Twin lattice towers supported a sign marking the beginning of the main span. "City of Chester Queen's Park Bridge 1923," it announced proudly. The suspension bridge soared high above the River Dee connecting the steep embankment where they stood with the riverside walk on the opposite bank. Drake stood and analysed the structure as Cynthia had taught him. It seemed to be having something of an argument with itself. The white balustrades with their latticework and curved stays spoke of lazy afternoon boating trips but the athletic leap right across the river and huge cable anchorages were testament to the serious engineering needed to connect the two halves of this bustling city. Drake gazed wistfully at the bridge, yearning for Cynthia to tell him what to think.

The little posse of policemen held back. He caught their awkward silence, shrugged his shoulders at Henshaw and followed him gloomily onto the wooden deck. It was narrow, perhaps little more than three metres across, curving tentatively up towards the centre. Double cables swept down in a more determined arc almost touching the handrail mid-span and then back up to the towers on the opposite bank.

As they emerged from between the trees, views opened up like proscenium curtains revealing a stage set. Chester could do history like almost nowhere else. It could be a Roman garrison or it could be a medieval city but here it chose neither. Here it was a genteel park, a generous sweeping curve of river, greenery and comfortable architecture. Downstream the Groves and the weir, the vista closed by Handbridge. Upstream trees jostled for the best waterside position on the right bank while redbrick and white stucco villas populated the higher ground to the left. A giant poplar tree was artfully positioned just as the river curved gently out of sight. Beyond it verdant lawns and a church completed the composition of the skyline. Here Chester soothed the ears as much as the eyes. The untroubled sounds of tourists in boats, children playing in the park and gulls calling from the roof of the café were all reflected up to the bridge by the acoustic mirror that is the River Dee.

Drake was enveloped by calmness for the first time that morning.

'What was Jimmy Cheung doing here, Henshaw?'

'The University driver dropped him right where we parked; he was going to walk across to his hotel. His daughter says he liked the bridge. He had taken pictures of it on the camera we found round his neck.'

'It's charming.'

'We had fun with it when we were kids,' grinned Henshaw.

'I forgot you grew up in Chester.'

'We used to run across and make it shake. The raw army recruits from Western Command up on the bank there, they marched them across trying to teach them to break step. They could never do it. Somehow they would all end up back marching together and in no time the bridge was swinging with 'em. The sergeant would bellow at them, stand them still until it settled down and try again. We used to clap and jeer. Used to make them real mad.'

'Beats me how they didn't know about that when they designed the new Millennium Bridge over the Thames,' growled Drake. 'Apparently that shakes just with ordinary folk strolling across it.'

A small open-cabin boat puttered its way upstream passing under the bridge just as they reached the blue scene-of-crime tent. Henshaw held the canvas flap open for Drake to enter. At least that worked! Apart from the chalk marks on the wooden deck where Jimmy Cheung's body had been found there was no sign of the awful sight that had terrified the two schoolgirls.

'I had to move the body, you know-exposed to weather-public place,' said Henshaw nervously. Drake nodded andstudied Henshaw's notes.

A Mr. Jimmy Cheung was found dead half way across the Queen's Park Bridge by Constable Katie Lamb at 19:26 on Tuesday September 12th 2000. She was patrolling in the park when two schoolgirls (Rebecca Evans and Deborah Grafton) ran into her, screaming having discovered the body when crossing the bridge. Control logged a 999 call at 19:23 from a man on a mobile phone down in the Groves who heard the two girls and thought there was a rape incident. We received a call from the manager of the Grosvenor Hotel at 22:47 after the victim's daughter, Janet Cheung, reported him missing.

Even inside the tent, Drake sensed the bridge grumbling as they moved around. 'Next of kin? This mentions his daughter. Any other relatives?'

'The son also works at the University. His wife died some years ago.'

'Was the scene-of-crime undisturbed?'

'Pretty sure, Sir. Constable Lamb was here within a minute of the girls' discovery.'

'She's still in training. It was her first solo patrol, like.' It was a more rustic voice.

Drake wheeled round to discover that the owner was a burly uniformed sergeant peering into the tent. The buttons on his tunic were engaged in an heroic struggle to keep it together as his chest heaved and wheezed. He wiped a dewdrop from his pockmarked nose just in time to stop it disappearing into the waiting moustache.

'This is Sergeant Denson,' sighed Henshaw.

'Some training exercise then,' Drake grunted.

'Freaked her out a bit it did, sir,' puffed Denson, 'but she's over it now.' He drew himself up to a height disappointingly little more than the crouch he had adopted to enter the tent. 'We've had people pushed off in fights. We've had several jumpers, some survived, a couple didn't but we've never had no shooting. The lads all chuck their caps off when they leave the Grammar school up there. But we've never had a murder.'

'Yes, thank you Denson,' snapped Henshaw.

'They've got some money these days, them Chinese.' Denson was getting his breath back. 'Saw a programme about them on the telly; got some of the richest men in the world there now they have. Who'd want to shoot an old fella like that and then just leave him; never even pinched the camera. Constable Jenkins says it's one of them triangle murders.'

'Triad,' muttered Henshaw.

'Unlikely,' growled Drake. 'Triad killings tend to be messy violent affairs usually involving meat cleavers or machetes and buckets of blood.'

Denson shivered. 'The city fathers want the bridge opened again sir.'

'Thank you for the history and theories,' snapped Drake, 'but the bridge stays closed until I'm satisfied.' He was rummaging through the case file, examining the photographs of the scene-of-crime. Several showed Jimmy Cheung's white shirt in close up focussing on the tear where the bullet passed through. Others detailed the open cuffs to his shirtsleeves.

'This is a fine cotton fabric and yet the cuffs look totally undamaged. But your report says one of his cufflinks was missing and the other found under his body.'

'Yes, it's silver and porcelain. Looks oriental. Henshaw pointed to a photograph of red Chinese writing. To Drake it looked like a collection of squiggles. On the left was something that could have been the number seven, written the way continentals do sometimes with a line through the upright. To the right was a small square and below it a rectangle sub-divided like a window. It clearly stood for something and yet it was meaningless to Drake.

'Could this be his name?'

'I have no idea, sir,' admitted Henshaw. 'There are also no fingerprints on it either.'

'So exactly how do you put on cufflinks without leaving fingerprints? I can fiddle for ages with them. What are we missing here?'

'We're certainly missing the other cufflink. We've hand searched the bridge deck. There's no sign of anything interesting but a few cigarette ends, a couple of bus tickets.'

Drake examined the gaps between the planks of the deck perfectly devised to infuriate anyone accidentally dropping small items of value. 'How deep is the river?'

'It's enough for them pleasure boats,' volunteered Denson.

Several craft were attached to buoys in the middle of the river and another was just mooring at the bank of the Groves where a brass band was tuning up.

'Flows quickly too,' groaned Drake. 'It doesn't look at all promising but you'd better get the divers in.'

Henshaw signalled to Denson who relayed instructions to the radio clipped to his chest. The radio issued several baffling crackles apparently understood by Denson who nodded back at it. The brass band was now well into a Viennese waltz. The octagonal bandstand was a permanent but summery structure that looked as one with the bridge. Its rusticated stone plinth interrupted the continuous rows of steps separating the path from the river. Sprouting from this were white painted columns of delicate cast iron holding up a slate roof.

A bright flash of light dazzled Drake. It was as if someone down there was using a mirror. A thickset figure moved out of sight behind the bandstand. Drake's instinct told him that the movement was deliberate. He stared waiting to see if the figure reappeared. It did not. The musicians were enthusiastically reaching one of Strauss's accelerando endings.

'It's difficult to talk here, Henshaw. Take me to the hotel.' A man with a binocular strap over his left shoulder waddled hastily away from the bandstand. He scuttled up a flight of steps in the wall behind the footpath before Drake could point him out to Henshaw.

'I want to see the girls who found the body. I dare say they're still upset so handle it carefully. You can use Grace Hepple for that.'

'Who is Grace Hepple, sir?'

'Ah yes. She's a young Detective Sergeant I have in the Unit. Very promising. She's on her way up by train. She's a pretty tough kid on the inside Henshaw so don't be misled by her appearance. I guess they told you I can't be here full time, so she'll cover for me while I'm away.'

Alarm bells jangled inside Henshaw's head. It was bad enough being mentored by Drake but some young ambitious girl, in his old job, watching his every move and reporting back! Would this Grace Hepple take instructions or would he find himself in an impossible pincer trapped between Drake and his sergeant? And what did Drake mean by not being 'misled by her appearance?'

'What did they say?' Drake continued, 'these girls.'

Henshaw looked blank then frantically thumbed through his notebook. 'Rather a lot and yet nothing; they gabbled on for ages,' he said stalling. You know how they can be, girls of that age.' Henshaw eventually found the page and read aloud. 'Rebecca, that's one of them, said he was slumped on the deck against the side. They noticed him as they got about a quarter of the way across. They thought he was dossing down. This area attracts that sort of character in the evening. When they got closer they could see he wasn't moving and Rebecca prodded him with her foot. Then they realised he was dead, screamed and ran off.'

'This was about half past seven in the evening,' mused Drake. 'There would be signs of dusk but the girls saw the body from some distance. So why did no one see or hear the murder actually happen?'

'Very strange it is, sir,' muttered Sergeant Denson, 'Yer in full view up here.'

'Would there be many people around at that time, Denson?'

'A fair few, sir. Earlier in the day it'd be thronging but by then not so many. There'd be folk down in the Groves. The bridge is a good short cut if yer on foot. It's a mighty long way round using Handbridge.'

Henshaw was still examining his notebook. 'The girls saw some boy from school; they couldn't say if they passed anyone else.'

Drake began talking to some imagined and distant audience. 'How would you plan a murder here? His camera wasn't stolen so it's not a typical crepuscular mugging.' Henshaw and Denson exchanged shrugs of bemusement as Drake continued, 'how do you shoot someone, not exactly in broad daylight but certainly not in the dark, and still be sure of getting away? Where was he shot from?'

Henshaw was still wondering what he had done with the dictionary he used to keep in the top drawer of his desk when working for Drake. 'I assumed it was someone else on the bridge,' he stumbled.

'Not good enough,' growled Drake, looking around. 'You may be right but there must be several locations where a sniper could have hidden down there. Have you asked the pathologist for an opinion?'

Henshaw shook his head feebly and wrote in his notebook. 'And why, Sir,' he asked carefully changing the question, 'that's what puzzles me. Why take the risk of doing it here?'

'Exactly. Why here?' Henshaw waited for Drake to suggest possible reasons but none came. Instead Drake began his lumbering walk off the bridge and back to the police car.

‘This fax arrived from London for you, Sir.’ Denson held out a brown A4 envelope. Henshaw was staring at the back of the receding Drake. This was not the man he knew; the shoulders were more hunched, the gait more halting. He used to command situations. Now his eyes seemed distant and full of uncertainty. The old Drake would have rebuked Henshaw for posing questions without offering a range of possible answers. He began to wonder if Drake was really going to contribute much to the case.

‘The hotel then,’ said Drake as they reached the car. ‘What did you say it was called?’

‘The Grosvenor, sir. It’s a pretty posh affair. Actually it’s fairly close to the other end of the bridge but it will take us a while to get back across the river and through the city.’ Henshaw opened the fax that Denson had delivered, read it, let out a puzzled grunt and passed it to Drake. It was from the oriental consultant at the Met.

I have examined the photographs you sent me. It is a Hanko. It could be Chinese but this one looks much more Japanese.

The Hanko is a personal seal used in Japan (also common in China and Korea) in place of a signature. The Japanese can own several Hanko and use them in different situations. This one I found on the Internet is very similar. It is sitting in a slim wooden case lined in red and gold material. Also in the case is a small inking pad. This is very common. You would ink the seal and stamp a document in place of your signature or as part of it.

The Hanko is thought to be of Chinese origin. There are many legends about Hanko but the most popular says that the first Hanko was presented by a Chinese emperor to a Japanese king some two thousand years ago. One of the oldest known Hanko is dated at least back to the fifth century and was made in gold. Part of the cultural mystique of the Hanko suggests that the material and the way it is fashioned can bring either good fortune or bad. The simplest ones are made from boxwood but the most auspicious materials include the horn from water buffalo and, regrettably, ivory. This one looks almost certainly to be of ivory.

Hanko have recently become collectors' items and many collectors are now to be found in the Europe and America rather than China or Japan. It may thus be carried as a lucky charm rather than a working item. When found on someone outside Japan this would seem the more likely explanation.

We are getting the Kanji characters on the end translated but this is not always a very accurate or informative process.

'So Jimmy Cheung carried this around as a talisman,' suggested Henshaw.

'It didn't work very well then did it?' grunted Drake. 'Where did you find it?'

'The left hand hip pocket, the right hip and the two back pockets were still stitched up as were the jacket pockets. The jacket was found in his university apartment.' By now Henshaw had his notebook open to check his facts. 'Dr. Cooper, our local pathologist said the threads on the left hand trouser pocket looked torn rather than cut.'

Drake stared out of the window for a few seconds deep in thought. 'So he put on this new suit for the ceremony, found the pockets still stitched up and was so desperate to carry this Hanko thing that he ripped one pocket open.'

'If so,' Henshaw said slowly, 'he must have been very superstitious.'

Drake grunted. 'Or he needed it for a specific purpose that we don't yet understand. Do his family know that we found it?'

'No, it had been removed before his daughter formally identified the body.

'OK, let's keep it up our sleeve until we have a translation.'

‘Do you think it could have something to do with the case, Sir?’

Drake offered no reply, his eyes fixed yet misty as they drove high above the riverbank and across the Grosvenor bridge into the city. He appeared to stare intently at the castle as they passed but Henshaw could never tell what was in the man’s mind. He had tried to work this out before and had concluded that Drake must have two brains; one monitored the surrounding world taking in every single sight and sound while the other worked on the case. It was the only explanation. In fact Drake was trying to correlate the world out of the window with the map of Chester in the case file. It could not be done. The inscrutable one-way system ingeniously crafted by the local traffic engineers was just too devious for him.

He abandoned the struggle and thumbed through the scene-of-crime photographs, returning repeatedly to one particular image. The body lay slumped on the deck of the bridge collapsed against the balustrade. Drake met Jimmy Cheung’s dead stare and felt the eyes penetrate to his core. They spoke of the unexpectedness of death and Drake felt it. He sensed a shortening of his breath and a thumping in his heart. This was a new experience. He had always dealt with bodies like a plumber searching for a leaking pipe. Death was a daily fact of life, a practical matter. Philosophical debates about deities and the meaning of existence had never managed to command much space in Drake’s brain. He was here to catch villains and bring them to justice; that was what gave meaning to his life. Victims had not been the focus of his attention so much as the perpetrators of crimes. Recent events had changed him, perhaps irrevocably. The unfairness of death, especially when early, made him angry now. That professional detachment had been blown away. His intention to retire was vindicated and he should have stuck to it. He shouldn’t be here. Could he ever be effective in this job again?

A soft lilting sound broke the silence. It was gentle at first but rose in volume until it turned into the irritating warble that only mobile phones seem to have mastered. A crescendo was developing with each reprise. Henshaw ignored its bungled classicism; Drake fumbled with one jacket pocket after another.

The phone was by now as insistent as it knew how without actually giving away its whereabouts.

'Perhaps it's in your coat, sir.'

'Yes. Hello. Oh Lucy how wonderful to hear you. I forgot that you messed around with my mobile last week. I've just worked it out; it's the flute entr'acte from Bizet's Carmen isn't it? That ballet adaptation of the opera you danced at college.'

By now Drake's daughter was already in full spate. 'Listen Dad, we had an injury so I had to step up to solo here in Amsterdam and now they want me to go on the Far East tour. Isn't that fantastic? And I can meet up with Tom of course!'

'Mum would have been so proud of you.'

'Aren't you proud of me too, Dad?'

'Yes of course I am. Oh Lucy I didn't mean that…'

'I know. Yes she would.'

Drake thought he heard a tremble in Lucy's voice that he wasn't meant to and tried to suppress the memory of the first time he and Cynthia had watched Lucy dance at college. Then it had been Cynthia who was in tears.

Lucy was still talking. 'Tom suggests you come out and visit him while we're in Singapore. My first night there will be on your wedding anniversary. Do please say you can make it Dad. Tom and I are worried about you and if you are all alone back in London you will just get upset, I know you will.'

'I'm not in London, I'm in Chester and I look like being too busy to get upset but I'll think about it I promise.' Drake snapped his phone shut. Henshaw instinctively glanced across the car but Drake's eyes did not invite conversation.

It was three months now. The weeks before he had been so busy looking after Cynthia. After the funeral he had felt like a deflated balloon. Everything was empty, an overwhelming numbness. Of course he knew it was coming but he was still totally unprepared for life without her. Well-meaning friends told him that time would make a difference. The Met had been very good over his compassionate leave but it was not the same. Almost every day Cynthia ambushed him; some event triggered a memory of her. It might be quite trivial and often it was the way his job demolished family life. A phone call to say he was late and would she mind going to the school play by herself, or that he couldn't join her on the next overseas trip after all, or, sorry but he could not make their lunch date at that nice new Italian.

This drove him into the darkest of moods. Not only was he unable to put Cynthia out of his mind but now he also felt remorse for the neglect of her that he had not been aware of when she was alive. Now he could travel for the first time in his life but she was not there to come with him. So 'the retirement' had not worked either; each day was one long lunch but there was no Cynthia to share it with.

He closed his eyes and fought to imagine her. Already he was forgetting! The realisation that he had never carried a photograph induced more feelings of guilt. If only he could remember her clearly and on demand. Instead her memory kept coming up behind him, saying 'boo' loudly and then fading back into the recesses of his mind. Darn the woman!

'This is the Grosvenor Hotel, sir,' whispered Henshaw tentatively.

Across the pavement from the open car door, and set back under a colonnade, the normal paving gave way to a diamond black and white pattern. A huge doormat carried dignified letters that proclaimed 'The Chester Grosvenor'. Two manicured box trees cropped into simple cones planted in cube pots framed the doorway in an unassuming, matter of fact sort of way. A flunky in a grey frock coat hung around by the door on the off chance that Drake would ever get to his feet. Henshaw finally arrived from the other side of the car to help him up to something nearing his full height.

Inside the lobby the commotion that was Eastgate was hushed to a soft rumble and, while Henshaw reminded the driver to get a Range Rover, Drake looked around. Oak panelling and buttoned leather sofas, soft rich fabrics and an abundance of flowers were all as evident to the nose as the eyes. The whole interior welcomed and seduced the visitor without any one item arresting the eye. It was luxurious rather than opulent, calm and confident but not brash or assertive.

The manager of the hotel appeared from nowhere and miraculously knew exactly who they all were.

'James Montcrief,' he said offering a hand. 'We're all very upset about this. Nothing like it has ever happened here. Please come this way I've closed the 'Library' to guests this morning especially so we can meet there. We can discuss how I can help.' The 'Library' surprised Drake by living up to its name; high backed chairs were surrounded by arched openings, polished wood bookcases and leather bound volumes. Blending seductively with them was the aroma of coffee and Henshaw, exhausted from his sleepless night and early rise, slumped appreciatively into one of the armchairs.

Montcrief wafted the pot in front of his guests expansively. 'Black or white?'

'Perhaps later,' said Drake still standing. 'I want to see the Cheung family first.' Montcrief bowed and waved away the hovering waiter. 'But you might just tell me if anyone here noticed anything unusual about Jimmy Cheung or his daughter.'

'Not really. They are ideal guests, exactly the sort we encourage here. Maybe there's one thing though. Our doorman never misses anything. He thinks that Mr. Cheung was being followed. He saw the same person in the street on several occasions when Mr. Cheung came in, a rather bulky oriental individual. Our doorman wondered if maybe it was some sort of minder or bodyguard.' He giggled.

Drake frowned and turned to Henshaw who was trying to get to his feet without anyone noticing that he had sat down. 'See if you can get a better description from the doorman. If someone was watching Jimmy and is now following us, we need to know.'

# 3 - Leather

Two heads of spiky black hair were just visible over the back of the green leather Chesterfield in front of the fireplace on the other side of the living room. As Drake and Henshaw crossed the intervening space the heads turned in mirrored unison to reveal Chinese faces. The left, more refined set of features was topped with slightly longer hair. The heads turned away and their owners stood up coming either side of the sofa to greet the policemen. The fatter face was now recognisably male, the other female. Henshaw made the introductions.

'This is Mr Jimmy Cheung's daughter Janet and his son Sheng Tian.' The woman dipped her head slightly. Her features were classically oriental; elegant high cheekbones sculpted in flawless skin contrasted her deep black eyes. Her demure but unblinking gaze told Drake she was no stranger to the niceties of social etiquette. She was at once both delicate and yet strong. He had to reach down to shake her alabaster-white hand; he estimated she was less than five feet tall.

'We are doing everything we can to discover exactly what happened to your father, Miss Cheung. The British Government is anxious that you should know all possible resources are at my disposal. The matter will be handled in the most discrete fashion.'

Drake had turned into a diplomatic apparatchik, thought Henshaw. A faint smile flicked across Janet's face as her head dipped in the slightest of nods, so subtle that Drake was not sure if he had imagined it. She maintained a calm dignity and was probably older than she appeared. He turned to repeat his assurances to Sheng Tian who looked as if he could be Janet's twin.

'We need no political interference,' spat Sheng Tian. 'Murder is murder, Chief Inspector.'

Henshaw just managed to stifle the nod of agreement that his brain had launched instinctively; perhaps Drake's diplomatic training had some way to go after all. Drake was wondering if it was possible for twins to have such different personalities.

'Mr. Cheung, you are quite right but when someone in your father's position is murdered in a foreign country there's always a concern that it may be political. It is for this reason that we have recently established the Diplomatic Unit of the Special Operations Branch of the Metropolitan Police Force. I must ask you both please not to leave the country unless I grant permission. As a matter of normal procedure, you are required to hand in your passports.'

'I have no reason to travel at this time,' growled Sheng Tian, 'but my sister will want to return to Singapore. You must allow this.' Janet looked embarrassed.

'I am sure we shall be able to return your passports soon.' Drake beckoned them back to the sofa and folded himself into a chair by the fireplace. Sheng Tian was only slightly taller than his sister but more thickset and the squarer line of his jaw lent him a pugnacious appearance. The effect was reinforced by the staccato nature of his sentences. Each syllable was fired at Drake like a bullet. Drake turned to his sister. 'Miss Cheung…'

'Please call me Janet, Inspector.'

'Janet, I believe you raised the alarm about your father being missing.'

'Inspector, Janet has already told your colleague all she knows.' Sheng Tian was firing words at him again from the far end of the sofa.

'Yes Mr. Cheung but I'd like to hear it first hand from your sister. I am anxious that we do not miss any detail, no matter how trivial it might seem to you.'

A mobile phone frustrated Sheng Tian's attempt to resume battle. It was immediately obvious that the caller was Chinese. If his English had been rapid fire, Sheng Tian's Mandarin was an automatic machine gun. To the English ears of Henshaw and Drake it sounded like outright verbal warfare. Sheng Tian covered the mouthpiece and continued in the same manner to Janet. Quite unconcerned by the assault, she smiled and nodded gently.

'Inspector, we expected you earlier. I am late for a meeting. My sister will answer your questions. Here is my card; please call me tomorrow I wish to talk with you.' He proffered a business card with Chinese characters on one side and English on the other. The card was held in both hands extended towards Drake, who mirrored the posture instinctively.

'Dr. Cheung, I am sorry but no one told me that you had a doctorate. I see you are a lecturer at the University.'

'No necessary for formality, this is England not Singapore. It is permitted to call me Sheng Tian. Now I must go.' He gave Janet a peck on the cheek, hugged her briefly and left the room grabbing a slim black leather briefcase from the coffee table.

'You must forgive Sheng Tian,' Janet said as the door closed. 'He sometimes seems gruff but he is a good man.'

'Of course,' Drake waved a hand invitingly. Janet resumed her seat, swallowed a deep breath and began in hushed tones.

'We had been at the University. My father was a Distinguished Visiting Professor in the South East Asian Business Unit there. He was getting an honorary degree. They made him a doctor.' The obvious pride in her voice tailed away as if the irrelevance of it all was only now dawning on her. The room listened attentively, even to her pauses. 'They held a small reception after the degree congregation but I was tired from the flight. I came back here to rest. My aunt Emily had already left straight after the ceremony to go back to her home in London.'

'Emily is your father's sister?' queried Drake.

'Yes, she is old now.'

'Who were the others who stayed for the reception?'

'I am not sure. One was certainly the Vice-chancellor, though he left early; I forget his name. There was the Registrar, Dr. Percival, and Professor Mallory. Then of course there were several people from the SEABU Unit, certainly Hamish McFadden the director. I get confused by all the names.'

'Understandable but perhaps you would let me know if you remember more. You said you left the reception early.'

'The university sent me here in a car and I came straight to my room. I read for a while, trying to stay awake to get over the jet lag. I think even then I might have nodded off until my handheld interrupted.'

'Excuse me, your handheld?'

She pointed to her phone lying on the coffee table next to the sofa. 'I think you call them mobiles. It was the university driver telling me that he had dropped my father by the bridge; he was going to walk back to the hotel. I gave up and went to bed.' She nodded at the left hand of two panelled doors opposite the window.

'The driver is a Mr. Johnny Davis, Sir,' said Henshaw. Janet nodded and continued.

'When I woke up there was still no sign of my father so I rang reception to see if he was in the bar. They couldn't find him. The manager called the police just to be sure.' She paused and sat in silence for a few seconds as the events replayed in her mind. 'Then early the next morning Inspector Henshaw came to see me and....' She coughed, and Henshaw went over to the bar next to the door and poured her a glass of mineral water. She took a sip and smiled her thanks.

'Who would do this thing. Why?' the question was directed at the empty space in front of her. Suddenly she seemed vulnerable but Drake could see there was an inner strength to this outwardly fragile woman. Not for one moment did he expect her to break into tears. Sure enough she sat motionless, staring ahead.

'That is what we are here to find out, Miss Cheung.'

'Everyone here so kind.'

Drake walked over to the window, parted the sheer curtains and surveyed the scene. It was Chester at its half-timbered best. Eastgate was a jostle of businessmen in suits, shoppers laden with bags and gawping tourists. People were weaving patterns along and across the full width of the cobbled street but a static figure in a doorway contrasted with all the movement. He seemed to be watching the hotel but it was his face that most interested Drake.

'Do you have any other relatives here for the ceremony?' Drake turned to see Janet's reaction to his question. She shook her head silently. 'Perhaps friends from home?' Another shake of the head. 'Did your father have any security staff?'

'Good gracious no, Inspector! Why do you ask?'

'Just checking all the angles.' Drake scanned the street, seeing only a police Range Rover carefully picking its way through the crowds. Letting go the curtain he turned his attention to the desk.

'Had your father ever been here before?'

'No. He was so excited about coming. He thought this would help Sheng Tian.'

'And you, Miss Cheung, have you been here before?'

'Yes of course; twice to sort out the details, once mainly with the University and then to finalise our accommodation.'

'The visit was well prepared then!'

'It is what I do. I organise my father's diary and prepare his visits on those occasions that I accompany him.'

'I see.' The mahogany desk under the window spoke of the Englishness of the place. A leather portfolio, decorated with the hotel crest, contained the usual headed notepaper and envelopes. The pristine emptiness of a cut glass decanter looked incongruous in this hotel of plenty. A silver strap around the neck explained all. It bore an inscription recorded the awarding of a degree to Jimmy Cheung by the university. Another leather folder was even more elaborately embossed with a coat of arms that Drake did not recognise. The insignia belonged to Deva University and inside were two documents. The first was Jimmy's degree certificate; the second was the oration that had been delivered at the congregation.

'I brought that back from the ceremony for my father,' explained Janet.

'Could I borrow it?'

'Yes certainly. It was a lovely speech. Professor Mallory such a kind man.'

'Professor Mallory?'

'The public orator at the university,' Henshaw said quickly, glad to be able to contribute.

'Tell me Miss Cheung, are you and Sheng Tian twins; you look so alike?' asked Drake.

Janet's eyes opened wide in an expression of astonishment, Drake thought almost of horror, which she held only fleetingly. Then she almost laughed; it was certainly more than the faint smile she had shown so far.

'No Chief Inspector, I am three years older than him.'

Drake wondered what caused her reaction but one of his inner voices told him not to pursue the matter further just yet. 'One final question Miss Cheung, sorry Janet, can you explain to me why you use an English name and yet your brother uses a Chinese one?'

'The family always use my Christian name. It seemed silly to change.'

The answer puzzled Drake again. The clipped language was slightly odd, perhaps that was all but he thought there was something else and he wished he could tell what it was. He was beginning to realise that these subtle cultural difficulties were going to be central to the Diplomatic Unit's work. He made a mental note to get some help.

'My Chinese name is Zhi Nuan; you can use that if it is easier.' There was an embarrassing silence of several seconds before Drake realised that she was teasing him.

'One last thing,' he stuttered, 'one of your father's cufflinks is missing. We found the other lying on the bridge beneath his body.'

'No, this cannot be.' Janet was frowning. 'What did it look like?'

'A silver bar with a white ceramic face printed with a red Chinese character,' replied Henshaw, pulling out a photograph and showing it to her. 'We assumed it was your father's since both of his were missing.'

'Oh no,' said Janet firmly. 'He never wore such a thing. These are tourist souvenirs. Actually my father was well-known known for having his shirtsleeves undone. I cannot say why; he wore them that way all his life. He would not use this.'

'So that is not his name printed on the cufflink?' queried Drake.

'Oh no.' There was a definite laugh this time. 'This is the Chinese character "fu". It means good fortune; this is a cheap trinket. Now Inspector if that is all, I have a headache and would like rest.'

'Of course. Henshaw, we need to speak with the hotel manager.'

'This cufflink business,' said Henshaw as they walked along the hotel corridor, 'maybe our murderer is Chinese.'

'It's too much of a coincidence to be irrelevant,' mused Drake. 'But then your reports show no evidence, either on the body or at the scene, of the kind of violent scuffle necessary to tear a cufflink from a shirt. I assume you've searched their apartment?'

'Just the usual; clothes, grooming accessories, a couple of books and magazines and their luggage,' replied Henshaw. 'They travel light.'

Montcrief was already sitting in the Library engaged in conversation with a high wing-backed chair. He rose to greet them and a smart young woman emerged from the chair. Henshaw initially thought she was a member of the hotel staff but seeing the smile she directed towards Drake, he guessed that this must be Grace Hepple.

Montcrief poured coffee from a white china pot offering cream from a matching jug. Drake accepted, Henshaw wanted his black but was more interested in assessing his new colleague, Detective Sergeant Grace Hepple. Now he understood what Drake had hinted at. She was striking rather than pretty, fascinating rather than conventionally beautiful. It was a well-groomed and calculated appearance and she seemed at ease in these opulent surroundings. Her movement was almost balletic and invited observation. Without ever making eye contact, it was apparent that she knew she was being watched. Henshaw wondered just how she did that. He tried not to stare at her and concentrate on what Montcrief was saying.

‘I have checked with our doorman who, I am afraid, cannot tell us any more. He is a bit embarrassed that he might have imagined the whole thing and embellished the story to impress colleagues. He cannot give any reliable description. Of course while we will help in any way we can, we do ask you to respect our guests here. Some of them inevitably are aware of what has happened but we are most anxious that these rumours do not spread around. I am sure you will agree the murder has nothing whatever to do with the Hotel.’

‘At this stage Mr. Montcrief we have very little idea who might be involved. What are these rumours?’ Henshaw stole another sidelong glance at Grace. She was fixed on Montcrief’s face while opening her briefcase and taking out a notebook. Henshaw felt stupid. Of course he should have been taking notes but now he let the more junior Detective Sergeant make the record.

‘Well,’ said Montcrief confidentially. ‘I can only tell you what members of my staff have reported. Some say that Mr. Cheung was trying to rape two schoolgirls but personally I think that extremely unlikely. Another story is that we have some Chinese turf war on our doorstep. Either way round, it is all very unsavoury.’

‘Is there anything else you can tell us about the Cheungs’ behaviour, Mr. Montcrief?’

‘Not really, except that Mr. Cheung liked a whisky here in the library before retiring to bed.’

‘And he had the means to pay for all this.’ Drake waved his hand in the air around him.

‘We never had any worries on that score.’

‘Thank you for your help, Mr Montcrief. We need not detain you any longer.’

Montcrief rose to leave. ‘I have made one of our best rooms available to you for as long as you wish. There will of course be no charges.’

‘That won’t be necessary but thank you,’ said Drake. Fergus had already booked him into a nearby hotel and he did not want to have Montcrief watching over his shoulder.

'Creepy man,' said Henshaw.

'I think he is just doing his job,' said Grace Hepple, 'He was professional. I would have taken exactly the same approach in his position.' Henshaw hardly had time to feel miffed at this put-down when Grace threw him again. 'You must be Inspector Martin Henshaw. I have been looking forward to meeting you, sir. They told me you were the outstanding sergeant under Inspector Drake at the Met, and I hope to follow in your shoes. It is a fantastic opportunity to work with both of you.'

Henshaw groped around for something to say, not helped at all by the smirk on Drake's face. She was going to be a handful, no doubt about that. Now that he was able to look directly at Grace he could not take his eyes off her. 'Amazing Grace,' he thought to himself suppressing the awful pun in his mind.

'I don't understand this Chinese name business,' said Drake. 'There's something odd about it.'

'It's simple, sir,' said Grace, 'the Chinese put their names the other way round to us. The family name comes first and is usually followed by two given names chosen by the parents and sometimes the grandparents. I have looked them up. Jimmy Cheung's full name is Cheung Jun Ming, his son is called Cheung Sheng Tian and his daughter Cheung Zhi Nuan.' Drake smiled to himself. He guessed Grace Hepple had always finished her school homework the day it was given out.

'Yes, yes; I understand that but why do they also sometimes use English names and how do they decide which to use?'

'That is usually because they are active Christians; especially this might happen in Singapore or Hong Kong, and they have literally been given a Christian name. It is also fairly common practice among those who come frequently to the West as they find it easier than trying to explain all this to us every time.'

'I still don't understand the way Janet answered my questions. More importantly I think someone else is taking an interest in us. Have you noticed Henshaw?'

Martin Henshaw was busy mentally undressing Grace Hepple; her combination of flattery and challenge was curiously seductive.

'Really? No I can't say I have!' he spluttered, 'what gives you that idea sir?'

'When we were on the bridge there was someone down below on the riverbank watching with a pair of binoculars.' Henshaw's grunt conveyed a certain lack of conviction without being entirely dismissive. Drake continued. 'Just now there was a man down in the street watching the hotel. I don't think the doorman was imagining things at all. I'm fairly sure it was the same man, rather square and almost certainly Chinese.'

Grace Hepple turned to Henshaw, who was still looking unimpressed. 'It must be a possibility we should take seriously,' she suggested. 'Perhaps the murderer is anxious to remove some evidence that we are not aware of yet.'

'Come to think of it,' said Henshaw, 'I felt I was being followed next to the churchyard on the night of the murder.'

'What did you see?'

'Well nothing actually, it was just a feeling.'

'Probably ghosts,' grunted Drake. 'The question is was the man trailing Jimmy setting him up and was he the same man who has been taking an interest us? It could be one, two or even three people. In any case I want to know who is following us. So keep your eyes open you two but don't frighten him off and remember we might be in delicate diplomatic territory here; I've got the FO on my back. We only have one copy of this degree oration so Henshaw, why don't you read it to us?' Henshaw picked up the leather portfolio from the floor under the table and opened it, running his thumb across the heavily embossed university crest. He read aloud making occasional gestures and gradually warming to his performance.

Doctor Jimmy Cheung.
Chancellor, you see standing in front of you a man most suited to be honoured by this university. Jimmy Cheung was born of humble stock in 1925 in the city of Johor Bahru, now part of Malaysia. Within a few years his parents had moved to Singapore, his father looking for employment in the port.

For a man of enterprise this was a good time and place to be born. The young Jimmy began to make his father's newly formed company more business-like and helped him to employ more of the coolies operating the shallow bottomed boats plying their trade between the seagoing vessels in the port and the warehouses along the Singapore River.

Two years before Jimmy Cheung was born, British engineers were engaged in two great enterprises. One was the building of a naval base in Singapore; the other the Queen's Park Suspension Bridge in Chester! It was of course the former that was to set the young Jimmy Cheung's career going. His father had started to work on the great George VI dry dock, the largest anywhere in the world at that time, and Jimmy was soon to follow suit. By the start of the Second World War Singapore was heavily defended from the sea by this huge complex with its own artillery, searchlights, and even an airfield. Singapore was described at the time as the "Gibraltar of the East."

But the British had fatally miscalculated. The invading Japanese entered Singapore in 1942, not by sea at all but just as the Cheung family had, by land from the north. Jimmy Cheung bided his time and when the British returned in September 1945, exactly 60 years ago, he soon found himself working for the British Navy and quickly became an indispensable part of the logistics of our operation in South East Asia.

Largely self-taught, Jimmy Cheung was to become one of the leading entrepreneurs who drove forward the astonishingly successful economy of Singapore. He was to start and establish many businesses; most of them successful, and at the latest count well over five thousand people are in gainful employment. The history of the Cheung empire mirrors the development of Singapore from a port trading the raw materials of tin and rubber from the Malay Peninsula through a British naval base to manufacturing computer components and now a modern information technology and banking centre.

It was no surprise that in 1985 Jimmy Cheung was made a member of parliament. Since then he has been a leading figure in the development of trade between Singapore and the United Kingdom and he is equally at home in Raffles Place and Whitehall. Jimmy Cheung has been of enormous assistance to Deva University in setting up our South East Asian Business Unit and takes up the post of Distinguished Visiting Professor to help us drive it forward.

Modern Singapore declared its independence on 9th August 1965 and was recognised by the United Nations as a sovereign country in September 1965. Singapore is therefore exactly the same age as this University. It is entirely appropriate that we celebrate the fortieth anniversary of the founding of the college that became Deva University by awarding an honorary degree to a leading Singaporean.

Chancellor, I present to you Jimmy Cheung as entirely worthy of the degree of Doctor of Letters Honoris Causae.

'Pompous lot these academics,' sniffed Henshaw at the end of his recital.

'In this case there is some justification,' grunted Drake. 'Our victim was obviously influential; the university was clearly basking in reflected glory. I can see why Whitehall is a bit touchy. We'll start with the Registrar.'

'Forgive my ignorance,' Henshaw interrupted, 'but I'm not entirely clear what a registrar is.'

'More of the pomposity I fear,' smiled Drake. 'I think it's just the name they use for the person who manages all the administration. Professor Mallory, who should be a real academic, is worth a visit since he did the research on Jimmy Cheung for this oration. I want to have a longer talk with Sheng Tian. Make sure you set all that up Henshaw, and it's about time you saw that driver, Johnny Davis. He's the last person known to see Jimmy Cheung alive. Now I'm going to catch up on the sleep I missed while my plane was performing pirouettes over the Peak District this morning.'

At first he couldn't place the jangling in his head, then he realised it must be the alarm clock. No, he had not even brought one. Brought one where? Drake gradually took leave of his night and made tentative contact with the harsh world of day.

There had not been a crazy night like that for many months, perhaps the best part of a year. Didn't someone say we are all mad at night? Perhaps it was Mark Twain. But Drake's nights were not so much madness as adjusted reality. The characters of a case would parade through his semi-conscious mind playing absurd roles in fantastic situations. On such nights he never really knew if he was awake, sleeping or drifting between the two. In the morning he would ask himself what was real and what fabulous but he knew not to seek the answer too soon. These were no arbitrary images but productive thought that his brain liked to perform when he left it alone.

So he lay in his bed wondering why Lucy and Tom had appeared as Jimmy Cheung's children. His family had rarely appeared in these concoctions of the night. Was there any particular significance in that? Then Cynthia had rung him to say she was worried about how Janet and Sheng Tian were getting on overseas.

Was that her calling again now? That dratted telephone!

'Yes. Drake.'

'I am sorry to wake you, sir but I thought you would want to come with me.'

'With you where, Henshaw?'

‘Jimmy Cheung’s apartment at the university, sir. The cleaner there has reported a break-in overnight. Scene-of-crime people are already there.’

There were few personal possessions in the rooms and no signs of habitation save for an empty whisky tumbler on the low coffee table in the bay window and Jimmy’s suit jacket hanging over the back of a dining chair. In the wardrobe were the discarded informal clothes Jimmy had worn earlier on the day he died. Fingerprinting was still going on but Mrs. Partridge had cleaned the room before reporting the damaged door to her boss so there was a general lack of optimism among the scene-of-crime team. There was no sign of any damage other than to the door, which had been crudely forced open.

Drake gave Henshaw an inquisitorial stare.‘There are three questions here. Firstly who is interested in this crime apart from us? Was our thickset Chinese male responsible for this break-in? And what was he looking for? Apparently he took nothing but he must have had reason to believe there was something here, perhaps incriminating.’

‘The University has taken an inventory,’ added Henshaw. ‘Apparently no University property is missing. I rang Janet. She is sure her father left nothing of value or interest here except his clothes.’

‘Just look at them!’ exclaimed Drake pointing to Jimmy’s informal clothes on a hanger in the bedroom wardrobe. Henshaw scanned the scene for some feature that Drake might be interested in and, shrugged his shoulders helplessly. ‘The trousers are folded neatly over the rail and the shirt buttoned over them, every button done up except the top. Only their owner would take such care. There is something else I should be seeing here, something important, something that should be obvious. The intruder made no attempt to conceal the break-in; it is amateur, clumsy even. Yet apparently nothing was taken. Nothing is missing. What are we missing? OK let's see what the cleaner has to say for herself.'

A short, rather stout and balding man with a wave of baby-fine ginger hair lapping over his shirt collar rose to meet them as they entered the adjoining apartment. He was wearing brown corduroy trousers, had a tweed jacket over his left arm and clutched a manila file. He held out his other empty, rather podgy, hand.

'Watson,' said a voice, unexpectedly squeaky and high-pitched. 'Director of Estates.' He turned to a frail white-haired woman wearing a light blue cleaner's overall sat on a sofa. 'This is Mrs. Partridge who cleans all eight of these Fellows' Apartments together with Mrs. Johnston who is off with flu.'

Drake nodded to the cleaner who had remained sitting bolt upright on the very edge of her seat twisting a handkerchief around her fingers repeatedly. 'Tell us what you found this morning, Mrs. Partridge.'

'There's nothing to tell, sir. When I got here the door was open and I just thought Mrs. Johnston had started to dust like, so I came in but she wasn't here. So I just cleaned and when I came to lock the door, I saw the damage and called Mr. Watson straight away.'

Drake let out a grunt of frustration. 'You did not see anything else unusual this morning?'

Mrs. Partridge shook her head as the handkerchief weaved its agitated way between her fingers. 'Well there is something else, Sir. I know I should have said something before but I just didn't make the connection you see. I am sorry, Sir. It was the day poor Professor Chan was murdered. It was when I came to clean that morning.'

'You saw something?' squeaked a frowning Watson.

'No, sir; not quite, it wasn't so much what I saw as what I heard. Then I thought to meself it was nothing 'til I found this door broken today and it just like came back to me, like.' The handkerchief twisting reached a fever pitch.

Drake held out a calming hand. 'It's quite alright Mrs. Partridge. Take your time.'

'It was Tuesday morning. I came to clean Prof Chan's room. He was supposed to be staying here but he hadn't been you see; that's why I didn't knock, like.' She looked across at Mr. Watson. 'I do, Sir normally, Sir but I just thought he wasn't there again like before.' Watson wiped a bead of sweat from his brow.

'About what time was this, Mrs. Partridge?' asked Drake.

'Oooo I suppose it would be around half nine,' said the cleaner. 'I come here after I've done me other work in departments you see.'

'And you heard something, Mrs. Partridge?' prompted Drake.

'It was a shoutin' match, no two ways about it. Almost screaming they were. I thought for a minute it was the telly. You know them soaps they're always shoutin.' But then somebody started crashing and banging. I got a bit frightened, like, so I went out quick. It was then I worked out as how I had left my things inside so I waited in number five and watched out of the window. About ten minutes later this man came out and dashed off. I recognised him straight away.' There was a silence while Mrs. Partridge sat twirling her handkerchief.

'It wasn't Professor Cheung then Mrs. Partridge?' prompted Drake.

'No it weren't Prof Chan.'

'It's Cheung, Mrs. Partridge, Professor Cheung,' insisted Watson emphasising the pronunciation.

'No I said it weren't Prof Chan,' said Mrs. Partridge frowning. 'It was Dr. Cheung. I am dead certain it was. I recognise him, you see, I used to clean his room in the Politics Department. I'd know him anywhere.'

'Let me be clear about this, Mrs. Partridge, you mean Dr. Cheung Sheng Tian, Professor Cheung's son?' asked Drake.

'I had no idea he was Prof Chan's son. No idea at all. But it all adds up don't it. I should have put two and two together, like. I mean they're both Chinese.'

Drake quickly abandoned the logical analysis he had begun. 'Mrs. Partridge, you say you waited in number five, is that empty?'

Watson read from his list. 'Yes, we are in number five now. We have eight identical apartments here of which only three, four and six are currently occupied.'

'So, Mrs Partridge, could you hear what they were saying?' asked Drake.

'That's the whole thing you see, they was talking in a foreign language. Sounded like Chinese to me. Well I suppose it would have been wouldn't it?'

'Mandarin,' corrected Watson. 'In Singapore they speak Mandarin.'

'Oh no I am sure it was Chinese like,' insisted Mrs. Partridge, 'not that I can speak it myself of course.' Watson drew breath and Drake, fearing he was about to deliver a lecture on the relationship between written and spoken Chinese languages, raised a hand. 'It probably means nothing at all then,' continued Mrs. Partridge, 'if it's his son. It's just a family squabble I dare say.'

'Probably nothing as you say Mrs. Partridge. Even so, for now please don't mention it to anyone else,' said Drake tapping his nose, 'just between ourselves.' Drake nodded to a woman constable from the scene-of-crime team to help the now shaking Mrs. Partridge back to Watson's office.

'So,' said Drake sucking in a long breath, 'Sheng Tian argued violently with his father on the morning he was killed.'

'Maybe he came back here last night to remove something he had left,' added Henshaw. 'What was he anxious that we didn't find?'

# 4 - Silk

Lunch all to himself had suddenly become a luxury again. The demands of so many people depending on him created a buzz that he had missed but like too much alcohol, it left a hangover. Drake instinctively sought the privacy that a crowd offers without the fearful loneliness of solitude. He found himself wandering aimlessly along Foregate hoping he would think of a reason before reaching the end of the street. A gaudy display of posters in a travel agent's window came to his rescue. Pictures of Cynthia's favourite cities elbowed their way past the rest; Sydney, Amsterdam, Kuala Lumpur, Rio de Janeiro and of course Singapore. Her success with a major firm of architects had suddenly propelled her into projects round the world and she had so wanted him to go too. It never happened; either it was too short notice or he was at a critical point on a case.

Standing looking in the window he had no forewarning of the idea; it just sneaked up on him. Perhaps now he was 'retired', he would retrace Cynthia's footsteps. She would have insisted that they both jet off to watch Lucy perform on her first foreign tour. A strange coincidence that her first stop was Singapore. It had been one of Cynthia's favourite haunts and now their son Tom was working there for an investment bank.

If he did go would it help or would he just miss her even more? Could he face the long journey? The prospect of a whole day stuck inside an airplane was horrific. Perhaps he could stop off en-route to break the journey but his geography was so embarrassingly poor that he searched the display for a map. A delivery boy dashing into the shop almost knocked Drake over and somehow he too was inside before he had actually agreed with himself about taking any real action. It was just a silly idea after all.

The place was little more than a wide corridor terminated by a blank wall, paradoxically a tunnel to nowhere. Customers sat on pairs of chairs at an eccentric angle to the long reception counter. Assistants in garish yellow jackets prodded at keyboards and frowned at computer screens. The brochures plastered over the walls were obsessed with either beaches or ski slopes. Drake browsed aimlessly for several minutes with over-excited children chasing each other around him.

He had little idea where you could visit on the way to Singapore but neither swimming nor winter sports would be on his agenda. Suddenly a feeling of being out of place overtook him and he made his exit without anyone noticing. Everyone seemed so young. He had never felt old before. Was that how it happened then? There you were one day quite normal then, without any notice, you were old. It was a worrying thought.

In danger of being late for his arranged pickup to go to the university, Drake quickened his step from amble to scuttle. Perhaps it was time he learned to use the Internet. Maybe he was just not cut out for long distance travelling. Besides he had a feeling that this case was going to keep him here for rather longer than Fergus Marshall had suggested. Lucy would manage perfectly well and she would have Tom to keep her company anyway.

The British Racing-Green police Range Rover waiting at the barrier contained three policemen and two briefcases but no uniforms. The sign in front of them read ‘The Deva University of Chester’. Drake wondered how many students would understand the significance of ‘Deva’. Even the football club was cashing in on the heritage angle these days with its ‘Deva Stadium’. It sounded more cultured than the old Sealand Road but would it do more to intimidate the opposition? It ought to. After all ‘Deva’ started its life as a Roman garrison, hardly a place of lightness and jollity.

The gatekeeper had obviously modelled himself on the Praetorian Guard. Empowered by his peaked cap, the wretched fellow was demanding to see warrant cards. Drake's insistence that they maintain an incognito presence had backfired. The constable driving had got so excited by this that he had left all his identity behind in his discarded uniform.

A character two cars back in the queue behind them was convinced he could resolve the situation by blowing his horn repeatedly. The peaked cap went back to 'sort him out,' while Henshaw searched for his warrant card.

The campus architecture was more "industrial estate" than "seat of learning" but Drake could discern a subtle change in the main administrative building. Cynthia would have described this as "decorated shed."

The porter at the main building forewarned of their arrival by the peaked cap, pulled out a plastic card stamped with the university crest and swiped it to allow them access. The interior had its own grisly architectural surprise. Marbled wallpaper, grey below and pink above a gold dado line contrived to imitate a cheap motel. The pink was trying to be grey and the grey was trying to be greyer still. Everything was apologetic about its existence. The ubiquitous 'brass' fittings were so obviously not solid that they fooled no one and obviously knew it. All round the walls were portraits of senior officers of the university every one of them wearing academic robes. The paintings were intended to establish history but looked remarkably like a job lot.

'Good afternoon, I'm Sally Brown, Dr. Percival's P.A.'. Drake had no idea how the young woman had so suddenly appeared. She was already bustling off as he started to get out of the grey leatherette chair he was still subsiding into. 'Dr. Percival should return from degree congregation any moment. He has a meeting of academic planning committee in ten minutes. He should be able to see you briefly.' Only half way to his feet by the time she disappeared round the corner, Drake was already in danger of getting lost. Henshaw hovered roughly halfway between him and their guide who had disappeared down a long corridor.

'I thought you'd fixed us an appointment,' Drake grumbled.

'So did I. I didn't realise it was this tight.'

The panelled door carried a wooden plaque with recessed Roman letters picked out in gold leaf that simply read 'Registrar'. Sally Brown opened it, waved an arm at two chintz-covered chairs and a sofa in the bay window and disappeared through an unmarked door. Across the room was an imposing desk in dark polished hardwood. Behind it a high backed rocking chair was incongruously stuck on a chrome swivel base. The desktop was empty save for a large blotter, an intercom and a triangular wooden name holder that read 'Dr. J. Percival'. Across the bay window were heavy chintz curtains held back in swags by rope ties fixed on the dado line. On the opposite wall were a series of watercolours swamped by ornate gold frames. On the side wall to the left were three historic maps of Chester. The remaining wall beside the door through which Sally Brown had disappeared, boasted four degree certificates. A grandfather clock was doing its best to relieve the silence with an insistent tick. In the corner a bent wood coat and hat stand was empty even on this chilly morning. Out of the corner of his eye, Drake saw the door to the corridor open.

'Good to see you again Inspector. You must be Chief Inspector Drake, I hope Sally has been looking after you.' Dr. Percival was standing framed by the doorway illuminated from behind by sunlight streaming through a window across the corridor. He was wearing black academic dress with gold wire detail on the shoulders along the reveals and on the buttons holding up the gathered sleeves. He was carrying a large black hat that was floppy save for a stiff almost circular rim. In all it was the kind of apparel that most men would be embarrassed to wear but Percival obviously revelled in it. Sally Brown appeared from her side door to help him remove this regalia. He clung firmly onto the reveals of the gown while she lifted the heavy hood over his head.

'We commissioned Ede and Ravenscroft to create an original design for our anniversary celebrations.' The muffled voice came from under the hood initially but then he was free and carefully smoothing back what remained of his fine ginger hair. At last he could shake the hands of Drake and Henshaw and motioned that they should resume their position on the sofa, as he took one of the single chairs. 'Some coffee please Sally, Oh and those special biscuits.' A half suppressed giggle suggested that he thought this was as naughty as it was possible to get mid-morning. 'Now I should be glad to hear how far your investigations have proceeded. We are anxious to have an end to this awful business as soon as possible, though I am sure it is nothing to do with the University. Are you near to making an arrest?'

'Dr. Percival,' began Drake with a thinly concealed air of irritation, 'things do not often happen so quickly. So far we have not been able to find the weapon that was used and we have no evidence that anyone saw the murderer. The last person known to see Jimmy Cheung alive was your driver and we would appreciate being able to talk to him as soon as possible. I'm going to speak with Mr Cheung's son this morning. I also want to interview Professor Mallory. Finally I would like a list please of all the people who were at the honorary degree congregation for Jimmy Cheung.' Percival's expression darkened while Sally Brown made notes. Drake continued. 'I understand that there was a reception afterwards and I want a list of the people who attended that too please.'

'Of course Chief Inspector, Sally can do that but I would ask for discretion; we had a number of important guests. This is a very sensitive matter.' Sally Brown whispered in Percival's ear, and he nodded. 'Sally points out that degree congregation list would be very long and may not be correct. We know who was invited but not necessarily who attended. However she is certain we can provide you with a correct list of people at the reception.'

Sally Brown spoke, interrupting Percival. 'Professor Mallory's secretary tells me that he is not in and she's tried both his home and mobile phone without success. She thinks he may have gone abroad. He travels a lot and she says a call from him in some country or other is often the first she knows of a trip.' Percival looked about to explode.

'Make a note Sally. I must issue a memorandum about staff notifying us where they are; we just cannot have people like Mallory gallivanting around the world out of contact like this.' Sally wrote assiduously only to be interrupted by an insistent buzz from the intercom on Dr. Percival's desk. She rushed across to it, her hand pausing just over the machine.'

'It's the V.C.' This news galvanised the Registrar. Nearly tripping over the coffee table in his dash across the room, he made a lunge at the desk and pressed the button.

'Yes, Vice-chancellor.'

The speaker spluttered into action. 'You're late for academic planning Percival. What are you doing?' Dr. Percival tried to explain the proceedings, speaking in lowered tones. 'These anniversary celebrations of yours are in danger of going belly-up in a grand way, Percival,' snapped the machine, 'this is not going to help our colleagues in SEABU one little bit. I need a report from you on item two so we'll change the running order of the agenda; for goodness sake sort it out and get down here as soon as you can.' The machine clicked off and Percival looked helplessly at his guests and shrugged his shoulders. Drake nearly felt sorry for him. Henshaw was trying hard not to grin through his biscuit. Sally Brown dashed out into her office and brought in a large folder labelled 'Academic Planning Committee'.

'Thank you for your time, Dr Percival,' said Drake levering himself off the sofa. 'I just need to know where you were after the degree congregation.'

'Of course, yes. I went to the reception for Professor Cheung. I seem to remember he left for his apartment and after a discussion with Hamish McFadden and the Vice-chancellor I immediately drove home.'

'I assume someone can verify that for us?'

Percival looked flustered, 'my wife would confirm that I am sure.'

'Thank you, Dr. Percival. We may wish to come back again when you have more time. For now I think we had better go and see Dr. Cheung.'

'Yes, yes, quite so. Mr. Watson will show you to the Politics Department.'

'One final thing, Dr. Percival.' Drake turned as he reached the doorway. 'Exactly what is this SEABU thing?'

'That is our South East Asian Business Unit. It is mostly a post-graduate research and consultancy unit that is very successful. Jimmy Cheung had been helping us establish it and was going to be the first Visiting Professor. It is directed by Hamish McFadden. I am sure he would be very willing to show you around their new building. He is very proud of it; we all are.'

It was one of those days when nothing runs to time and things go wrong that you did not even know were there to go right. Detective Sergeant Grace Hepple was mopping up detail, oiling the wheels of the machine and checking that everyone was working to the same systems and procedures. A key task was to get the updated pathology report from Professor Wilson.

'Has the post-mortem been more difficult than you expected?'

He shook his head. 'This city is impossible to get around; terrible traffic. Actually the local pathologist has done a pretty professional job. I'll write you a report but I know you people always want instant answers.'

'We are under some pressure to get results ourselves,' smiled Grace. 'So you are confirming that he died of a shot through the heart?'

'The shot through the heart caused him to die.'

'Is there a difference?'

Wilson stood clutching his lapels as if about to deliver a lecture. 'He probably died of shock. Forensic pathology is usually not that precise, Sergeant. There would have many consequences of the shot through his heart, several of them would eventually lead to death. Which of them did so first is a matter of speculation without a much longer study. My guess is that he died of a massive shock that, combined with the physical damage to the heart resulting from the bullet wound, caused him to lose consciousness. The bullet entered the chest, passed straight through the aorta and on a route that appears straight and uninterrupted out of the body without meeting any ribs. There is evidence of a significant amount of alcohol having been consumed. The victim was of an age that, under these circumstances, it would not be surprising if he became unconscious more or less immediately. Although there is remarkably little blood evident externally, there was very substantial internal bleeding from the damage to the aorta. This would certainly result in a loss of oxygen arriving…look do you want me to go on with this?'

'Thank you, Professor Wilson; I get the message.'

'My report will not add much to what you already have, except perhaps for one thing.'

Grace expected another sentence but it was not forthcoming. 'What is that, Professor Wilson?'

'I'm not exactly sure yet. I need to consult my references. The indications are that the fatal shot was at very close range but the damage to the tissue is much less than I would expect to see. So clean is the wound at the point of entry that it suggests the bullet was not of the expanding variety and probably did not mushroom on impact. Relatively little of the kinetic energy has been transferred to the tissue. I have a vague memory of seeing something about this somewhere but I have never seen it first hand before. I have taken some photographs and if I can offer you anything further, I will call you. I don't suppose you have the weapon or the bullet?'

'We were rather hoping you might help us out by telling us what to look for. Just one more question. I suppose you are certain this is murder?'

'I can only see two other logical alternatives,' said the pathologist laughing, 'either it was an accident or it was suicide.'

'Could it have been suicide?'

'I think we would still have the gun in that case, Detective Sergeant!'

'Unless someone else took it.'

'Hmmm OK; well it's technically possible. I've never seen a case of someone shooting themselves in the heart. This demands a most unnatural posture. Imagine trying to hold a gun away from you, pointed back at your chest and firing it.' He demonstrated the awkward movements. 'It is far more likely to be a shot to the head in the case of suicide.' Again he illustrated this holding his hand with a forefinger pointing to the side of his head.

'Thank you, Professor Wilson.' Grace felt that she had given as good as she got in the exchange. No sooner had the pathologist left than there was an impatient knock on the door, which opened as she began to speak. The flustered figure of Sergeant Denson appeared, grasping a piece of paper in his large red hand that appeared to be shaking uncontrollably.

'Dave, our technician, just brought this in.' An enthusiastic young man in a dark blue overall coat was standing on tip toe looking over Denson's shoulder nodding vigorously 'Dave says it's from one of those anonymous email addresses.'

'Yes,' said Dave. 'You won't be able to trace it but I thought you'd want to see it as soon as the Professor had gone.' Grace read the paper. It was full of all those apparently meaningless headings, filenames, dates and routing details that computers delight in adding to even the simplest message. The body of the email was short and very direct.

SEABU and McFadden not what they seem

Henshaw was standing at the first floor window of the Facilities Department watching the University limousine sweep up the drive outside. The driver's door opened and a uniformed man got out, opened the rear door, took out his cap and an A4 diary, locked the car and disappeared from view into the building below.

'This is Johnny Davis,' said Mr. Watson, opening the door a few minutes later. 'He drove Professor Cheung everywhere. I will leave you to it.'

Davis sat down, took out a cigarette and started to light it. 'Do you mind if I smoke? I'm not allowed to in the car and I get a bit frantic for one if I don't get a break.'

Henshaw opened the window and sat down opposite him at the small table in the middle of the room and took out his notebook. 'Tell me about your work for Professor Cheung.'

'He was a bit of a devil that one. Don't get me wrong; nothing out of order or anything but he liked the good life and no mistake. I'm really sorry about what happened to him; quite liked the old bugger. I took him to a couple of places that I'm sure he wouldn't want his daughter to know about.' He gave Henshaw a knowing wink. 'Very good to me he was though; nice tips. He must have been a jack-the-lad in his younger days!'

'What about the day of the murder?'

Davis opened his huge diary. 'I picked him up in the morning at the hotel a bit before 9. He wanted to come to the Fellows' Apartments. He brought a suit in a bag with him to change into for the degree congregation. He said he had a reception to attend that would go on at least until 5. I remember suggesting I came for him a bit earlier to avoid the rush hour. It's really dreadful here; you have to go all the way round this insane one-way system. About 4:45 I got a call from him to say he wasn't ready so I said I'd call for him at 6:30 to let the traffic die down again. I got called to do another job so I was late. When I came for him I had to knock on the door loads of times so I think he might have been asleep. When he came out, he had no jacket on and I remember saying to him that it might get a bit chilly for him. He just smiled, I don't think he was taking it in. He smelt a bit of whisky.'

'He didn't have anything else with him?'

'Not as I remember. The traffic was worse than ever; an accident I think. We didn't move for ages. He got a bit impatient. Then he started asking about the suspension bridge. He said it was just about the same age as him and he wanted to go there again. I really don't know much about the bridge I'm afraid but we were close to it and he told me to duck out of the traffic and drive him there so he could walk back. He might have thought the fresh air would sober him up a bit before he met his daughter. He said they were having dinner together and she was always trying to stop him drinking. She was really devoted to him; you could tell. I pulled up Queen's Park Road and showed him where to go to find the bridge. I could see he wasn't that steady on his feet so I called Miss Janet at the hotel to let her know he was on his way. That was the last I saw of the old fella.'

'And where did you go then?'

'Home. I took the car. I had an early pickup the next morning.'

'Can someone verify that?'

'My wife and kids were in. I can't say exactly what time that was.'

Henshaw rose as if to leave. 'Is there anything else at all you can tell me about Professor Cheung? Did he ever mention anything about having any enemies or being in danger?'

'Oh no, he never said anything like that. He was a pretty cocky sort of a chap, perky for his age and obviously used to getting his own way and all that. I've picked up a fair few of these SEABU visitors; they're a bunch of wide boys if you ask me. Not the usual sort of visitors we get to the university; put it that way. Wheelers and dealers they are. By all accounts there's big money involved and some say not all of it is entirely above board. You might say that's just talk but then there's no smoke without fire, as my mother says. I never expected anything to happen to Prof Cheung, not at all but then I'm not surprised that something has gone wrong in SEABU. That McFadden has been heading for a fall.'

'Can you give me anything more specific to go on?'

'Perhaps I shouldn't have said that. There's nothing concrete at all; it's just talk around the place you know. Sometimes I think these high and mighty ones like the Vice-chancellor and the Registrar would do better to listen to us humble drivers and porters and cleaners. We sort of pick things up and talk among ourselves. We have most of them summed up, and they have no idea.' Davis grinned and winked.

Drake liked to get 'the sniff of the place' so he turned down a lift to the Politics Department. Now he was regretting it. There was little about this place worth sniffing. The only remarkable thing was how it contrived to be unremarkable. There was nothing you could latch onto. No memorable buildings or places. Everywhere looked the same and Drake had a nasty feeling he might be lost, though he was not prepared to admit this just yet. There were few students about except for the group who demanded money from him in a jovial fashion. It was 'rag week' and they were collecting for charity. Apparently they were planning a mock kidnapping of one of their lecturers and thought they would rehearse on Drake. He wondered what would have happened if they had realised they had a member of the Special Operations Branch in their grasp. In exchange for a fiver they told him where the Politics Department was, which was just as well since he had already walked right past it.

Inside things were no better. This was a building of internal corridors that occasionally turned through eccentric angles obviously designed to disorientate the visitor. Virtually all the doors were shut and Drake had no idea if they were occupied or empty. The impression was more of a monastery than a collegiate building for sharing ideas. Luckily a passing lecturer confirmed that Dr. Cheung's office was just around the next corner.

'Come!' He recognised that staccato Chinese voice from deep within the room. Drake opened the door slowly to reveal a scene from the Orient. A huge chest of drawers in a black lacquered finish with organic inlaid mother-of-pearl detail occupied half one wall. Opposite was a daybed in the same material with sweeping curved ends and an ornate carved back. The seat was scattered with cushions covered in red shot silk with tassels at the corners. Standing on the floor by the window was a gigantic bamboo plant in a blue and white china vase. In the middle of the room were several semi-transparent silk banners decorated with hand embroidered oriental scenes. They were looped over black rods at the top and bottom held by ornate frames which were tensioned to the floor and ceiling with steel cables. There were books everywhere; they were on shelves covering most of the wall surface and in piles standing on the floor. An assortment of vases, woodcarvings and other oriental ornaments shared the shelves. Every item in the room was exquisitely crafted and beautiful in its own right. Drake could just make out Sheng Tian through the banners. He was sitting on a wooden chair at a simple plank desk.

'Welcome to my office, Chief Inspector,' Sheng Tian indicated the daybed as a possible place to sit.

'What an amazing room you have here!'

'Little haven in empty place.' Sheng Tian gestured around the room with his left hand and out of the window with the right. 'This room important to me for several reasons,' he added.

'A piece of China in a Roman city,' observed Drake. Sheng Tian smiled and bowed his head to acknowledge Drake's neat phrase. There was less aggression in the atmosphere than in their first encounter at the hotel. Even so Sheng Tian exuded the impatience of a scholar surrounded by people of lesser intelligence.

'Sheng Tian, I wonder if you can help me? I see such similarities between you that I asked your sister if you were twins. She seemed to find the question amusing. Can you explain that?'

'You English always think we always look the same,' Drake was not sure if he was being teased again. Then Sheng Tian broke the silence laughing. 'She cannot be my twin unless she is also my sister.'

'Janet is not your sister?'

'Correct; she is my cousin.' Drake looked baffled.

'Janet was adopted by my father so she is legally my sister but not so by birth.'

'I understand, Sheng Tian. Forgive me for being so slow.'

'Janet is only daughter of my father's brother. He went missing in Second World War, presumed dead. Her mother was ill for long time and was not able to look after Janet. Naturally my father adopted her. Chief Inspector, you need to understand something; my sister is devoted to my father. She has spent nearly all her life working for him and looking after his affairs. Do not think she resents her position. She is very grateful. Why do you need to know all this?'

'Just normal enquiries.' Again the smile and nod. Drake was anticipating this response now. 'I understand your mother also died some time ago?'

'She passed away when I was twenty-one. Then it was Janet's turn to look after him; my father never remarried.'

'I am sorry about your mother. I get the impression that although Janet is not your natural sister, you are very fond of her.'

'Of course, we believe in the family. It is big part of our culture. I would do anything to protect her. This has not always been easy.' Drake made a mental note of another slightly enigmatic sentence.

'Why do you think anyone would want to kill your father?'

'I cannot imagine.'

'He had been a member of parliament; did he have any political enemies?' Sheng Tian let out a guttural laugh though he looked far from amused.

'Not of the kind you imagine.' Sheng Tian sat back in his chair touching the fingertips of his hands together as if delivering a corrective tutorial to a group of lazy students. 'The Singaporean Parliament is not the same as yours, Chief Inspector. My father has been a nominated member, so he did not campaign against an opponent in an election. Our parliament can be seen as a sort of cross between your houses of Commons and Lords. Our culture values collective responsibility and duty as much as individual freedom. The Singaporean version of democracy reflects this. There is no single powerful opposition; we have a much more stable Government.'

'I assume your father supported this political system but what about you, Sheng Tian?'

'Of course not; I was my father's main opposition.'

'So you used to have arguments with your father?'

'We had disagreements sometimes.'

'When was the last time you had a disagreement with you father.'

'I can't remember. It did not happen all the time.' One of Drake's internal voices told him not to ask directly about the argument the cleaner had overheard.

'Why do you choose to live here? Is that because of your political views?'

'Oscar Wilde described your democracy as "the bludgeoning of the people by the people for the people." It is interesting to observe the British system for a while. I am preparing a critical monograph on modern European political history from Asian perspective.' Drake understood every word but was not convinced he got the sentence.

'You are lucky that your father was able to support your academic studies.'

'Able yes; willing no. I support myself entirely.' This sounded like a raw nerve.

'I imagine your father becoming a visiting professor would be a help to you?'

'I have nothing to do with SEABU. They exploit the economies of South East Asia for the benefit of the West.'

'Surely with your knowledge and expertise you could be of great assistance to SEABU.'

'If that was my choice; this is not why I am here. I would not work with McFadden.'

'Hamish McFadden is the director of SEABU isn't he?' asked Drake.

'You should ask him where all the money came from for that new building he is so proud of.'

'What are you suggesting Sheng Tian? Is there something improper?' There was a studied silence and it was obvious the Singaporean was not going to break it. Drake changed tack.

'Sheng Tian, would you please tell me your whereabouts on Tuesday evening between 6 and 9 p.m.?'

'I was working here; I had a conference paper to finish.'

'Are there any witnesses who would be able to confirm that?

'Not that I know; most people here have gone home by then.' Sheng Tian's voice was rising and getting more aggressive. 'You are accusing me of killing my father because I don't support his politics?'

'I need to eliminate you from our enquiries.' There was another silence. It hung around awkwardly until another rendition of Carmen broke it. Drake looked at his phone and saw it was his daughter again. He did not want to talk about Singapore in earshot of Sheng Tian. 'Excuse me please' He rose to leave the room but with little effort, Sheng Tian easily beat him to it.

'Please Inspector. I need to collect something from the porters' lodge.' He was gone before Drake knew it.

'Lucy. Hello. Lovely to hear you.'

'Dad, just thought I would call you before I go to Singapore tomorrow. I'm not sure if this phone will work there. I shall be very cross if you don't come. I'll call you from there if I can. Tom says he will make arrangements for you. Must dash, byeee.'

Drake sat recovering from the whirlwind that was his daughter on the phone. He looked around the room. The books seemed to be split almost equally between Chinese and English. Among the spines he could read were titles covering political theory from the middle of the twentieth century. There were biographies of great figures from varying political and religious persuasions; there was Marx, Churchill and Hitler. A book on the war over the Falkands, one about Nelson Mandela, many on Lee Kuan Yew, and a whole slew of books about both first and second world wars. The collection gave the impression of belonging to a scholar rather than a bigot.

There was no sign of Sheng Tian so Drake closed the door, retraced his steps and found the porters' lodge. They had seen nothing of Sheng Tian. Asking them to lock his room, Drake stepped outside into the afternoon sun. Sooner or later he was going to have to have a proper conversation with Sheng Tian and on his terms not those of the elusive Singaporean. Why was Sheng Tian so quick to terminate the conversation at that point, and why had he not mentioned the argument with his father?

# 5 - Wood

A watery sun had just crept over the buildings to his south, as Drake sheltered from the early autumn breeze on a bench in the centre of the courtyard. A blackbird perched in a maple tree above chirped out territorial defiance with increasing gusto. Its neighbour's repost sounded rather disinterested, perhaps more out of duty than enthusiasm. All three were all deep in the labyrinth that masqueraded as the campus of Deva University. Peering through the branches to see the duettists, Drake contemplated the attractions of avian life. There was something to be said for having simple objectives instead of the complex morass of demands imposed by his world. Besting your neighbour through nothing more threatening than a song on a sunny day was as a blameless an existence as Drake could imagine.

He performed a mental role call of the characters he had met so far in the Jimmy Cheung case. They were a fascinating bunch. How many secrets was each hiding and how did their lives cross? He prided himself on his ability to read people but oriental cultures presented a new challenge. A flapping of leaves signalled the departure of the more timid bird and silence fell on the courtyard.

Drake had always thrived on the variety and unpredictability of his life. Cynthia kept hijacking him unexpectedly but his taste for investigation was returning. He was no longer being carried by colleagues; he was in charge again. How tedious to be a bird predestined to repeat the same song in the same tree every day!

The now familiar excerpt from Carmen broke the newborn silence just as it was getting established. Drake even knew where to find his phone. It was Grace Hepple telling him about the anonymous email.

'That's the second time we have been given this message,' said Drake. 'Sheng Tian made a very pointed reference to SEABU and

McFadden. He obviously dislikes them intensely. Get our technical people to try to find the source of the email.'

Drake watched another gaggle of students lurking with obvious intent around the entrance to the building opposite. He had always envied academics their life. He might be OK at research but he would not relish trying to hold the attention of a group of teenagers more interested in their rag. It was bad enough bringing on a couple of detective sergeants. Drake looked at his watch.

Right on cue, Henshaw appeared in the open corner of the courtyard between History and Modern Languages. Good. Sometimes you need a listener to explain your thoughts to before you understand them yourself. Sheng Tian had major differences and even arguments with his father but he had more or less denied Mrs. Partridge's evidence that they had rowed on the morning of the murder. When to confront him with their evidence about the incident? SEABU had a working relationship with Professor Cheung that Sheng Tian disapproved of. What was that? A plan of action was formulating in his mind.

Drake looked up again, expecting Henshaw to have joined him but he was nowhere to be seen. Then there he was again, this time in a gap in the opposite corner between History and Archaeology. Henshaw's purposeful walk had given way to a puzzled stumble only interrupted by Drake's energetic waving.

'I've been going around in circles,' groaned Henshaw.

'Squares.'

'Beg your pardon, sir?'

'Squares. You've been going round in squares not circles. I did the same. This place numbs the mind,' growled Drake. 'Not exactly what you need in a university.' Henshaw recovered his breath between exchanges about their interviews, and the email.

'I hesitate to be too definite,' said Drake pointing, 'but I think SEABU will be through there.' Each 'quadrangle' had a name on the map but there were no such signs in the real world. 'Yes that corner over there behind us I think.' Henshaw wanted to disagree but felt on too shaky ground. Unbeknown to them, while they were walking, the buildings had all rearranged themselves between the 'quadrangles' with the specific purpose of confusing them further. Or so it seemed, when ten minutes later they recognised the bench they had started out from; at least it looked like the same seat.

Henshaw wanted to ask someone the way; Drake argued that was tantamount to being beaten by a second rate architect. 'You can't miss it,' said a young woman when Henshaw finally won. 'It's totally different from every other building. It's made entirely of wood instead of all this nasty concrete.' The two policemen set off again with renewed confidence. Several more wrong turns later, they emerged from the labyrinth to find themselves in a grassy opening. They could see countryside in the distance. Two buildings were visible. The first, a small plain brick construction of three storeys with flat roofs, was signposted as the 'Fellows' Apartments'.

'We must have been on the other side of that yesterday,' grumbled Drake. Standing in open space to the right was a single storey building hovering above the ground. It was topped with tiled roofs that sloped steeply down until they flared out at the eaves. It beautifully relieved the modernist disorientation induced by the courtyards and they were drawn towards it. The sign above the door confirmed that this was SEABU.

Disappointingly, the building did not hover at all but was supported by timber posts obscured by the deep overhanging roof and projecting wooden walkway that surrounded the whole structure. Drake nodded inwardly to Cynthia who had loved the vernacular architecture of most places eastern, tropical, and Indonesian in particular.

The front façade of the building was much the same all the way across; panels of diagonal timber boarding interspersed with glazing occupied the spaces between the wooden posts. Edging the deck was a balustrade of flat vertical timber slats with curved outlines topped by a smooth moulded handrail. The whole structure was constructed from a reddish-brown wood that got darker where it had been touched frequently. The building told you how to use it.

A sudden contrast with this oriental vernacular startled the policemen. As they approached, two doors of frameless glass set in the main façade slid open smoothly disappearing into the walls on either side. There was a 'swish' made with a rising tone the way Australians turn ordinary sentences into something sounding like a question. Henshaw, being in the lead, took half a step back in alarm, and the doors closed in disappointment. Drake reached the top of the steps and the doors obligingly opened with renewed enthusiasm. Inside, the colours and materials of the building continued seamlessly. An entirely glazed wall ahead revealed a courtyard heavy with exotic plants.

'Can I help you?' Henshaw spun round quite prepared to believe that the doors could talk. The reality was more prosaic. So transfixed had they been by this refuge of calm that neither noticed they were standing next to an internal window opening onto an office to the left of the main door. One section of the window was pulled aside by the owner of the voice, a very smart looking woman.

'We are looking for the Director,' said Henshaw, 'He is expecting us.'

'I am his P.A. Sheila Wilkins; and your names, gentlemen?'

'Drake and Henshaw,' interjected Drake, not wanting to start rumours of investigating policemen crashing round the building.

'Please take a seat and I'll track him down' said the disembodied voice of Sheila Wilkins, who had disappeared back into her office. Casual chairs by the courtyard windows were constructed from a woven rush material and scattered with cushions in geometric stepped patterns of bright reds, oranges and greens. Above them Drake and Henshaw could see high up into the soaring roof. One of the wicker seats creaked as it adjusted to the weight of Henshaw; Drake thought better of it. Next to the seats were three towers, made of rush and square in plan but twisted like liquorice allsorts. They contained sparkling miniature lights. A Balinese gamelan orchestra was playing quietly over loudspeakers in the roof and there was the faintest whiff of oriental incense in the air.

The wooden deck continued briefly outside in the courtyard, which was landscaped with a combination of pebbles, plants and water. Mostly the planting was low, save for the occasional dramatic bamboo with bright red stems holding up a canopy of gently swaying leaves. Strategically located in this landscape were stone sculptures, some rising up to the eaves level. Although unique, the sculptures acknowledged each other in form enough to suggest they were from the same hand. A smaller version of these sculptures was between the entrance and the area of seats where Henshaw was now sitting. On its plinth was a label with three interlinked letter 'A's.

A burly figure strode purposefully towards them along the corridor bordering the courtyard.

'Inspector Drake?' it enquired holding out a hand exactly halfway between the two policemen.

'Dr. Hamish McFadden?' responded Drake, taking the sizeable paw.

'Yes and no. I am Hamish McFadden but I do not have a PhD. I am too busy for silly research degrees; I am an MBA.'

'MBA?' queried Henshaw only just audibly to Drake.

'Master of Business Administration,' muttered Drake. Hamish McFadden was a large man in every respect. He was not excessively tall like Drake, nor was he fat. He was just large. He had blonde hair combed flat, a bullying jaw and blue staring eyes. He looked like a man used to giving leadership and expecting others to follow unquestioningly. He was wearing a pale blue shirt with a button down collar trapping a red tie. Dark blue trousers suggested that they belonged with a jacket hanging over the back of a chair somewhere. The shoes were black and highly polished. There was no sign of the Scottish accent the name suggested.

'Harvard Business School,' added McFadden meaningfully, 'Please follow me.' He led them to the end of one side of the courtyard and round the corner where the corridor wall disappeared. They found themselves in an open space running right across the building. Beyond it, fully glazed walls looked into a series of small offices where people could be seen working. A couple had pulled down wooden Venetian blinds presumably to get some privacy. Off the other end of this space was a small kitchen area partly shielded by a partition and partly by a counter supporting promising looking gadgets for making tea and coffee. There were groups of different kinds of seating; here a sofa with occasional low tables, there some more business-like tables and chairs, beyond a group of smaller and higher circular tables for standing at. Separating the various areas of seating were a series of tall glazed display cabinets each containing carefully illuminated artefacts.

They sat on the dining chairs around a table already laid with cups and a pot of coffee. As McFadden plonked his hands firmly palm-down on the table, Henshaw and Drake looked at his wrists and then at each other. The cuffs of his shirt were turned over and clipped into place with porcelain cufflinks each marked with a Chinese character.

'We call this the 'Hive,' said McFadden with a sweeping gesture of his right arm, 'it's based on the latest theory about office working patterns. We study each person's pattern of working; whether they spend their time mainly here, or in other parts of the university, out on the road, abroad and so on. Each of us is then classified and given accommodation to suit our needs.'

'Which is your office?' Drake asked.

'I don't have a personal office at all as I'm a 'Nomad' so I am more often out of the building than not, and for that matter more often out of the country. I do not waste space by leaving an empty office behind. I will happily show you around the whole building and explain the theory behind it later. The idea is to combine the art and science of business practice, and to harmonise the values of the cultures of the East and the West.'

Drake felt that the charm of the place was already evaporating and that it might be lost entirely on a tour guided by McFadden. The man had an air of bombast about him; he was a talker rather than a listener. 'I am sure we would enjoy that later, Mr. McFadden. To begin with, could you explain the role of Jimmy

Cheung here? I believe he was about to become Visiting Professor?'

'*Distinguished* Visiting Professor actually. The title is awarded only to the most senior people. It is well understood in Singapore and that part of the world but not normally used here. We have permission to use it from the Senate since it indicates appropriate status in ASEAN where we mostly operate.'

'ASEAN? Can you explain that,' asked Drake.

McFadden let out the sigh of a man who found this kind of ignorance rather tiresome. 'The Association of South East Asian Nations. It's a bit like the European Union only at a much earlier stage of development. It seeks to develop political and economic cooperation for the mutual benefit of the member countries. It does not have the bureaucratic sclerosis of the EU nor do its members have aspirations towards political unity. It was founded by Singapore, Malaysia, Thailand, Indonesia and the Philippines. Other countries with generally smaller economies have since joined, such as Vietnam, Cambodia and some others. It represents a total population of half a billion people so it is a very significant international player and some of these economies have been growing considerably although various difficulties have seen this decline recently. There's a huge amount of business to be done there.'

McFadden sat back and paused as if to see whether his audience was still paying attention. Henshaw thought they could walk around the courtyard once and still find McFadden talking to empty chairs. The one spare chair at the table looked as if it had heard it all before and was thinking much the same thing.

'Malaysia and Singapore are influenced by their past association with Britain and one must remember that Indonesia is actually the fourth largest country in the world. Our job here in SEABU is to assist by enabling opportunities for UK business to develop technologies and skills in ASEAN countries. Jimmy Cheung was of enormous help in making links, introductions and networking for us, particularly in Singapore but also in other countries. He was not only a hugely successful businessman in his own right but also well connected to governments. He was invaluable and his death is a disaster for us. He will be impossible to replace.' Drake thought these comments suggested a concern for Jimmy not much different to the crocodile shedding tears for its prey.

'Could you explain then to a couple of humble police officers why Jimmy Cheung deserved this special title of "Distinguished Visiting Professor"?'

'People in the UK are so isolated. It's too easy to be dismissive of the amazing contributions people from the ASEAN countries have made.' Drake and Henshaw exchanged glances of mock guilt unseen by McFadden who was on autopilot. 'A remarkable change has taken place in Singapore during Jimmy Cheung's lifetime. The Singapore he was taken to as a young boy was a thoroughly lawless place.'

'Wasn't Singapore part of the British Empire?' asked Drake.

'The British totally failed to understand the complex make up of races, religions and cultures they were governing. Within the Chinese community, secret societies ran protection rackets on a grand scale. Then we deserted the country during the Second World War leaving them to the invading Japanese for more than three years.'

'I see.' Drake made a mental note to get some basic history books.

McFadden was still lecturing. 'You'd have thought we'd done enough damage but even after the Japanese surrender we mismanaged the transition to independence with riots between Muslims and Chinese taking place as recently as the fifties. Mostly these were reactions to clumsy British governance.'

'I hadn't realised we made such a mess,' admitted Drake.

'Today it isn't. Singapore is an economically successful country positioned at the cutting edge of modern technology that has also provided extensive infrastructure and housed the great majority of its population. All this has happened since independence from the British in the last thirty-five years. Jimmy Cheung has helped to create that economic and social miracle. It is we who must learn from him, not the other way round.'

Drake decided it was time to end the lecture. 'How much time did Professor Cheung spend here at the University?'

'Not a great deal. He was more useful to us when he was back in our target region. He had only just become DVP and was to come more frequently to lecture and lead seminars.'

'Have you any idea who might have wanted to see Professor Cheung dead?' Drake looked very directly into the blue eyes of the director to see if there was any involuntary response. The face was impassive but, Drake thought, in the calculatingly fixed way of a poker player.

'I've no idea. Very successful men often have enemies.'

'Who were Professor Cheung's enemies, Mr. McFadden?'

'I know of none who would murder him. It was a generic observation, Chief Inspector.' Drake held the silence deliberately for a few seconds, and it worked. 'Unless….' McFadden tailed off into a shrug. 'I am told that most murders are committed by members of the victim's family.'

'Have you any reason to suspect any of Professor Cheung's family?'

'No.' Drake held another silence wondering if perhaps McFadden might mention Sheng Tian but this time to no avail.

'This is a very beautiful building,' said Drake looking around him.

'Very special isn't it?' replied McFadden proudly, 'of course all of this is necessary to do the job. There is nothing lavish or wasted I assure you.'

'Academic friends of mine tell me that universities are not generously provided with funds these days. Deva University, being so young, must find it difficult to raise funds for buildings like this.'

'In this case no. We have many friends in the Far East who are willing to have their names associated with us. There is a list of sponsors in the main entrance. You will see many major industries represented.' Drake thought more 'digging around' was necessary before continuing this line of questioning.

'Thank you Mr. McFadden. I expect we'll want to come to speak with you again in due course but that's all for now. Unless you have anything else to tell us?'

'If I think of anything I'll call you. You are very welcome here at SEABU at any time. We are anxious to see the perpetrator of this awful crime brought to justice. I am away a great deal but my P.A. Sheila Wilkins or my deputy Dr. Elliot will be at your disposal.'

As they began their return journey to the entrance, Drake noticed a surprising display of weapons in the nearest cabinet. McFadden recognised his interest and began another well-rehearsed description.

'There are two themes in these cabinets, both illustrated by artefacts from the Asean region. This one is personal defence and has examples of weapons throughout the ages. It begins with precious examples of the Keris Malay dagger, characteristically having a wavy blade. The cabinets on the other side display items connected with personal communication ranging from early Chinese calligraphic devices such as bamboo brushes, right up the latest personal computers manufactured in Singapore.' Drake's gaze had settled on a cabinet with several pistols, and McFadden moved to stand proudly next to it.

'Various sponsors have lent us items for these cabinets but most of the pistols here are from my collection; shooting and collecting historic pistols is one of my hobbies. I hold a firearms license Chief Inspector so perhaps I should be your chief suspect.'

Drake did not return the smile that McFadden had directed at him to accompany this last remark. 'Obviously you were at the degree ceremony and the reception afterwards in honour of Professor Cheung?'

'Of course.' McFadden quickly returned to his characteristic belligerent stare.

'Were you still there when Professor Cheung left?'

'I had some important business to discuss with the Vice-Chancellor and the Registrar.'

'And that I presume was the last time you saw Jimmy Cheung?'

'Yes.' The voice was unemotional.

'And after that, Mr. McFadden, where did you go next?'

McFadden closed his eyes, apparently replaying the events in his mind. 'I came briefly back to this building, collected some papers and drove to my house on the Wirral.'

'Would your wife be able to confirm what time you arrived home,' asked Henshaw, pencil poised over his notebook.

'Unlikely. I divorced my wife some years ago,' snapped McFadden.

'Thank you, Mr. McFadden,' said Drake as he struggled out of his chair and Henshaw closed his notebook. 'By the way, I could not help but notice your cufflinks.'

'Neat aren't they? Given to me by one of our sponsors. One is my first name and one my second but I have no idea which is which. I might be back to front today.' He growled with laughter at this obviously well rehearsed joke. Drake and Henshaw smiled dutifully.

'OK,' said Drake, shaking McFadden's hand. 'That will be all for now but I am sure we shall want to see you again in due course to follow some of this up.'

Drake was silent, apparently devoting all his energy and attention to the business of walking across the open space in front of the SEABU building. In fact his brain was rehearsing the names of the sponsors listed in the entrance of the building. He did not want Hamish McFadden to see him writing them down. The list was surprising. There were some international companies and many unfamiliar oriental names. One that stood out was Cheung Anglo-Asean Enterprise Pte Ltd. Now that the term ASEAN had been explained to him by McFadden, he had noticed several other companies on the list using it in their name.

'There's some more digging to do there,' he said suddenly. Henshaw looked at Drake's face. That word again. Invariably when Drake talked of 'digging' he thought he was onto something, ahead of the game, in control. Sure enough Drake's face had that look about it. The case had got to him.

'Call Grace; get her to meet us somewhere we can eat. We need a conference.'

'I know the very place, sir. An old school friend of mine runs a pub in Handbridge, and he has a room he will let us use.'

Two notebooks and three pints of beer were on the round table with Henshaw's left foot firmly clamping one of the wrought iron table legs to stop it rocking. The table stood by a window looking into a small tidy rear garden boasting several benches and a solitary children's swing. A large recessed fireplace generated more noise than heat but still managed to warm a settle large enough for two. The walls displayed a selection of hunting scenes. Four irregular oak beams dominated the ceiling, yellowed from years of cigarette smoke. Periodically the room would darken and shake as a bus or lorry passed right outside.

'I don't know about you,' exclaimed Drake, 'I've had my fill of academics for the day. Our Registrar friend, Percival, is certainly full of invented pomp and circumstance with portraits and gowns aplenty. As for Hamish McFadden, I can't say I like the man at all. I bet he's hugely ambitious and doesn't care who he tramples on. He seems to have been very happy to exploit Jimmy Cheung and shows no emotion at all about his demise. A very cold fish.'

'The cufflinks are odd too,' said Henshaw. 'They looked almost identical to the one we found on the bridge.'

'But he claimed they spelt his name and he was wearing two of them. Janet told me that the cufflink we found was printed with the character for good fortune.'

The publican was waiting politely in the background, hopefully holding three copies of the bar meals menu. Grace reported on the pathology report from Professor Wilson and Drake briefed her on their enquiries at the university. Henshaw elaborated from time to time. He was rather pleased when Grace giggled at his impersonation of McFadden.

Grace continued. 'I checked out Dr. Percival's wife to confirm his arrival home after the degree congregation; a timid little housewife who doesn't look as if she sees the light of day. Surly, unhelpful and oddly unsupportive but I think it's just the way she is. She said that Percival has no regular routine. She has no idea what time it was that night, and as she put it, she doesn't keep records.'

'Well if I was married,' spluttered Henshaw through his beer, 'I'd hope my wife could do a better job at providing an alibi than that.'

'I don't think a wife's alibi makes a great deal of difference one way or another,' said Drake. 'Still it seems odd that she is so indifferent about it. Any more news, Grace?'

'This is the anonymous email that I called you about, sir,' said Grace handing the computer printout to Drake.

'Mmmm,' groaned Drake, 'McFadden and his cronies at SEABU have made enemies. I'm not surprised. The man seems a bit of a bully to me. I think we have to take such things with a large pinch of salt unless we can get to the actual source. Is that all, Grace?'

'One final thing; the Hanko, that cylinder thing found in Jimmy's pocket. Apparently they're really struggling to translate the characters on it. They reckon it's some form of his name. They are pretty sure it is a personal signature stamp.'

'OK,' drawled Drake, 'it's time to ask his daughter about that.'

A warbling sound interrupted the conversation. Two fumbled for their phones; Drake sat back wearing a smug expression.

'Yes, speaking,' said Henshaw, standing up and walking away from the table. The table rocked and Drake's beer spilled as Grace dived to save the notebooks from flooding.

'Now that is interesting!' said Henshaw returning a few minutes later. 'That was Sally Brown. It seems that after we left, Dr. Percival began to replay Jimmy Cheung's degree ceremony in his mind, and he couldn't remember seeing Sheng Tian at the ceremony or the reception. Then Sally Brown rang to say they have checked with their ceremonies office. Sheng Tian did not accept the invitation. He was not at either event!

'What's the significance of that?' asked Grace.

'I'd say it's very odd!' exclaimed Henshaw, 'your father comes all the way from Singapore to visit your university and get an honorary degree and you don't even go to the ceremony!'

'Well there could be many plausible explanations that we can't think of right now,' said Drake cautiously, 'but one more thing is definitely odd. I specifically asked Sheng Tian where he was after the ceremony. He told me he was working in his office. It is curious that he didn't tell me then that he had not been to the ceremony?'

'Seems like he didn't want us to know that for some reason then,' said Grace. 'Of course he still doesn't know that we have heard about his argument earlier with his father.'

'Exactly,' said Drake emphatically, 'and that we know he was in the university earlier. It certainly needs a bit more digging here.' Henshaw grinned at Grace. He had already warned her about the 'digging' word. She acknowledged by tapping his knee under the table and there was a telltale shake of the beer in the glasses above. Henshaw froze while he contemplated the significance of Grace touching his knee but Drake was still in full flow.

'Each time we have talked to Sheng Tian so far he has escaped before I have finished with him. I want a proper go at him.'

'I guess he must be our prime suspect so far then?' asked Grace.

'We shouldn't be thinking of anyone as a suspect in that way yet, Grace. That can be very dangerous and close your mind to other possibilities. But we certainly need to get answers to some pretty obvious questions. Henshaw, will you call him and ask him to come into the station tomorrow morning please. Make it absolutely clear that we are asking him to do that of his own free will but that there are a number of matters we would like to clear up. That should set him thinking. Grace, get search orders in place for his home, and ask Sally Brown if we can search his office. I might have another word with Janet. Now where's that publican friend of yours Henshaw? That whiff of pies cooking in the kitchen has made me even hungrier.'

Drake limped along Foregate Street head down but as he passed through the gate in the city walls, the ornate Victoria Clock tower above drew his eyes upwards. People walking along the historic city wall over the gate seemed to pause under it apparently unaware of the glory above their heads as they looked down along the street. What would Cynthia have said about this?

Her impatient voice chided him gently. This one device provided a unique landmark by which you could navigate, conveniently, told citizens the time of day and allowed pedestrians safely to cross the street below. It also neatly separated Foregate from Eastgate, enabling them both to develop their own individual character. Drake sniffed an acknowledgement of Cynthia's spectral lecture. He added a confident note of his own that while the clock was Victorian the much plainer arch supporting it must be Georgian. Actually he had cheated by looking this up in a guide at the hotel but he was so smug about being able to recognise the stylistic differences that he forgave himself this minor deceit.

The hotel doorman pulled the door open for him, greeting him by name, an impressive personal touch that probably required a deal of practice. This operation needed careful timing. Janet must not be able to tell Sheng Tian about the interview so he must be already waiting at the police station under supervision. The whole process that morning had to run like clockwork.

'Good Morning, Chief Inspector. Please come in; I have called for Chinese tea to be brought up. How are you getting on with your investigations?'

'At this stage we do not have any clear suspect, any motive or any weapon. We do have some lines of enquiry that we are working on. This is really just a brief visit as I was passing. How are you feeling now, Janet?' She still looked like a woman grieving and the question seemed to upset her.' She smiled but did not reply. A knock at the door heralded the arrival of a maid with a tray of tiny white teacups with a squat matching teapot.

'Could I ask you about your brother? I am told he did not attend the honorary degree ceremony for your father. Is that true?' Janet looked up from pouring the tea.

'Yes certainly this is true. He is a man of principle and as a holder of higher degrees I understand he resents them being given away to others.'

'Even to his father?'

'I tried hard to persuade him to come. It upset my father but I could not get Sheng Tian to change his mind. He can be very stubborn. He is just like his father.....was.' The last word came only after a painful hesitation. 'Tell me, Chief Inspector, why does this matter. Surely it has nothing to do with my father's death?'

'Probably not but we still do not really know what is important and what is not at this stage.'

'Chief Inspector, if you are suggesting that Sheng Tian may have had something to do with the murder then I can tell you categorically it is not the case. He is a good kind man. I do not believe he has ever hurt anyone.'

'How can you be so sure? Surely your brother was not here at the time?'

'No of course not, I did not see him that day. He may sometimes be difficult and stubborn and sometimes even angry but I assure you he did not kill his father. Like any son, he wanted his father's approval. Sadly the father also desperately wanted respect from his son. Neither of them could tell the other, and now they will never will.' She paused reflectively for a moment. 'I think that may be why Sheng Tian is angry now. He is angry with himself. I also feel a little angry; I should be able to help you more.'

'When we found your father, he had virtually no possessions with him,' continued Drake. 'He was not wearing a jacket and his trouser pockets still had the tailor's stitching across them. The jacket has been found in the University. We also found quite an expensive camera around his neck so it seems unlikely to have been attempted theft.'

'Yes, Chief Inspector. I found his wallet and credit cards here in the hotel,' said Janet.

Drake nodded and continued. 'In one trouser pocket was a small case with a stamp. Our experts tell us it is probably a Japanese Hanko. Can you explain this?'

Janet looked both angry and puzzled. 'Really? I had no idea. I do wish he would not carry that thing. He has…had, a small collection of them. They were around as long as I can remember. I'm sorry to say they are made from ivory. Making these things is banned now in Singapore.'

'Why do you refer to it as "that thing", Miss Cheung? You obviously do not like the object but it seems harmless enough?'

'Harmless perhaps but it is Japanese. We do not like Japanese things.'

'Why is that?'

'You do not live in a country that was occupied by the Japanese, or you would not ask this question,' Janet almost spat out these words.

'You mean the Second World War? That is a very long time ago now and you surely cannot remember it yourself?' Janet did not reply but sat motionless with the blackest expression that Drake had seen on her delicate face.

'So why would he be carrying the Hanko?' asked Drake.

'This I do not know.' Again there was a pause that intrigued Drake. 'Maybe he considered it lucky.'

'Thank you Miss Cheung. I am sorry to keep troubling you. I would be grateful if you would not mention this conversation to anyone, even Sheng Tian.'

Janet frowned. 'I will do as you wish Chief Inspector. If you have finished with the seal, I would like it returned.'

'Of course, in due course but why would you want it?'

'It must be destroyed. It has my father's name. Effectively it is his signature. That is the traditional way after death. A Hanko must be destroyed; in the wrong hands it could be misused.'

Grace Hepple stood in the open doorway of Dr Cheung Sheng Tian's university office. Mr. Watson the Director of Facilities had accompanied her to avoid rumours spreading through the portering staff. She sensed his sweaty body hovering behind her.

'Thank you Mr. Watson. I may be here some time. Perhaps I could call you when I have finished so that someone could lock the door again?' Watson reluctantly waddled off down the corridor, pulling out his mobile phone, no doubt to report back to the Registrar.

Although it was still early in the morning the room was stiflingly hot. Grace pulled a cord and the blind rolled up with an angry rattle to reveal a late summer sun blazing over the building on the far side of the 'quadrangle'. The sun had been taking advantage of the east-facing window from long before Grace had even got up. She opened a window and pulled the blind down again to obstruct any prying eyes as she went about her business.

She painstakingly removed every book on the first shelf, examined it and returned it to its original position. Getting bored with this, she turned her attention to the filing cabinet, which was obligingly unlocked. Grace sampled, at first methodically but increasingly randomly. The top drawer contained mostly dry reports of what had probably been extremely heated university meetings about nothing very much. The lower drawer was full of academic articles. She couldn't make much sense of the first three so guessed she wasn't going to do any better with the remainder. The furniture and silk hangings were much more interesting, just as Drake had said. After another hour of equally fruitless activity Grace sat in Sheng Tian's chair and helped the limited breeze from the window to cross her face. She desperately wanted to find that piece of killer evidence that would advance the case. It was not going to happen here.

The interview room was not designed for walking but the Singaporean was doing his best, repeatedly pacing up and down. The uniformed constable told Drake that he had been getting increasingly agitated.

'Dr. Cheung, I am so sorry to have kept you waiting. This city is not built for the motorcar and it seems worse than ever this morning,' started Drake. Sheng Tian grunted as Drake sat in the chair across the small table from him.

'Dr. Cheung, when we met the other day in your office, I asked you where you were after the degree ceremony.' Sheng Tian nodded. 'Would you like to answer that question again for me please?' A look of bewilderment crossed Sheng Tian's face.

'I was working in my office at the university.'

'And you have no way of proving that to me since there are no witnesses.'

'No.'

'Why you didn't tell me that you never even went to the degree ceremony.' Sheng Tian shuffled his feet under the table.

'You not ask me that.'

'Don't you think it's a little odd not to tell me in response to that question?'

'I never intended to go to the degree ceremony. It was false. I do not approve of such things.'

'So if you were not at the ceremony and you worked in your office afterwards, when did you last see your father?'

'I can't remember.'

'I find that hard to believe. Surely when your father was murdered you would automatically think back to the last time you saw him?'

'It might have been the day before.'

'Dr. Cheung, we have reason to believe you saw your father on the morning before the degree ceremony and that you had a serious argument with him.'

The defiant expression slowly drained from Sheng Tian's face and he held his head in his hands. It was several seconds before he spoke. 'We argued about the degree congregation.'

'My understanding is that the argument was rather violent and there was a lot of shouting.'

'Shouting, maybe a bit, violence, no,' spat Sheng Tian.

Was the degree ceremony that important?'

'It was to my father.'

'Why have you concealed all this from me, Dr. Cheung?'

'Because I think you have me on your lists of suspects, I have no alibi and if you knew we argued it would look bad.'

'You're right; it does look bad.' Drake's phone rang and he decided to leave Sheng Tian to stew gently for a while under the gaze of the duty constable.

A net curtain twitched in the next-door front window. Henshaw led his small team up the step drive to Sheng Tian's house. A larger than average semi-detached affair, it was set back and high above the Whitchurch Road almost in the village of Christleton. The police locksmith flashed a supercilious smile to the others having opened the front door in record time. He was dispatched to do the same to the double wooden garage doors, while Henshaw went inside with Katie Lamb. Now over the shock of finding her first dead body she could barely conceal her excitement at being at the centre of the action. Henshaw took the ground floor and dispatched Katie up the carpeted staircase to explore the three bedrooms and a bathroom.

The house exuded affluence and good taste with a mixture of western and oriental furniture. The landscape paintings on the walls and the china ornaments were exclusively Chinese. The whole place was clean and tidy. On the ground floor were two sizeable living rooms. A large curved bay window in the front room looked down over the road. The room to the rear had a French window into the garden. Alongside this was a generous kitchen with another outside door. The locksmith quickly reappeared through this door having entered the garage that ran the whole length of the house to the side. Henshaw could hear Katie Lamb moving methodically around in the bedrooms above.

The locksmith reported that the garage was empty and he assumed that the owner had gone out in his car. Henshaw nodded an acknowledgement without taking his eye off a beautifully crafted wooden box on a shelf over the empty fireplace in the rear room. It was made from what looked like a polished hardwood, the corners were elaborately tongued together and the lid was decorated with inlaid mother-of-pearl. On the front was a silver clasp held by a padlock.

'How about that?'

'Oddly it may prove more difficult than the doors,' admitted the locksmith. 'It's very small. I could easily break it.' He set to work and Henshaw continued with a more systematic search. Constable Katie Lamb appeared from her search upstairs to report she had found nothing of interest and definitely no cufflinks of any description.

'What did you say a minute ago?' asked Henshaw suddenly to the locksmith.

'This lock is small and fiddly and easily broken.'

'No. Before that, about the garage. You said the car was out.'

'Yes sir. The garage is empty.'

'But what makes you think he has a car?' asked Henshaw.

'I dunno I just assumed I suppose. No wait a minute; I trod in some fresh oil on the floor,' said the locksmith.

'I have the same problem,' said Henshaw. 'My sump leaks overnight but Sheng Tian arrived at the station in a taxi. I saw him standing outside paying the fare.'

They went out and examined the oil patch and Henshaw noticed a faint smell of petrol.

'I couldn't say for sure it was dropped last night,' said the locksmith. 'It wouldn't be more than a few days old.' Henshaw phoned Drake.

'Sorry about that,' said Drake bringing in two cups of coffee and placing one in front of Sheng Tian.

'Tell me, Dr. Cheung, do you own a car?'

'No, why?'

'You have quite a journey from where you live to get to the University, and you must be able to afford one on your salary.'

'I did have a car but I have decided to sell it and use public transport.'

'When did you sell it?'

'Last week.'

'Was that to a dealer or a private sale?'

'Private.'

'I assume we could establish that and that you could give us details of the new owner? Just write the registration number here for me.' Drake handed him a small notebook and ballpoint pen.

Sheng Tian was flustered now. The wind had gone out of his sails and his hand shook as he wrote. 'Chief Inspector, I have a right to be told if you are arresting me, and if so why?'

'No Sheng Tian you are voluntarily helping us with our enquiries. You came here of your own accord and are free to leave at any time.'

'I wish to leave now please. You should concentrate on catching my father's murderer instead of persecuting me.'

'Is there anyone you suggest we should be investigating?'

'Not for me to say but I suspect the SEABU people. Hamish McFadden is not all he seems, Chief Inspector. I have never trusted him. My father did and perhaps he was mistaken.'

'Ah yes, Dr Cheung, you sent us an email about that.' Sheng Tian looked startled and puzzled.

'No, I sent no email. What is this email?'

'We received an email saying something very similar Dr. Cheung, I thought perhaps you had sent it.' Drake thought his eyes revealed a genuine puzzlement.

'No. I know nothing of an email.'

‘Well can you give me any more to go on?’ asked Drake. ‘Why would Hamish McFadden want to see your father dead?’

‘I have no idea; maybe my father discovered something he was not supposed to but I am not doing your job. It is not for me to say more. I wish to go now.’

‘Of course but I should be grateful if you would please stay in Chester or notify us before you intend to travel anywhere. We may need to talk to you again.’

The padlock sprang open with a clunk and the locksmith stood back and winked at Henshaw who carefully lifted the silver clasp and opened the wooden box. Henshaw, Constable Katie Lamb and the locksmith all stared open mouthed. The box was lined with deep blue plush velvet and nestling neatly into this was a pistol. It was old, weary from use even. It was an unusual rather spindly affair with a thin barrel about 10 centimetres long, projecting at a sharp angle from a square chunky section behind, all fashioned in a blueish metal. The grip had a diagonal chequered appearance with wooden side faces. There was a serial number stamped on it.

Henshaw photographed the gun in its wooden box, put on his rubber gloves and lifted it out carefully. He took several more pictures from various angles, and then returned the gun to its velvet nest. The locksmith tinkered for a while and pronounced the padlock closed.

# 6 - Iron

Grace Hepple was reporting on her inconclusive search of Sheng Tian's university office when Henshaw burst in.

'I think we should have detained Sheng Tian,' he snapped. 'We found a gun in his house.' Drake frowned.

'So where is it?'

'You told me to leave no sign of our search.' The furrow across Drake's forehead deepened. A constable entered with prints from the Henshaw's camera and laid them out on the table.

'Where did you find this?' demanded Drake studying the pictures.

'In a box on a shelf in the rear living room.' Henshaw pointed to a picture of bookshelves.

'So the gun wasn't hidden?'

'It was hidden in a locked box.'

'This looks more like a collector's item than a working handgun,' said Drake, 'and the box adds to that impression; perhaps it's a precious antique.'

'It looks in perfect working order and could still be used to kill someone.'

'I could email these images to our firearms experts,' suggested Grace Hepple breaking the febrile atmosphere.

'OK get identification,' said Drake.

Henshaw was not finished. 'Sheng Tian fits the description we have from the hotel doorman, and for that matter the sightings you had, from the bridge and the hotel room.'

Drake frowned. 'He's not likely to be the man I saw from the hotel window. It was too soon after he left and too bulky but for the time being we should put Janet Cheung under protective surveillance. Sheng Tian seems to have a temper. If there is some dreadful family dispute behind all this, we would look pretty stupid if we hadn't taken precautions. I just don't see anything even remotely like a case against him, not yet anyway.'

Drake stood up preventing a riposte from Henshaw. 'Now I might go down to have another look at that bridge. Henshaw, check on the progress made by the divers and join me there in a couple of hours before we see the girls who found the body.'

The swish of passing traffic on the main road below almost masked the chime from deep inside the house. On her way to pick up the two girls and their mothers, Grace had stopped off at the house next to Sheng Tian's. The address database indicated a single occupant. A vague shape moved through the obscured glass in the front door followed by twitch of the curtains in the front room bay window. A more body-like silhouette appeared in the hallway and it eventually opened the door on a short security chain. Part of a small wrinkled face appeared only just above the door handle.

'Yes?' said the face in a questioning sort of way.

'Mrs. Tranter?' asked Grace.

'Yes,' said the face tentatively.

'Detective Sergeant Grace Hepple, Mrs. Tranter.' Grace held her warrant card up to the face. 'There is nothing to be concerned about. We are making a few enquiries. Could you spare me a few minutes to talk please.'

'Oooh yes.' The face glowed with enthusiasm. 'Come in dear, don't stand out there.' In contradiction to the invitation the door closed and, after some shaky rattling, reopened to reveal not just the face but the rest of Mrs. Tranter who had set off unsteadily down the hallway muttering about cups of tea. She waved a walking stick at the rear room and disappeared through a door into what Grace presumed was a kitchen. On the wall at the end of the hall was a pair of tubular doorbell chimes descending nearly three feet from the yellowing Bakelite box that held the hammers. Much of the house harked back to the fifties, and Grace guessed its owner had lived there ever since.

A musty odour left little doubt that the windows were mostly kept closed. An arched-top mantle clock over the fireplace ticked a gentle duet with a television whispering in the corner. Crossing the room Grace looked through the French window into the back garden. In truth this was not easy. There were locks on the doors and bolts into the frames with a security grill across the windows. The garden was neat and tidy in an old-fashioned conventional sort of way.

'Was them your friends that was poking around next door then?' Mrs. Tranter rattled her way into the back room with a tray, two cups, a pot of tea and two walking sticks. Grace hopped across the room to help and put the tray on a square coffee table beside the high-backed chair that was pointed at the television. The television and the coffee table shared a common passion for the crocheted mats draped over them.

'My grandmother did crochet, Mrs. Tranter,' said Grace.

'I don't do as much now as I did. My hands shake you know.' She held them out for Grace to inspect. Her joints looked arthritic and there was a distinct shake in her right hand even though Mrs. Tranter gripped its wrist with her left. 'Fancy you being a policeman, dear,' exclaimed Mrs. Tranter as she slid onto the high-backed chair. 'You don't look a bit like one but you can never tell these days can you?' Grace smiled. Mrs. Tranter picked up the remote control in her shaky hand and started waving it around the room though generally in the direction of the television that had so far been playing to a disinterested audience of empty chairs.

'We always turn Telly off when we have visitors don't we,' muttered Mrs. Tranter as if to pacify the machine. At last one of her waves was good enough and the television obligingly shut down. 'I'm by myself now, and it's company for me but we always turn it off when we have visitors. So was it your friends next door then?'

'Do you know your next door neighbour, Mrs. Tranter?'

'Not really no dear. He's Chinese you know!' these words were uttered leaning forward with a hushed and confidential voice. 'Keeps himself to himself he does. He's very polite, beautifully spoken he is; must be nicely brought up. I see him come and go. Normally I don't hear him though. He's very quiet. Not like that the other day, now that was a commotion. Standing in the front drive shouting he was. They were taking his car away. There were two of them; big burly fellows and this woman. She was trying to calm him down I think. They backed the car down the drive and he ran after them shouting and banging on the window of it with his fist.'

A swan family paddled sedately downstream undisturbed by the more frantic efforts of a couple of rowers practicing racing starts. Drake meandered along the Groves. The rowers' voices carried across the water shouting mutual encouragement. Nearby, rather noisier swans were being fed by two shrieking children, their father providing bread from a plastic bag. The swans became a touch too enthusiastic for the younger child. One spread its wings and rose almost out of the water. The poor kid stepped back in alarm and dropped his ice cream. Howls and floods of tears brought the mother scurrying across from an iron bench where she was reading in the forlorn hope that her partner would entertain the children for a chapter or so. She gave the crying infant looks of sympathy and her partner stares of disappointment. He took to showing the older child how to skim stones across the water. The swans, sensing their free meal was over, joined the other group way out in the middle of the river. Drake's gaze followed them and on up to the deck of the bridge where the murder had been committed.

'She's over 80 years old sir and as handsome as the day she was opened. I call her my Iron Lady.'

Drake spun round to see a weather-beaten man wearing a flat cap at a slight angle, oil-stained jeans and a check shirt under an unbuttoned black leather waistcoat. He gave off a slight smell of diesel.

'Designed by Mr Charles Greenwood, City Engineer and Surveyor to replace one that lasted a mere 50 years, which was held up by iron chains. This one has wire steel cables, with a main span of 275 feet and was officially opened on 18th April 1923. We hold a sort of anniversary party for her every year on board the boat and a special cruise in her honour, we do sir.' Drake could now see the pleasure cruiser moored against a jetty downstream of the bandstand. 'Next trip to Eccleston Ferry and the Iron Bridge leaving in ten minutes; round trip about two hours.'

Drake's dismissive wave got enough of the message across to the boatman who turned his attention to the family deserted by the swans. Drake ambled upstream as far as the steps leading to the bridge. He turned and set off across the bridge towards the side of the river where he and Henshaw had parked the car the first morning he arrived in Chester. The wooden deck echoed back the noise of each step and the bridge shuffled irritably.

He reached the centre of the span. He could tell this by the way the catenary suspension cables on either side had curved their way down almost to meet the balustrades. The remnants of the chalk marks were just visible on the wooden deck where the scene of crime team had drawn around Jimmy Cheung's body. It had lain slumped against the diamond lattice balustrade on the downstream side of the bridge exactly in the centre of the span. Drake peered over and looked down at the River Dee washing its way quietly on its journey seawards. The water skipped and gurgled at Drake mocking his inability to solve a puzzle that it knew the answer to perfectly well.

Upstream the river curved gently out of sight as it came down through the town. Spacious homes built by past generations of gentry sat high on the banks to the left. It was picture postcard stuff. The pleasure cruiser was setting off from its mooring at the Groves and steadily making its way under the bridge. He must take that trip some time.

The very centre of the span! What was the significance of that? It had not been so obvious when he first visited the bridge because the scene-of-crime tent masked the curve of the cables. Perhaps it meant nothing. There was something else struggling to find its way out of his mind. There was something that did not quite make sense.

'The divers have drawn a complete blank, sir.' Drake looked round to see Henshaw. 'The mud on the bottom is all stirred up from recent rain and the river is flowing quicker than you might think. There's little chance of finding anything.' Drake looked blankly back him saying nothing. Henshaw recognised that look. The old devil was working something out, he could tell. It was pointless asking him what it was until Drake had sorted it out to his own satisfaction.

'Grace has arranged for the two girls who found the body to come to the station. It was a struggle; one of the mothers is a real busybody.' He looked at his watch. 'We have about an hour and a half before they arrive.'

'Excellent,' said Drake, 'I want to take the walk from here back to the hotel.' The two men set off along the bridge in the direction of the city. Passing between the twin towers they continued along the wooden deck over its shorter span, sloping gently down to meet the high ground behind the Groves. From there a flight of steps up to a footpath took them up past the park on the right and a ruined church on the left. Henshaw pointed out a curious coffin high up in the gable wall of the ruins let into the stone in a vertical position. 'Poor sod', growled Drake, 'wouldn't be surprised if that wasn't to be my fate. Not allowed to lie down even in death.'

Skirting around the uncovered remains of the Roman amphitheatre, they turned right up a side street and soon found themselves back on Eastgate by the hotel. Drake looked at his watch and noted the time. The walk had taken less than ten minutes.

The two girls were sitting in the lounge at the police station. Grace would have preferred Drake to see them at home since they were only fifteen. Drake reckoned that they were more likely to open up together than separately. As usual, he was right. All the way there in the car, Rebecca's mother, Mrs. Evans, had complained at the treatment they were receiving, how traumatised the girls were, and how they shouldn't have to go through it all again. Deborah's mother had obviously heard all this before and sat quietly in the back looking out of the window holding her daughter's hand. The two girls nudged each other and smirked.

'This is Chief Inspector Drake, who is in charge of the investigation,' said Grace. Mrs. Evans repeated all her complaints to Drake. He smiled, bowed slightly and allowed her to generally run out of steam.

'I do understand that this is difficult for you,' he said eventually, looking at the two girls. 'It must have been a very nasty shock and I am sorry we have to ask you to remember it all again.' Deborah nodded, swallowed hard, and the giggles drained out of her. Rebecca sat looking around the room wearing a sulky, confident expression. Drake guessed she would use such a look on aspiring boyfriends to test them out. He nodded to Grace to begin the questioning.

'Can you please tell us again what happened that evening?' Mrs. Evans took a deep breath ready to set off again and Drake held up a hand to stop her.

'Becky, why don't you start?' said Grace.'

'There's not much to say really,' said Becky, looking at her friend as she spoke. 'We'd been at a late rehearsal for the school choir and we was just going home like normal, only a bit late; well a lot late really.' There was a hint of a giggle from both girls.

'We always walk across the bridge; we can get a better bus that way,' added Deborah in a tiny voice.

'As we was going across we saw this man; well to start with we didn't know what it was, we thought he was a wino. You get them there sometimes,' said Becky.

‘There’s one we sort of know. He’s often there, Terry they call him,’ added Deborah.

‘So when he didn’t move,’ continued Becky, ‘I sort of pushed him with my foot, only gentle like; honest I didn’t move him. Then we saw it wasn’t Terry.’

‘And he was dead,’ sobbed Deborah. Grace held Deborah around the shoulders and patted her. Drake took up the questioning.

‘Becky, you said you didn’t move him. Are you sure about that?’

‘Of course she’s sure,’ interrupted Mrs. Evans. ‘What sort of a question is that? Now look here….’

‘Mrs. Evans, you are very welcome to be here but I must ask you to allow Becky to answer the questions herself.’ Becky looked at Deborah, who burst into tears again. Drake allowed Grace to calm things down and then began on another direction that he knew had to be covered.

‘There is another possible explanation of events that I must put to you. It is that the victim was trying to molest you; that you fought him off and in the struggle the gun went off and you both ran away.’

‘That’s tantamount to accusing them of murder,’ screamed Mrs. Evans.

‘It could easily have happened by accident in which case it would not be murder,’ said Drake as sympathetically as he knew how.

‘No it’s not true, we didn’t kill him, honest,’ said Becky, while Deborah burst into tears again. Becky turned to her mother and repeated her denial. Mrs. Evans sat nodding her head in a told-you-so sort of way. Becky turned back to Deborah.

‘Tell him, Debs. We didn’t kill him did we. He was already dead. We never saw no gun.’ Deborah’s tears subsided to sobs and Drake paused to allow more comforting from Grace. Eventually it was the sobbing Deborah who spoke first.

‘We got to tell them, Becks. We got to tell them now.’ Drake nodded to Grace.

'Tell us what, Becky?' she probed.

Becky looked at Deborah and then at her mother. Finally she started speaking again. 'Well it wasn't quite like we said. He was actually leaning over the side of the bridge so we thought it was Terry being sick. We've seen him do that before. So Debs shouted at him but he didn't move. I did touch him with my foot, well I suppose really I kicked him; just gently like on his leg. He started sliding and me and Debs caught him.'

'It was awful,' sobbed Deborah, he fell over me and he was staring at me.'

'We couldn't hold him so he sort of collapsed onto the floor but his neck was caught. His camera was twisted round the bit of the bridge, the handrail like, and he was hanging by his neck. Debs was screaming that it was strangling him, and I pulled it over his head and he fell down. Then we realised he was dead, so we got the camera out of the side of the bridge where it was stuck and stuffed it back round his neck. Then we legged it.'

'We didn't kill him. We didn't. We didn't,' sobbed Deborah again.

'You should have told me all this before, Becky,' shouted Mrs. Evans.

'Becky and Deborah, listen to me carefully,' said Drake firmly. 'I do not think that you killed him. He was already dead; he had been shot.'

'We saw all this blood and I thought we'd choked him and he was spewing it,' said Becky.

'Did either of you notice a cufflink lying around on the bridge?' asked Drake changing the subject.

'What's that when it's about then?' asked Becky cheekily.

'Men use them to tie their shirt sleeves together,' said Grace showing the girls a photograph.

'Nope didn't see no cufflink,' said Becky looking at it and sniffing. Deborah shook her head silently.

'All very dramatic but does it change anything?' asked Henshaw after they had gone.

'It might,' said Drake cautiously. 'Maybe the camera didn't get tangled at all; perhaps it was tied over the handrail to hold him in place.'

'That would enable the murderer to escape without appearing to leave a dead body behind,' added Grace.

'Exactly,' said Drake. 'That could be why no one saw our murderer running away. Just shot him while he was leaning over the rail taking a picture, tied the camera up and walked off calmly. Who knows, perhaps many people passed noticing only a man leaning over the rail. That stainless steel camera is square, an ideal object to use for the purpose. It would lock nicely like a toggle and hold the strap tight around the body. He was a short slim man, I am sure you could make his body stay that way. Even so…' Grace and Henshaw waited for the next sentence but it didn't come.

'Have we got the pictures off the camera?' asked Grace.

'I'm not sure what they will tell us,' answered Henshaw as he went off to get the technician to print copies of them.

'What have you discovered Grace?' asked Drake.

'Mrs. Tranter, the next door neighbour, obviously doesn't know Sheng Tian at all well but being an old-fashioned sort of soul she is suspicious of him because he is Chinese. Sheng Tian definitely did have a car and very recently. She thought it was a very expensive one; we are tracking it down from records at DVLA. Three people, two men and a woman, came and took it away the other day and she thought Sheng Tian was arguing with them and trying to stop them.'

'I wonder,' reflected Drake. 'Maybe it was being repossessed. Perhaps Sheng Tian has got money problems.'

'That occurred to me too,' said Grace. I have set some checks going with banks and finance companies. HQ said they should be able to trace it from the registration number.'

Henshaw had returned by now and overheard the last part of the conversation.

'So Sheng Tian argued with his father, was in debt, probably would have come into an inheritance and has no alibi,' summarised Henshaw.

'It's the beginnings of a case to be sure,' said Drake cautiously. 'Keep a watch on him, Henshaw. Now what about this cufflink? Janet tells me Jimmy never wore cufflinks and then we see very similar ones on McFadden's shirt. Janet says the one we found says "good fortune" and McFadden claims his have his names on them.'

'So was our cufflink worn by the murderer and torn off by Jimmy when he was attacked,' speculated Grace.

'There's no evidence of a scuffle,' said Drake. 'The lack of finger prints is puzzling.'

'If McFadden was the murderer and had lost a cufflink, surely he wouldn't wear another similar pair to be interviewed by us?' chimed Henshaw.

'Something doesn't add up,' admitted Drake. 'What have you found Henshaw?'

'There are pictures in the city then half a dozen pictures of the bridge and a couple of views down the river,' said Henshaw. 'We're getting them printed.'

'This is Dave, our technician,' said Henshaw, introducing a young man in a dark blue overall entering the room and nodding.

'Technician!' exclaimed Drake, 'I didn't know we had one here.'

'Well sort of,' said Henshaw, drawing the young man forward. 'He is on a basic forensic science grade so really we should call him a scientist. He started with us straight from school on a youth employment scheme and he's managed to make himself so useful that we've kept him on.'

By now Dave was nodding even more ostentatiously. 'But you can't call me a scientist,' he said sulkily, 'scientists have degrees and I don't. They wear white coats and I've got this blue overall.'

'Let's not go into all that again just now,' snapped Henshaw.

'All what?' Drake sensed one of those delightfully trivial spats about uniforms.

'I have been hoping that the police would sponsor me to go to university to do a science degree,' said Dave very loudly.

'Well do a good job for me on this case and I will put a word in for you. Now let me see these pictures.' Dave spread the prints on the table.

'They don't seem to tell us anything,' said Henshaw.

'Maybe *they* don't but all the same I wonder?' Drake tailed off into silence again and the others sat waiting for him to continue. 'Doesn't it occur to you that it's odd that Jimmy Cheung had just come from his degree ceremony and there are no pictures of that on the camera?'

'What are you suggesting, sir?' asked Henshaw.

'I don't quite know yet. I think we need to do some more digging. Dave, can you see if you can discover any way of telling when these photographs were actually taken. We are assuming that Jimmy Cheung had taken them just before he was killed. It would be good to have that confirmed. Grace, see if you can track down Professor Mallory who prepared the honorary degree citation He must have done more research on Jimmy Cheung to write all that. It's a long shot but worth it.'

# 7 - Brass

There was silence as Drake read his copy of the fax from the firearms expert for the second time. Pictures of the pistol lay on the desk in front of him. Grace was busy sending a copy of the report to Professor Wilson.

Fax received 9:38  Monday 18 Sept 2000

This is an example of the Japanese Army Nambu Type 14 pistol that was standard issue in the Second World War. It was designed by General Kijiro Nambu around 1925 (hence the name). The type 14 designation refers to the year of its original manufacture corresponding with the 14th year of the emperor of the time. It is a recoil-operated, locked breech, semi-automatic pistol using a peculiar type of 8mm bottlenecked brass ammunition with 8 rounds held in a single column magazine in the handle. Although superficially this pistol appears similar to the more-well known Luger Parabellum pistol of the time, it actually uses quite different mechanisms. Although it was accurate it had low power and was not popular. However the Nambu had previously always been used by Japanese officers as a symbol of loyalty as opposed to better foreign alternatives.

It was thought to be suitable for close range fighting in forested theatres such as those often encountered by the Japanese Army in its South East Asia campaigns of the Second World War. This one is an early version; later models had an enlarged trigger guard to allow for gloves to be worn in cold climate arenas. The 8mm brass ammunition is virtually unique to this pistol so if we can find some at a scene of crime we stand a very good chance of making a firm identification. These pistols are now collectable though this version was made in such large quantities that even a good example such as this is unlikely to fetch more than a few hundred pounds. Its predecessors, the so-called 'Papa Nambu' and 'Baby Nambu' had much shorter production runs and can sell for well over £1,000.

'Notice that bit about low power, sir?' said Grace to Drake. 'Professor Wilson made some references to low levels of wound damage in his report and I want to see if he thinks this pistol would be capable of producing the effects he identified.' Drake spoke quietly.

'I think some pistols displayed in the SEABU building were similar. We even had a little lecture from McFadden about his collection of historic pistols. I can't quite see what the connection might be here but it certainly seems odd. Perhaps Henshaw will find something during his visit today.'

'Mr. McFadden is overseas at the moment,' the SEABU receptionist said. 'Could his deputy, Dr. Elliot help?' Henshaw nodded.

'I'll see if I can track Dr. Elliot down.' While he waited, Henshaw made a list of the names of SEABU sponsors on the wall in the entrance. This was all that Drake had asked for but Henshaw was anxious to make some more progress so starting with a new member of staff was worth a try.

'Mr. Henshaw?'

'Henshaw turned round surprised to see a short woman standing next to him. Her blond hair streaked with ginger wisps was swept back into a bun. A pair of red-rimmed spectacles appeared too large for her stern face. She was wearing a plain black suit over a white blouse and flat shoes that accentuated her lack of height. Everything about her was tidy, perhaps obsessionally so. She spoke with an American accent. It was a gentle twang, definitely not New York or the deep south; somewhere round Massachusetts, New Hampshire or perhaps Maine.

'I'm Dr. Marcia Elliot. I am the deputy director of SEABU.' Her tone could be interpreted as impatient, certainly unwelcoming. So far the SEABU world had seemed rather macho and Henshaw had automatically assumed Dr. Elliot would be male. He guessed that this was now apparent and that Dr. Elliot was the sort of woman to disapprove of such chauvinism.

'Could we go somewhere to talk confidentially, Miss… Dr. Elliot?'

'Perhaps you could give me some indication of the nature of your business with Mr. McFadden?'

Henshaw pulled out his warrant card and lowered his voice. 'It's in connection with the murder of Jimmy Cheung.'

'I see. Come this way.' She strode off down the sunlit corridor followed by Henshaw while the receptionist strained her neck to follow their progress. They passed sculptures and trees in the courtyard to one side and the display cabinets to the other. Unlike McFadden, Dr. Elliot had a private office. The building must have fought her all the way but somehow she had managed to create a stark and unloved place in its midst. The only contents were essential furniture and a computer. There was a planning chart on the wall behind the desk but no pictures, ornaments or mementoes.

'I thought you didn't believe in individual offices here,' said Henshaw.

'Who told you that, Inspector?'

'Mr. McFadden gave us quite a lecture about it.'

'You've already met Hamish? He didn't tell me; but that's nothing new. Of course I have my own office. What Hamish believes is a matter for him. There is more than one school of thought about such things.'

'Could you tell me a little more about Professor Cheung's role here?' asked Henshaw, as innocently as he could.

'Mr. Cheung was useful to us in making contacts in the Far East.'

'You refer to him as Mr. Cheung.'

'He had not actually taken up his post and there was still a matter of obtaining Senate approval for his title. That is not a formality, even after we had given him a degree to make it respectable.'

'You don't approve of the title?'

'What I approve of doesn't seem to be of any consequence here.' She sniffed and Henshaw followed Drake's practice of allowing a silence to develop. Dr. Elliot broke it. 'In my country all senior academics use the title Professor. Here they give it away to some selected privileged people as a bribe. I don't think you can have it both ways. Either it is a title that has to be earned or it is not.'

'You don't think Jimmy Cheung had earned it then?'

'What exactly has this to do with the murder investigation?'

'We are anxious to discover who might have a motive for killing Jimmy Cheung?'

'You cannot seriously think I would kill him to stop him getting a professorial title?' Dr. Elliot laughed but did not look amused. 'You seem to have a low opinion of both academics and women, Inspector.'

'Not at all.' Henshaw searched around for a direction that would not end in more disapproval from Dr. Elliot but he need not have bothered.

'To tell you the truth,' said Dr. Elliot, 'from my perspective Jimmy Cheung offered very little. He knew nothing of modern management theory and could contribute little to our research or our masters' courses.' Henshaw nodded encouragingly feeling at last that he had got her onto a topic she wanted to talk about. Sure enough she continued, now more rapidly. 'He promised to give one lecture to the undergrads next session, and he was going to speak to the masters about the Asian Tiger Economies this month. Other than that, he offered nothing. I tried to point this out to Hamish but then he isn't exactly the greatest theoretician either. Sure he talks about theory when it suits him. It sounds like he gave you the office layout stuff from what you said earlier.' Henshaw nodded again. 'You should ask what significant publications Hamish has produced since we started SEABU. Mostly he's just a fundraiser but not proper research grants; it always seems more like commercial sponsorship to me. Not that I object to applied research of course.' Marcia Elliot was now in full flow needing no further encouragement from Henshaw.

'As for those two doctoral students he has from China. Several times I've tried to get them to give seminars to the graduate school. Goodness knows what they actually do apart from a lot of travelling. Don't misunderstand me, in a way I am grateful to Hamish. Give him credit; he certainly generates funding. Some of it obviously has strings attached. You could say Jimmy Cheung was one of those strings.' She paused to see if Henshaw was getting the message.

'So he gets a professorial title. I had to put the whole MBA course together myself and I'm not deserving of one. Well that sucks, Inspector. Academic disputes can get vicious but the idea that any of us would want to shoot Jimmy Cheung is ludicrous. I think you need to look outside the University for your killer, Inspector. From what I've heard it's pretty surprising that someone hasn't knocked off our Jimmy years ago. The stories are that he has used some pretty ruthless business practices and left a fair few people damaged in the process. There is a theory that says any man who has risen so far so quickly must be standing on some injured parties.'

Henshaw was caught out by the sudden end to her outpourings but eventually got his act together again well enough to probe further. 'So are there any directions in particular you think we should be looking, Dr. Elliot?'

'Look, I haven't got any direct evidence to give you. I am as surprised by the whole episode as everyone else.'

'We saw your display cabinets on our previous visit and McFadden seemed particularly proud of the pistols.'

'He's a leading member of the local shooting club, and I would love to think he had finally seen through Jimmy Cheung and taken a pop at him but sadly I cannot offer that as a serious hypothesis for you.'

'Well if anything comes to you, this is my number Please give me a call.' Henshaw passed her his card. 'I'm afraid as a matter of procedure I must ask you not to leave Chester without checking with us and to hand in your passport.'

'Sure. My passport is always with me when I'm overseas.' She opened a slim briefcase on her desk. 'Let me walk you back to the entrance. It's easy to go round in circles in this place.'

'No need at all; I can find my way but on that score, isn't this a very expensive building for a university like Deva? I expect all this art cost a fair packet.'

'Well there you go! Exactly. I wasn't here when it was built but I hear stories of several hands being in a number of tills,' said Dr. Elliot with a wink and a nod that seemed out of character to her previously angry countenance. Henshaw rose, shook hands and left, deliberately turning the long way around the courtyard to get a better look at the building. He passed the display cabinets starting with the Keris collection with its wavy blades. He shivered imagining the damage they could do as he read the label describing them as from Malaysia and Indonesia where they were thought to have magical powers. The label acknowledged an organisation known as AAA for the loan of the items on display. The gun cabinet had so many pistols, Henshaw lost count but one looked very similar to Sheng Tian's.

He stepped down into the courtyard and along a stone pathway that meandered between the plants and sculptures. It could easily have been an oriental art gallery for some eastern spa with the sound of water splashing on pebbles. Getting close to the largest sculpture for the first time, Henshaw was surprised by its size. Art was not something he had either studied or wanted to particularly and certainly not oriental art. This was a concoction of dragons, fish and humans. He could not tell whether it was old or precious but he guessed both. The path reached another set of steps back up onto the deck and he found himself back in the foyer area. Facing him was the screen with all the sponsors' names. He was pretty sure he had them all in his notebook but Dr. Elliot's arrival had surprised him and he just wanted to make certain. It was then that he noticed something odd. He wondered why he had not spotted it before. All the sponsors' names were on individual brass plates screwed to the wooden panel. But there was a gap. There were even screw holes suggesting a nameplate had been removed.

The phone rang on Grace Hepple's desk. At least she thought it did. Her desk, and all other surfaces around were covered in sheets of paper on which she had written all the pieces of knowledge they had about the case. It was a trick her previous inspector had taught her but she was embarrassed to try it in the presence of Henshaw and Drake. The idea was that each sheet of paper contained only one item of information. There were different coloured sheets for established facts, suspicions and questions. You surrounded yourself with these pieces of paper and then shuffled them around looking for patterns. The technique had given her some success before. Now she was less sure. Everything just seemed confusing but she was getting an uncomfortable feeling about Sheng Tian. So many pieces of paper could be brought together to make a case against him but not one of them was convincing in isolation. She realised Drake felt the same way but that Henshaw was becoming convinced of his guilt.

Right now the problem was to discover which piece of paper concealed the phone that was ringing. The phone had become more insistent and irritable. Pieces of paper were moved to reveal books, files and maps. The ring stopped with the inevitable result that the next piece of paper she moved exposed the phone. She had returned to surveying the scene hoping for some inspiration, when the door burst open. It was Sergeant Denson.

'Ah Hepple, we've been looking all over for you, and you were here all the time. There is a Professor Wilson been calling you; says it's very important but that he won't leave any message. Rude blighter he is. Won't trust anyone else he says.' By now Denson had paused to take in the scene around him. 'What's happening here then?'

'It's just an idea I'm trying out.' Denson grinned and chuckled.

'I'd better get this Professor back for you then; try answering the phone this time.'

'Grace Hepple.'

'Ah Sergeant Hepple,' said the pathologist, 'Got your fax. You might have something. I looked up a couple of papers. The early Luger Parabellum leaves a very clean entry point and transfers little energy to the tissue. One paper also refers to the Japanese Nambu pistol as having similar characteristics. The brass bottle necked ammunition has good penetration but causes little damage. Unless it manages to hit a critical organ, in this case the heart, it could leave the victim relatively unscathed. Painful I dare say but far from fatal. If this happened here then either it was darned bad luck on your Jimmy Cheung or a pretty good shot on the part of our murderer. I am not saying that this gun or even one like it was the murder weapon. I am merely saying that the evidence we have is consistent with that. You do understand?'

'Yes Professor Wilson, I understand precisely.' The phone rang again. It was Sergeant Denson.

'We've got that Chinaman, Dr. Cheung on the phone,' said Denson. 'He's bin holding for one of you; says it's very important. I'll transfer you.'

'This is Cheung Sheng Tian. I want to speak to Drake. This is very urgent.'

'I am afraid Chief Inspector Drake is not here just now and I am not at all sure when he will be in next. Can I help you?'

'Since I last talked to him, I have found that one of the porters, Charlie Smith, will confirm that I was working in my office at the University all evening when my father was murdered.'

'Thank you Dr. Cheung,' said Grace, 'we'll check with Mr. Smith.' She was making a note of the name in her notebook when the phone went dead. She would have asked Sheng Tian more about this but as usual the Singaporean had terminated the conversation on his terms.

Grace had only just managed to clear away all her papers when Henshaw came back, full of his interview with Marcia Elliot and his discovery of the missing sponsor's nameplate. Together, Henshaw and Grace poured over the list of names in his notebook. Some of the names were international companies and they made a separate list of them. Grace was charged with running checks on all the others through the computer at Specialist Operations. Henshaw was about to leave when she told him about her phone calls.

'How very convenient for Sheng Tian,' exclaimed Henshaw; 'a suddenly discovered alibi. Drake will probably want to get him back in pronto.' He picked up the phone. 'Denson, where is Chief Inspector Drake? Can you contact him for me?' Grace could hear Denson's voice as Henshaw held the phone slightly away from his ear to protect it from the sergeant's booming voice. 'What? The old blighter, what is he up to? Would you come in Denson please?' Henshaw put the phone down. 'Drake's gone away.' Henshaw and Grace Hepple were still staring at each other in astonishment at this news when Denson crashed into the room.

'Where's he gone then, Denson,' demanded Henshaw.

'Said he was going away for a while. Something about visiting his daughter and killing two birds with one stone. Dave's set him up with a laptop and showed him how to use email.' Denson chortled. 'Dave says how he ain't sure the old man has got it though. Went through it with him half a dozen times he did. Chief Inspector Drake told me to be sure to say to you, Sir that he was leaving the Cheung case in your hands like. Said he was very confident in yer.' Denson nodded vigorously in agreement with himself. Grace thought Henshaw's chest puffed out just perceptibly for a split second. 'Said he would call in a couple of days.'

'Awkward timing,' said Henshaw. 'What's the old man up to? Grace, go to the University and find Professor Mallory, the public orator. If you can't see him, make arrangements for us to do so pretty darned quick.'

Henshaw had to admit to himself that he was fascinated by Grace. He had caught himself looking at her ever since that first meeting in the hotel. It was all very awkward and complicated; he had no idea how to handle this situation. Now Drake had gone away they were going to have a lot of time together but he had to maintain the proper distance; darned tricky. 'Now Drake has disappeared I am strongly inclined to haul Sheng Tian in.'

'You mean arrest him, sir?' queried Grace. Here we go again, thought Henshaw, she doesn't agree. Henshaw suspected she was not impressed but he was going to manage this case the way he felt right. He was in charge again.

'Yes of course, arrest him. We need a proper period of interrogation. He'll crack when pressure is applied and so far he has been able to end proceedings when he feels like it under Drake's gentle touch. Let's see how he responds under tougher stuff.' Grace said nothing but the silence spoke for her. Henshaw picked up the air of disapproval. 'You don't agree then, Sergeant Hepple?'

'I am not so sure, sir. I don't think Drake would make an arrest on such evidence in a case as delicate as this. I think he would want more than circumstantial connections.'

'OK you go get this alibi checked out and then I'll decide,' said Henshaw gruffly.

The porters' lodge at the Politics Department of Deva University was a jovial sort of place. There was a small window onto the lobby of the building and people passed by exchanging greetings and jokes with Fred, the head porter. On the wall was a huge chart showing the rooms in the building that had been booked by members of staff on particular days. Along one wall were a series of mail trays and hanging high up in the corner was a television set that was showing a golf tournament somewhere in America. Fred and his two mates from another building were sharing their sandwiches and joking about their own limited golfing ability. On a worktop below the television, a kettle was furiously whistling its readiness to make Grace Hepple's cup of tea. Fred had insisted that this took precedence over any discussions. It was not often they had such a pretty young woman in their lodge.

'Now then, Sergeant,' he said flipping through a large desk diary and turning to his mates. 'Lo and behold, it should have been Charlie Smith.' The other porters collapsed in roars of laughter. This went on for some time with them all nodding to each other to confirm just how hilarious the joke was.

'Why is that funny,' asked Grace.

'You don't know our Charlie then? How do we put it lads?'

'Swings the leg,' said one without taking his eyes off the television.

'Didn't his third grandmother die that day?' said the other and they all fell about laughing in another bout of porter bonding.

'He is ill a lot then?' Grace asked when it all died down enough to make herself heard.

'Ooo I don't know about actually ill,' said Fred, 'but somehow whenever we have some special work to do or heavy weights to move, he isn't here.'

'So are you saying that Charlie Smith was not on duty that day?' Fred was thumbing through another book that he had pulled out of a drawer. The crowd on the television set roared its approval of a golf shot and all three porters paused to watch the replay and tell each other just how difficult that sort of thing really was. Fred returned to his research.

'Here we are,' he said at last. 'Went home with a bad headache just before lunch.'

'Ah,' said the other porter, 'just when all the new furniture arrived in that big wagon. I had to come over and help.' Grace looked at the book. Tuesday 12 September, Charlie Smith, unwell with bad headache. Went home 11:45.

'So where could I find Charlie now then?'

'Pub or the bookies?' Fred enquired of his mates. After some argument, they reached consensus; the bookies was thought the more likely at this time of day.

Grace Hepple studied a display showing embarrassing portrait photographs of staff in the History Department. Professor Peter Mallory's picture stood out. He looked easily the most at home in the photographic studio and Grace read off the number of his office, 243. No one seemed interested in her so Grace decided to find the room for herself. That would be Drake's tactic, she thought, avoid unnecessary contact with people who could spread rumours. Guessing that the first part of a room number indicated the floor level, she climbed two flights of the stairs and found Professor Mallory's office. She knocked and waited. There was no answer. She tried the doorknob. The door was locked. Bother! They were getting a bit desperate to see Mallory. She had to resolve this situation but she wasn't sure how to proceed.

She decided to call Henshaw. This would have the added benefit of making him feel she depended on his advice. She had easily picked up the signs that he was in denial about being attracted to her. Grace Hepple was used to such looks, especially in this male dominated police world. Henshaw had tried to get a conversation going the other evening in the pub before others arrived to interrupt them. He had told her a little too obviously how he had recently split up with his girlfriend. Why ever do men think that this is good news to a woman?

Henshaw answered the phone and Grace told him about Charlie Smith's invented illness.

'I knew it! Never felt right.'

'Well hang on, sir. I would just like to interview Smith and confront him with this before we can be absolutely certain.'

'Yes, yes OK. Anyway great work, Grace. What about Mallory?'

'There is no sign of Mallory and his door is locked. I think we should press on with this now, if you agree sir but this would mean going to the porters or the secretaries and revealing who I am and I don't think Drake would approve of that. What would you like me to do, sir?'

'Yes, for goodness sake let's take a look inside his room. Go to the main building and see the Registrar's P.A. Sally Brown and ask her to get Watson the Director of Facilities to let you into the office. That way we avoid a warrant problem and unnecessary rumours.'

'Right sir; will do.'

'And Grace….well done, good work all round.'

'Thank you, sir.' It was probably just as well that Henshaw couldn't see the smile on Grace Hepple's face as she put away her phone; it was just a touch too knowing.

'Oh Dr. Percival,' Sally Brown said as The Registrar passed through on the way into his office, 'this is Detective Sergeant Grace Hepple. She is working with Chief Inspector Drake on the Jimmy Cheung murder case.'

'I am very pleased to meet you, Sergeant. How is it going, and how can we help you?' asked the Registrar.

'We have a number of leads but I can't say more at this stage.'

'She is here to see Professor Mallory,' said Sally Brown, 'but he seems not to be in….again,' the last word was emphasised.

'Professor Mallory, like so many of our distinguished academics, is an international figure and he travels a great deal,' said Percival with a transparent pomposity that nearly made Grace giggle.

'I would like to know where he is, and when he will be available now please, Dr. Percival. We have been very patient and it's vital that we see him. Chief Inspector Drake is anxious not to spread rumours around the university so I have not asked his secretary so far. I would like to look around his office now.' Dr. Percival looked a little flustered by the confidence and authority of this young policewoman. She guessed that he had assumed that he would be able to dominate her. Sally Brown came to the rescue.

'Mr. Watson is on his way over to escort Sergeant Hepple to Professor Mallory's office. If you like, I can ask his secretary to let us have his immediate diary.'

'Yes Sally,' said Percival, 'of course. Exactly why is it so urgent that you speak with Mallory, Sergeant?'

'He was a key player in the honorary degree ceremony,' said Grace, 'and one of the last people known to have seen Jimmy Cheung alive. Because of the research he did for the oration, we think he may know some more background to Jimmy Cheung's life that might help us to identify possible lines of enquiry.'

'Ah I see; he is not a suspect then?' asked Percival sounding relieved.

'No one is a suspect, Dr. Percival but all connected with the murdered man have to be investigated.' Percival's eyes narrowed slightly and he let out a nervous laugh.

'Even me then Sergeant Hepple?'

'Even you, Dr. Percival,' said Grace with a straight face. Dr. Percival's face flushed noticeably. He turned and left without further niceties. Grace wished Drake was here; he was so good at reading these situations. Was Percival showing signs of guilt or anxiety? Was he trying to cover something up? Did he know something about Professor Mallory that he did not want Grace to discover?

If an office can convey the personality of its owner then Professor Peter Mallory was a neat and tidy sort of man. The room was a model of organisation; maybe he was even a control freak? Files were clearly labelled and stored away in logical positions in a series of filing cabinets under a long workbench. Shallow shelves above this held papers and reports all written by Mallory. On the workbench were sets of filing trays, mostly empty or containing a few letters or papers he was currently working on. On the other side of the room, a floor to ceiling bookcase was crammed with books on economic and social history with some modern politics thrown in. A large desk sat in the window. It proudly displayed several photographs of Mallory in the company of various other people, almost exclusively male. The body language spoken in these pictures suggested that Mallory was proud to be in this company and his companions thought he was pretty lucky too. Several photographs were autographed just in case this message had not been completely understood.

There was no sign of a computer but a power supply lurked under the desk waiting for its laptop to be plugged in. The top drawer of the desk contained the usual staplers, Sellotape, paperclips and envelopes. Grace was about to close it when the stack of envelopes collapsed and she pushed them back neatly. It was then she saw the first photograph underneath. In fact there was a dozen or so. These were not like the trophies in frames on the desk but Grace thought they might be trophies of another kind. They were all of women. Not once did Mallory appear in these but somehow Grace sensed his presence behind the lens. Without exception these women looked straight at the camera and smiled. Some were outdoors and some indoors but the background was never important.

Grace turned to Mallory's papers, which appeared to be on the value of different systems of economics in modern history. They spoke of people rather than commerce and about social justice rather than political ambition. Many of the papers referred to twentieth century events in eastern countries and specifically the Asian tiger economies. There was no diary or wall planner.

Grace rummaged around in Mallory's filing cabinets and eventually found a copy of the oration for Jimmy Cheung's honorary degree ceremony but there were no notes, earlier drafts or supporting documents. It occurred to her that this was odd. Of course the research material could be on his laptop. She was about to return the document to the file when her gaze caught a phrase in the first sentence "totally unsuitable". She rubbed her eyes and looked back at the document and read it through from beginning to end. She began to notice subtle changes to the oration they had all studied in the hotel. Almost every other sentence was not only different but strikingly so. The changes themselves might have been subtle but the effect was devastating.

Doctor Jimmy Cheung.

Chancellor, you see standing in front of you a man totally unsuitable to be honoured by this university. Jimmy Cheung was born of humble stock in 1925 in the city of Johor Bahru, now part of Malaysia. Within a few years of his birth his parents had moved to what is now Singapore; his father looking for employment in the port. For a man with few scruples this was a good time and place to be born. The young Jimmy soon began to exploit his father's operation and in particular the hapless coolies operating the shallow bottomed boats plying their trade between the seagoing vessels in the port and the warehouses along the Singapore River.

Two years before Jimmy Cheung was born, British engineers were engaged in two great enterprises. One was the building of a naval base in Singapore; the other the Queen's Park Suspension Bridge in Chester. It was of course the former that was to offer the young Jimmy Cheung his first opportunity. His father had started to work on the great George VI dock, which was the largest dry dock anywhere in the world at that time, and Jimmy soon to follow suit. By the start of the second world war Singapore was heavily defended from the sea by this huge complex with its own artillery, searchlights, and even an airfield. Singapore was then even described as the "Gibraltar of the East." The British had fatally miscalculated and the invading Japanese entered Singapore in 1942 not by sea at all but just as the Cheung family had, by land from the north. They established a brutal regime known as Syonan. During this period of occupation, Jimmy Cheung miraculously prospered and when the British returned in September 1945, exactly 60 years ago, he soon found himself working for the British Navy and quickly became an indispensable part of the logistics of our operation in South East Asia.

The streetwise Jimmy Cheung was to become one of the leading entrepreneurs who drove forward the astonishingly successful economy of Singapore. He was to start and establish many businesses, most of them successful, though often at a cost to his partners and employees. The history of the Jimmy Cheung business empire mirrors the development of Singapore from a port trading raw material such as tin and rubber from the Malay Peninsula through a British naval base to manufacturing computer components and now a modern information technology and banking centre.

His accumulated wealth and power was such that in 1985 Jimmy Cheung was made a member of parliament. Since then he has been a leading figure in the development of trade between Singapore and the United Kingdom and he is equally at home in Raffles Place and Whitehall. Jimmy Cheung has brought his business methods to Deva University and helped to build the South East Asian Business Unit in the image of his own dubious practice. In recognition of this we have made him a Distinguished Visiting Professor.

Modern Singapore declared its independence on 9th August 1965 and was recognised by the United Nations as a sovereign country in September 1965. Singapore is therefore exactly the same age as this University. Perhaps it accurately reflects the values of Deva University that we celebrate our fortieth anniversary by awarding an honorary degree to such a man.

Chancellor, I present to you Jimmy Cheung as entirely unworthy of the degree of Doctor of Letters Honoris Causae.

Grace read the document several times. She wished she could remember the version that was actually delivered in more precise detail but she certainly remembered its laudatory tone. The accusatory nature of this version stood out in stark contrast even though it was disguised by the formal language. Mallory seemed to be a bitter man who held both the university he worked for and Jimmy Cheung in very low esteem. There was no doubt now that they need to find him and quickly. It also suggested that more of a look around SEABU might be profitable. She was however pretty sure that Drake would not want her to go to Dr. Percival over that. It seemed likely that Percival and McFadden were close and she needed to avoid any warnings that SEABU was under investigation. Henshaw was so focussed on Sheng Tian that he was not likely to be interested. She read the false version of the oration one more time. This may be bitter but was it murderous? Perhaps Mallory was so angry that he confronted Jimmy Cheung and an argument broke out but then surely Mallory would not have a gun with him; that would indicate premeditation. The gun could have been Jimmy Cheung's. But a struggle on the bridge would surely have been noticed and reported.

Constable Katie Lamb stood by the door of the interview room trying to look important and doing a pretty good job of it. Sheng Tian was sitting nervously, shuffling his feet. Every few minutes he would get up and walk around the room, look of the window and then sit down at the small desk again. On the desk was a pad of paper that Henshaw had left for him to write his statement. Outside Henshaw and Grace Hepple were deep in conversation.

'I fully understand, Inspector Henshaw,' said Grace.

'But you still don't think I should have arrested him. He has a motive. He's struggling financially and would gain a very substantial inheritance. He's had his car repossessed. We know he had a furious argument with his father only that morning. He owns a gun that the pathologist says could be the murder weapon. He had the opportunity; he was not at the degree congregation. Then he invents an alibi that you have blown up. I am going to put some pressure on him and keep him overnight. You'll see he will crack and give us something we can really go on.' Grace nodded reluctantly.

Sheng Tian looked up angrily from his task when they entered. Henshaw collected the paper from the table and scanned through it.

'Inspector,' said Sheng Tian, 'you will see I cannot say anything different. There is nothing different to say.'

'We will come back to this later,' said Henshaw curtly. 'First I want to know about your financial situation. We have reason to believe your car was repossessed recently due to your failure to pay the hire purchase payments.'

'I am having some difficulties.'

'Is this because your father had withdrawn the financial support you have been receiving?'

'I did not want my father's money.'

'But you will now benefit substantially from his will, I imagine?'

'I have no idea what is in my father's will.'

'Oh come on. Do you expect us to believe that. You are his only son. Your mother is dead and Janet is the only other person likely to be a major beneficiary.' Henshaw was speculating here but he could see from Sheng Tian's expression that he was not far from the truth. 'Why did your father stop the payments he was making to you?'

'We had an argument.'

'You seem to have had many arguments. So what was this one about?'

'His honorary degree and visiting post at my university.' He stared belligerently at Henshaw for a few moments and then resumed.

'I disapprove of honorary degrees. I worked for mine. I have made a position here on my own ability and then my father comes here to embarrass me. I told him I did not need him here. He said that if I did not need him, I should not need his money. I can live without his money but he stopped it very suddenly. I could not afford the payments on the car.'

'So Sheng Tian, we seem to have established a motive.'

'I did not kill my father,' Sheng Tian was shouting and banging the table with his fist. Grace could see a tear in his eyes. Henshaw was not going to take the pressure off.

'We found a pistol in your house,' he continued. 'The particular wound that your father suffered is known to be caused by this kind of pistol.'

Sheng Tian looked startled. 'If you mean the old pistol in the box in my living room, that is an antique. I do not know how to use it.'

'Sheng Tian,' said Henshaw slowly. 'May I remind you where you are. Unless there is anything else you would like to tell us now, I shall terminate this interview. We will talk again tomorrow.' Sheng Tian sat in silence hunched over the small table in front of him. Henshaw performed the formalities of completing the interview, turned off the tape recorder and signalled to Constable Lamb to look after Sheng Tian.

# 8 - Electronics

At last the excitement was dying down in the cabin. Drake looked around relieved to see the other passengers were getting on with their own business and that he was no longer the centre of attention. The twelve hours flight to Singapore allowed him to think everything through without interruption. The space in business class meant he could stretch out his legs and he had discovered that his seat unfolded to become an almost flat bed. Unfortunately the discovery had been made at the cost of some embarrassment. He had pressed some buttons on the little illuminated diagram of the seat on the armrest hoping simply to lean back a little to savour the glass of wine in his hand. Somehow it got totally out of control and he had ended up lying flat on his back with half the wine down his shirt.

It is well recorded that most kinds of electronic devices have ganged up against Drake at some time or other. This seat was a signed up member of the conspiracy. A tiny Singaporean airline stewardess had eventually saved the situation and got him more or less upright. She delivered an illustrated lecture, complete with practical follow-up sessions, on how to use the seat. To her despair Drake had not been an excellent student.

What a strange scene this was, he thought. Here they were miles above the ground, hurtling through the air at a speed that would be lethal in most earthly locations, and yet all was calm and peaceful. His fellow passengers sat unmoving; the occasional stewardess wafted elegantly down the aisle. Even the drone of the engines added to the soporific quality of the place and so fitful sleep crept up on Drake. He drifted through a chaotic dream of Janet playing the role of Alice trying to reassure a frantic white rabbit anxious about being late for its degree congregation. He tried to draw some sense out of this and decided there probably wasn't any.

He read Mallory's oration for Jimmy Cheung, listing things he would follow up on his trip. Was there for example, any real connection between the history of Deva University and the history of Singapore? Drake felt that it was more likely to be a display of erudite academic investigation than to have any real substance. Even so, he could not help wondering if the murder of Jimmy Cheung had any connection with the anniversary not just of the founding of the university but with the creation of Singapore as an independent country.

Drake had lain awake all the previous night worrying about his decision to fly to Singapore. Would Henshaw jump in too heavily? He'd better call him as soon as he landed to make sure he didn't go straight out and arrest Sheng Tian. On balance it was still too early for that but Henshaw was quite likely to push events just to see what happened. Drake looked at his watch and tried to make sense of it. This wasn't a task with which he normally had a lot of difficulty but the longer he looked the more confusing it all became. The little television screen conjured out of his armrest by the stewardess was alternating between showing the times in Manchester, Singapore and their current location, wherever that was. In its enthusiasm for times of all kinds it was now also showing their expected arrival, in Singapore time of course. Drake was reduced to counting on his fingers and they told him that when he landed Henshaw would be asleep for at least another eight hours.

Time difference was going to be a problem. Drake's body was already giving advanced notice that it would require him to be fast asleep long before Henshaw got into the office. He would have to rely on email! The full horror of that dawned on him for the first time. Dave had spent hours setting it up on a laptop for him and explaining it, so it should be OK and yet…

Drake turned his attention to the clouds passing in a reassuring procession outside his window. The shifting canopy below was hypnotically fascinating and yet you knew where you were with it. He had found by prodding other buttons on his armrest that he could make the screen in front of him show a map of the journey rather than a film. This he liked far more than the combined output of all the Hollywood and oriental film studios at his disposal. They were now high above a current war zone in the Middle East. The clouds appeared to have no awareness of the special circumstances of the place; they seemed more or less the same as they had looked over a peaceful location half an hour previously. Drake's fellow travellers showed complete indifference to his discovery. Down there below, people were dying or getting kidnapped and tortured for goodness sake! The two characters to his right, who had barely concealed their amusement at his earlier seat battles, were laughing at their respective screens. Drake wondered just where you would decide that you were no longer in the West but in the East. It must have been so much easier when the British first sailed to colonise Singapore. His cabin was quaintly called 'Raffles Class' but Sir Stamford had taken months about the journey and never had to deal with time zones.

Drake's hosts had been extremely efficient and hospitable. They had been so almost to a fault. They had volunteered to set up his whole trip, organise his travel and accommodation and to provide him with a car and driver. There was no doubt that the Singaporean Police and their masters were interested in the Jimmy Cheung case but Drake sensed reluctance to share information. He emerged from the Cantonment Complex where the police had their headquarters and his contact was based. He had spent a couple of hours with Inspector Philip Lim. The level of technology available to his opposite number was truly astonishing. Computers were everywhere and databases of people, incidents and case notes were instantly searchable. The setup put Drake's office to shame and he was going to make sure that Fergus Marshall back at the Met was made aware of it.

Drake suspected that Jimmy Cheung's background was hardly whiter than white but so far he had been unable to get anything tangible out of Philip Lim. It was possible that either the

Singaporean Police had nothing solid on Jimmy Cheung or they had but Philip Lim was not party to it. Drake couldn't tell; he wasn't able to read the situation as easily as with a British police force. Philip Lim did suggest that Jimmy Cheung left the parliament rather against his own wishes but even that was not entirely clear. He was a nice chap, Philip, and obviously very dedicated and hardworking. He spoke with an authority that gave Drake great confidence in him. It was just that, on later reflection, his sentences seemed not to have actually said anything definite.

Jimmy Cheung's fortune was originally based on the early exploitation of coolies in the port. Certainly Jimmy Cheung had begun to develop his empire during the Japanese Occupation in the Second World War and there were rumours that he had collaborated with the government of the time but no real evidence of this had ever been produced. That was all a long time ago, as Philip Lim had dismissively observed, even before the country existed and the current legal system was put in place. Drake had showed Philip Lim the Mallory oration for Jimmy and got no reaction to it. The local man had thought it was as accurate as those sort of things go. No, he did not see any obvious connection with the anniversary of the founding of the country. It was after all not a particularly important anniversary. Philip Lim was only a teenager when the country was formed in 1965 and didn't have clear memories of it but he soon found a history book and pointed out a number of paragraphs to Drake. Singapore's independence did not come at the end of some long battle or campaign against the British. Drake was taken with a passage in the book quoting famous words from the first Prime Minister, Lee Kuan Yew.

Some countries are born independent. Some achieve independence. Singapore had independence thrust upon it. Some 45 British colonies had held colourful ceremonies to formalise and celebrate the transfer of sovereign power from imperial Britain to their indigenous governments. For Singapore, 9 August 1965 was no ceremonial occasion. 'We had never sought independence,' was the mantra.

Philip Lim explained how the politicians of the time had thought Singapore could not be economically viable as an independent country, and it seemed there were real worries about breaking away from what had since become Malaysia. Thankfully they had been proved entirely wrong but their concern had liberated a hugely entrepreneurial spirit of which Jimmy Cheung had been a celebrated example.

The local policeman briefly made less flattering references to some more recent suspicions of illegal trading by some of Jimmy Cheung's companies but this hardly sounded serious. Drake was certain there was more to discover about Jimmy Cheung than was revealed in the university oration and that he had managed to drag out of Sheng Tian or Janet. Coming to Singapore had definitely been the right thing to do. He left Inspector Lim thinking that the real Jimmy Cheung was yet to be discovered. He stepped out of the building under cover of the projecting upper floors. The driver had obviously been alerted by Philip Lim and the Mercedes car silently pulled up in front of Drake. Everything here was so smoothly organised, thought Drake as he eased himself into the back seat.

'I'm having lunch with my daughter at Raffles Hotel in an hour and a half. Where can I go to see some of Singapore on the way?' Drake asked the driver. The driver cocked his head as if thinking this over and then suddenly announced.

'We go Bugis; ten minutes.' With that the car was slowly moving off and Drake guessed he was not expected to argue with the driver's choice. They made steady progress up a street between towering buildings. Drake guessed they were getting into the Central Business District, or CBD, as his host called it. In London, it was unhelpfully described simply as The City. How would a visiting Singaporean make sense of that? They suddenly emerged from this architectural canyon into open space by the harbour, and to Drake's right the sea stretched away to the horizon. They crossed a bridge and headed up a wider more open street. North Bridge Road, said a signpost. Drake remembered this from Cynthia's descriptions. Reassuringly, they passed Raffles Hotel and several blocks further on took a turning off to the right, followed by one to the left. Suddenly the scene had changed. Gone were the multiple lanes of traffic and the rushing crowds. This was a smaller scale, much older and altogether calmer place.

'Arab Street, Boss,' said his driver with a grin. 'Funny place, yes?' This other more middle-eastern culture was obviously a source of strangeness and amusement to his Chinese driver. Drake was invited to view it like some fairground freak show. The driver pointed up the street and agreed to wait while Drake had a look around. He climbed out of the car into the dazzling sunlight. The contrast of midday in the tropics with the air-conditioned interior of the police car was overwhelming. He had never actually felt surrounded by air before but here it pressed in on him. The hot-damp smell of the tropics had hit him as soon as the plane doors opened at Changi Airport but in Arab Street it was tinged with a heady combination of musk and spice.

Drake found himself in the middle of a throng of people who all looked busy and urgent. He marvelled at how they moved so quickly in the heat and humidity of Singapore. He shuffled along, constantly distracted by the sights, sounds and smells of the place wondering which way to turn next. Although the mass of people engulfed him, he could easily see over their heads. Not since he was a teenager had he been so conscious of his height. It felt as if all the surrounding faces were staring at him and the bodies they belonged to were nudging each other and pointing him out. He caught himself accentuating his normal stoop.

How silly! The bodies surrounding him were far too busy to take any notice of his height. These were no petty-minded Lilliputians terrified of giants but sophisticated and busy people going about their daily commerce. Besides they had seen tall people before in this most cosmopolitan of cities. His attention turned to the longer view across the sea of heads down the street. Looking even higher above the buildings he could see a golden dome glinting in the sunlight.

He remembered Cynthia's practice collaborating with a local firm of architects based near the mosque. She described the streets around with a poetic enthusiasm that even Drake had been moved by. He ambled down a side street and found himself in a maze of narrower but equally busy streets. Every building was set back on the ground floor behind an arcade supporting the upper floors. Drake could walk along in their shade admiring the variety and yet similarity of the facades. All had shuttered upper windows, cornices and elaborate detail. Some were painted in bright colours that clashed and yet complemented each other at the same time. Other buildings looked faded and in need of repair. Most buildings were occupied by family businesses selling carpets, fabrics, wicker baskets or jewellery. Dotted amongst them were a few bars and newer looking enterprises pandering to the passing tourist rather than local customers. He came to a junction and turned left into a wider pedestrian street. The charming but regular buildings down either side framed the vista and deferred to the great yellow onion dome of the mosque.

The mosque was no stage set but a working building. Coming and going were many dressed to indicate they were Muslims and with faces to match. This was in stark contrast with the more predominant Chinese culture of Singapore. It seemed like a little lost and hidden world. Here an overtly Muslim community, Chinese traders and western tourists all went about their different business, each apparently oblivious of the others and yet sharing the same space. Chinese bells jingled in counterpoint to the call to prayers booming from the minarets of the mosque. The place was slowly but surely weaving its spell on Drake. This was surely one of the streets Cynthia had described so enthusiastically. He had heard her account but not understood it. At last he appreciated why she was so enchanted by it and why she so wanted to show it to him.

He took several more turns each revealing buildings different and yet all belonging to the same basic pattern. Then he saw the sign. “Asean Art and Antiques Pte Ltd”. This sounded very familiar; perhaps that was one of the names on the sponsor’s board at SEABU. He looked causally in the window. Inside he could see a cornucopia of oriental bric-a-brac. There was furniture, pictures, wall hangings, sculptures and smaller objects d'art of all kinds. He could see a figure hovering in the depths of the building, which seemed to go back away from the street by many times the width of the shop. He was not anxious to meet anyone until he was sure of facts. He would get Henshaw to check if he had indeed stumbled on one of SEABU's sponsors and return later.

To say Drake hastily returned to his car driver would be an exaggeration. By now he was beginning to feel the dual effects of the seven hours of jet lag and the stifling heat and humidity of midday Singapore. He turned and began steadily enough down the street but soon dropped his pace to a shuffle. He could by now feel the beads of sweat on his forehead and his damp shirt clinging to his back. His shuffle soon turned into a struggle. He remembered his earlier lesson of walking on the shady side of the street and crossed over. Never before in his life had he been so grateful to an overhanging building.

He passed a limousine like his transport from the police but all cars seemed to look that way in this affluent city. 'Hot today, Boss,' grinned the driver as the window silently wound down. The man had obviously followed him and anticipated his discomfort. Drake grunted, wiped his brow and flopped into the cool calm interior of the car. He could feel sweat trickling down the back of his neck. 'Hot everyday,' said the driver roaring with laughter. 'Not like England, eh Boss? Very cold,' He gave an imitation shiver. 'Raffles Hotel now then, Boss?' asked his driver.

'Yes please,' replied Drake, 'I have not seen my daughter for a long time so it may be a long lunch. You can leave me there and I'll call you when I need you next.' The driver nodded and began telling Drake about his own daughter in halting English. It was along the lines of the cost of daughters in general and weddings in particular. Although having his own police driver would in many ways make things easier, Drake was not at all sure he wanted his movements monitored by Philip Lim. He felt pretty sure this was likely to happen. The setup here was just too darned professional not to record his movements.

The car slowly set off and Drake sat back. By now the driver had returned to an earlier topic of conversation.

'I admire you English,' he said. 'Very tough, very tough. You live in cold place.' With that he gave another mock shiver and laughed again contentedly to himself. Soon the car was back on a major road and surrounded by the traffic of a modern metropolis. Drake marvelled at how Singapore could change so quickly and dramatically.

He had been looking forward to seeing Raffles Hotel and was not disappointed as they swept off Beach Road onto the curved gravelled drive. The crunch of the car wheels contributing to the air of exclusive luxury. The front of the original block was a three storey white building in a classical western style with symmetrical wings cranked forward on either side of a generous glazed and tiled porte-cochere. As the car swung up to the front door, an impressive Indian man in full regalia opened the car door. This made even Jimmy Cheung's hotel in Chester look small beer and did so without even trying. He thanked his driver as the hotel doorman helped him struggle to his feet. As Drake's head continued its skyward journey the doorman's eyes widened and he nodded an acknowledgement of Drake's superior height.

Drake was glad to get straight under the cool arcade and into the full height hallway. In front of him, a grand staircase offered access to the upper floors and high above large brass fans whirred reassuringly. Dotted around were armchairs and low tables. In the centre of the whole space was an oval table in highly polished dark wood. It groaned under the weight of a huge glass vase holding more orchids than Drake had ever previously seen in one place. To the left and deeper into the building, was an incongruous wrought iron railing complete with gate. It separated a side room that appeared jolly popular. The hum of conversation and the clink of cutlery were corroborated by a sign announcing that this was the Tiffin Room. Drake could see his daughter Lucy sitting at a table by the window. Recognising him, she gave a squeal of delight and rushed over.

'Oh Dad, it's fantastic to see you. I was really worried that you wouldn't come.' After the kinds of hugs and kisses that end the long separation of a father from his daughter they settled down to catch up and eat lunch. Drake began to take in his surroundings: high ceilings, tall windows, classical detailing and everywhere white with touches of bright red. Drake could imagine Somerset Maugham and his crowd holding court in this room. The cutlery, crockery, waiters' outfits and demeanours all reflected a colonial past. This was a hotel that would satisfy your every whim, and probably before you had even whimmed it.

'Dad you're not listening to me!'

'Sorry Lucy; this place is overwhelming.'

'I knew you'd love it. Apparently Rudyard Kipling said "when in Singapore, feed at Raffles".'

Drake smiled to see his daughter so obviously happy and excited at her recent career successes. Cynthia had described Raffles to him. Darn it, why wouldn't she leave him alone?

'Mum told me that some architect or other had said, "while at Raffles, why not visit Singapore?" Typical architect; they always think their buildings are the centres of the universe.' He laughed to choke back his emotion. Lucy, who had not been fooled, joined in with her infectious giggle and squeezed his hand on the table. A waiter brought the Mulligatawny soup that Lucy said was a specialty of the house.

The clever trick played by the soup was to sound vaguely Scottish and look quite inoffensive. It was of course neither as Drake discovered precisely three spoonfuls later. He took a long swig of cold mineral water to damp down the spices. He began to describe his day to Lucy, at least his brain did but his throat let out only a pathetic croak. Lucy roared with laughter and Drake had no alternative but to join in, shaking his shoulders, grinning and spluttering. An adjacent table threw carefully constructed looks of disapproval in an English sort of way. For the first time in his life Drake understood what his schoolboy atlas meant by colouring countries in British Empire pink.

Lucy took control of the situation. 'After lunch I am going to take you down to the river and give you a boat ride.'

'That would be lovely but look Lucy I have to....' She interrupted him.

'You need to slow down here Dad. You've done enough for today, the sun and the humidity will kill you otherwise. When we have finished our boat ride we'll be right by Tom's office and he'll join us for a drink at one of the bars on Boat Quay.' Memories of the last time he had seen Tom and Lucy together welled back up in Drake's mind. He did not want to think about that particular occasion just now. It was wonderful that they both had international careers but he missed having them around, especially since Cynthia had gone.

'OK Lucy, I give in. I can't imagine anything better than having my son and daughter take me for an early evening drink by the river. But perhaps after that I might need some sleep. I'm beginning to understand this thing they call jet lag.'

Drake wondered if the young Jimmy Cheung had used this very boat. The crackling recorded tape operated by the boatman explained how the vessel was a bum boat used throughout its earlier life on the Singapore River to ferry people and goods between the ships further out to sea and the godowns or warehouses. The boat was a solid-looking affair with a broad beam and shallow draft. It had a rising open bow section but a low gently curved roof protected the middle, in which they were sat. The boatman sat holding an old fashioned tiller in the rearmost section, again open to the sky. They were not alone. Many similar boats chugged past, each broadcasting a snatch of its commentary on the river scene. A particularly close encounter drew Drake's attention to the eyes painted on each prow. They might have been old but they were cocky little boats, in their element and every eye seemed to wink at Drake inviting him to guess if had belonged to the Cheung empire of old.

Between crackles of the tape and the splashes of the river Drake deciphered just enough to identify the museum and made a mental note to return. They sailed out under a low bridge into the harbour and Lucy proudly pointed to the theatre where she was performing. From out here, the central business district was visible as a mass of towering buildings huddled shoulder to shoulder like penguins in the Antarctic winter. As they returned to the landing stage it became obvious that the soaring structures began one block back from the river. All along the bank were old two and three storey buildings of a pattern that Drake recognised by now but here converted to eateries of one kind or another. The central business district was just as Tom had described it. Most buildings were so high that Drake could not see the top of them from under the roof of the boat.

There were some embarrassing moments getting Drake off the boat, which the boatman refused to tie up, preferring to keep the engine running with the prow bumping against the steps to the embankment. Drake lunged at it a couple of times just as the boat bounced back and lost his confidence. The Chinese boatman was yelling exhortations from the stern and the engine was revving angrily. Neither the Mandarin shouting nor the pungent scent of diesel did much to help matters. Anxiety soared but third time lucky. Drake made contact with dry land and they climbed the few steps up to Boat Quay.

Along the waterfront was a series of umbrellas and awnings allowing for outdoor eating. Boat Quay curved away from them, allowing the river to widen before it narrowed again to get under the next bridge upstream. Walking between the buildings on their left and the awnings and river to their right they were trapped. They had no choice but to run the gauntlet of restaurateurs. These were a highly specialised breed of reverse bouncers holding out menus for inspection, trying to persuade Drake and Lucy of the absolute necessity of eating their particular food. Each one gave off its own distinctive odours: Chinese of course but also Malay, Thai, Indian and some places Drake had never heard of and didn't like to admit it. There was even an Italian and most puzzling of all, a place masquerading as a London pub. Lucy had already learned the trick of not making eye contact and certainly not engaging any of the menu-holders in conversation but her father's slow pace endangered her strategy as the more desperate characters walked backwards alongside them, turning pages. They were saved by a figure waving both arms over his head from a table right next to the river. Tom had booked pride of place for them.

'This is our favourite haunt for lunch if we have time, and to wind down after work. What can I get you to drink?' Tom said as they collapsed onto seats, each under portable electric fans.

'What ever is local, long and cold.' Drake mopped his brow to laughter from his children.

'Three Tiger Beers; no make that a jug,' Tom instructed the waiter. Tom told them how the old buildings lining Boat Quay had been rescued from demolition with only days to spare. They watched more bum boats plodding up and down giving rides to tourists being instructed to strain their necks to see the historic terraces behind them or to admire the new parliament complex across the river. As Tom and Lucy chatted about their lives and jobs, Drake noticed a man standing leaning against the corner of a building talking on a mobile phone. It looked very like his police driver. If he had been followed it had been done pretty skilfully. Drake prided himself on his ability to spot a tail. He must be a little more careful tomorrow.

Tom and Lucy had given up on him and were talking about the coming weekend. They had often seen the blank expression that invited no interruption. Tom said that the Jimmy Cheung case had been given surprisingly minimal coverage in the newspapers in Singapore. He had noticed an obituary in the Straits Times but it was little more than an announcement. He showed Drake the issue of the day that devoted a couple of pages to the announcements of births, deaths, marriages, anniversaries and the like. Unlike the staid pieces of text in English newspapers, here family members and friends compete for the largest panels or even full pages to print photographs messages. Tom thought it was odd that such a significant figure had not received this treatment. He had found a small announcement about Jimmy Cheung's death in a Chinese language newspaper.

'So what does it actually say then, Tom?'

'It's tricky to translate directly into English but the sense of it seems to be something about how his shining light has finally gone out; it seems slightly poetic and romantic. It isn't signed. Jenny can probably give you a better translation.'

'Thank you, Tom that's really useful,' muttered Drake getting increasingly frustrated. He was trying to transfer enough lemon chicken or pineapple rice from plate to mouth to make chewing worth the effort. The chopsticks provided were in no mood to make the task any easier so a fork was brought from the kitchen across the road. Having been humiliated by food twice in one day, and with the time difference catching up on him, Drake decided it was time to retire.

'I had better go and get some sleep. Tomorrow I want to do some digging.'

'OK,' said Lucy. 'I'll fix you, Tom and Jenny with the best seats for my last night on Saturday when you won't be so tired. I don't want you nodding off in my big solo.'

'And then on Sunday,' added Tom, 'Jenny and I are going to hold a party for you. All our friends are anxious to meet the famous detective from Scotland Yard.'

To: m.henshaw@cheshire.pnn.police.uk
Cc: g.hepple@cheshire.pnn.police.uk
Subject: Testing this infernal email thing
From: c.drake@aol.com
Date: Wed, 20 Sep 2000 19:29:12

Hello Martin, have I finally got this email thing working?
Drake

To: m.henshaw@cheshire.pnn.police.uk
Cc: g.hepple@cheshire.pnn.police.uk
Subject: Testing this infernal email thing
From: c.drake@aol.com
Date: Wed, 20 Sep 2000 19:29:38

Hello Martin, have I finally got this email thing working?
Drake

To: c.drake@aol.com
Cc: g.hepple@cheshire.pnn.police.uk
Subject: re: Testing this infernal email thing
From: m.henshaw@cheshire.pnn.police.uk
Date: Wed, 20 Sep 2000 12:55:14

Yes sir…receiving you loud and clear…you sent the same message twice !
Where are you?
Martin Henshaw

To: m.henshaw@cheshire.pnn.police.uk
Cc: g.hepple@cheshire.pnn.police.uk
Subject: Good
From: c.drake@aol.com
Date: Wed, 20 Sep 2000 19:29:38

Oh sorry. I can't tell whether the message has gone or not. It is still all a mystery to me I am afraid.
I'm in Singapore. I came to see my son and daughter and to do some digging. I will tell you more about it tomorrow. I am going to bed now.
Drake

To: c.drake@aol.com
Cc: g.hepple@cheshire.pnn.police.uk
Subject: re: Good
From: m.henshaw@cheshire.pnn.police.uk
Date: Wed, 20 Sep 2000 13:45:05

Why what time is it there?
Martin Henshaw

To: m.henshaw@cheshire.pnn.police.uk
Cc: g.hepple@cheshire.pnn.police.uk
Subject: Time
From: c.drake@aol.com
Date: Thu, 21 Sep 2000 01:13:43

I have absolutely no idea what time it is! I don't even know what day it is!
I just woke up again. I thought it was morning but it's still the middle of the night.
Now I don't know if I am tired or not.
Can you check out an organisation called Asean Art and Antiques Pte Ltd. I found this shop entirely by accident and it sounds familiar. They use three letter A's linked together as a logo. I was wondering if they are one of the sponsors of SEABU. Have you checked out their notice board again yet?
Drake

To: c.drake@aol.com
Cc: g.hepple@cheshire.pnn.police.uk
Subject: re: Time
From: m.henshaw@cheshire.pnn.police.uk
Date: Wed, 20 Sep 2000 17:41:21

That could well be no sign of their name on the sponsor's board at SEABU but a nameplate has been unscrewed some displays/sculptures have AAA on them looks like you found something sir keep digging
Found Sheng Tian alibi false arrested him still wants to tell the same story think he will crack soon
Martin Henshaw

To: c.drake@aol.com
Cc: m.henshaw@cheshire.pnn.police.uk
Subject: see attached
From: g.hepple@cheshire.pnn.police.uk
Date: Wed, 20 Sep 2000 17:41:21
Attachment: MalloryOddOration.doc

Found the attached in Professor Peter Mallory's office. Pretty extraordinary stuff. Looks like Mallory has more to tell us. Obviously didn't like Jimmy Cheung but there are no notes and nothing in here is really hard enough to go on. Perhaps you can find out more while you are in Singapore sir. So far no sign of Mallory himself but we are tracking his phone now. Also think SEABU worth more investigation on this basis.
Grace Hepple

To: m.henshaw@cheshire.pnn.police.uk
Cc: g.hepple@cheshire.pnn.police.uk
Subject: Arrest
From: c.drake@aol.com
Date: Thu, 21 Sep 2000 09:53:23

I have just woken up and it really is morning here now but I guess you must be in bed asleep. How confusing all this is! I just don't understand all this time difference business.

Careful with Sheng Tian. Not sure arrest is wise. Unless you can assemble a case we can take to court, you cannot charge him and will have to release him. We are entitled to hold his passport. Keep me informed on that. Grace, the alternative oration from Mallory is particularly interesting. He might not have liked Jimmy but why prepare a whole document like this? Find and question Mallory as soon as possible. Keep me informed. Going digging in the sun.
Drake

# 9 - Pottery

Nature was playing that favourite English autumn trick of suddenly and quite without warning, producing a cold and dark evening. Grace shivered as she realised she really needed a coat. Drops of dew on the grass began glistening tentatively in the pale light cast from a half moon. The drooping habit of the ash trees surrounding the lawn added a ghostly quality. They swayed as the evening breeze occasionally rattled the lower hanging branches. The SEABU building hovered in total darkness, revealing a new character, sinister, almost haunting. It would make a wonderful stage set, perhaps the royal hunting lodge scene from the first act of Swan Lake.

Grace's mind wandered back to her childhood obsession with the ballet. When she joined the police force she still wondered if she could have made it as a dancer. Now she was so immersed in a successful career and she had forgotten those times, until meeting Drake's daughter last year. Lucy's excitement and enthusiasm rekindled Grace's interest. She had no regrets. This was the career for her but the romance of the ballet still haunted her.

She had no idea why she was walking this way to her lodgings except that she wanted time to think. She was at odds with Henshaw over Sheng Tian. She desperately wanted to be supporting him and to have his approval. The last couple of days had gone so well, and he seemed pleased with her work. But then they had parted with Henshaw showing a stiff formality and awkwardness that she had seen several times.

Men were so difficult. She realised that her assertiveness sometimes alienated them, so she tried to moderate it. She thought Henshaw was much less confident than his manner suggested. It was fine when they saw things the same way but when they disagreed! Grace thought they both recognised the problem but neither had found a way to communicate that understanding. All very difficult! With Drake it was easy. He simply played the father figure role; she the learning and dutiful offspring.

A flash of light from one of the SEABU building windows brought Grace to an abrupt halt. She stood on the path that hugged the line of the trees skirting the lawn in front of the building. There it was again, another flash and then a third in quick succession. The laws of probability told her they must be related to the same incident. She looked up at the sky searching for another source of illumination. She thought she heard the sound of a car driving away down the road forming the boundary of the campus. Perhaps it had been headlights. There was no further sign from the dark building. She heaved a sigh of relief and continued on her way. Then it happened again. The suspicion in her mind had only pretended to go away. Actually it had hung around for a while just in case. Now she was certain. Something was going on in there.

Cutting across the short-cropped grass, she reached the SEABU building in seconds. So far she had made no sound; her footsteps absorbed by the spongy manicured lawns in front of the steps to the floating balcony. The curving footpath towards the entrance was made from flagstones let into the grass. She could see clearly in the moonlight and stepped easily between them maintaining her silence. Now she had to climb the wooden steps without making a noise. She felt her heart thump against her chest. Then she was on the timber deck that surrounded the building. So far so good. The plate glass doors in front of her had no handles or locks that she could see. She wondered if she should look for another entrance. She moved forward slowly to look inside. Swoosh! It was the suddenness of the doors sliding open that startled her rather than the noise. In fact they hardly made a sound. Recovering, she stepped inside hoping the doors would close as quietly behind her. They did.

It was dark inside. Why then was the building unlocked? Perhaps it was a porter doing his security round. That suspicious feeling was now tramping around all over her brain. Her heart was beating even faster. She moved further into the building until the corridor came into view. The moonlight was playing on the sculptures in the courtyard, pretending to be a graveyard. It looked even more theatrical but she had no thoughts of the ballet now. Grace wished she knew her way around. Her eyes were now fully adapted to dark interior. Tiny emergency lights along the corridor ceiling glowed without illuminating much. They cast faint patches of light, creating a regular rhythm along the floor. She moved slowly down the corridor looking into each room she passed. They were all in darkness. She caught occasional glimpses through the landscape to the wall on the opposite side of the courtyard.

Then it happened again. There was a brief flash of light. It was subdued but there was no doubt about it. It came from the next side of the courtyard. She stopped and stood deep in shadow at the back of the corridor to watch. She saw it again, this time for slightly longer. She waited. Several minutes passed. She estimated perhaps three or four. There was no further sign. She could hear her own breathing. It was so deafening that surely anyone else in the building would hear it. It was a new emotion and it puzzled her. She was frightened, terrified even but she still felt in control. She was almost enjoying the situation.

She edged forward again slowly and turned the corner. Now she could clearly see the open area with the display cabinets that Drake and Henshaw had described. She looked inside each one. First the ghastly looking curved daggers. That didn't help much! Next were the pistols; further on a display of bamboo brushes and Chinese calligraphy. Then a case containing pottery was lit by moonshine from windows high in the roof above. She could clearly see a brass plaque on the cabinet; the collection was of Peranakan dinner services from Melaka. She had no idea what that meant but the bottom line of the plaque told her that AAA donated the collection. The same as in Drake's email!

She paused again and listened. The silence was so silent it was thunderous. It was a tense silence. The sort of silence that is wondering just what will break it. Swoosh. Grace recognised the sound. The front doors had opened for somebody. Whoever she had been tracking must have gone round the other side of the courtyard. She retraced her steps as quickly as she could until she reached the main entrance. The doors were shut but then they would be. She approached them and they obligingly opened with that normally reassuring but now terrifying, sound; yes that was definitely what she had heard. She scanned across the lawns between the SEABU building and the line of trees. Then she saw the movement. At first she hadn't noticed it but now she could see it clearly. A dark figure was moving across the grass in a jog. It was not an athletic run but the motion was definitely one of haste and it was not following the line of any path. Grace stood to one side to allow the doors to close. The figure reached the edge of the grass, looked over its shoulder and disappeared into the trees. Whoever had been in the building must have heard or seen her. Grace would stand no chance of following without being seen; any sort of pursuit would be fruitless.

She decided to take one more look around the building. If she had disturbed the intruder, there might be some signs left behind. She walked the other way round the courtyard, her heartbeat beginning to subside. At last she got hold of that suspicious feeling and told it to get the hell out of the pit of her stomach. Every door she passed was shut, except for one. The room looked like a record store, the wall opposite her was covered in filing racks. In the middle of the room was a small simple desk and chair. On the desk were three small piles of files. She opened the single drawer of the desk. It was empty. One pile of files seemed to be lying awkwardly; she lifted the corner of the top file. Underneath she saw finely crafted wooden nameplate that read "Asean Art and Antiques Pte". One of the filing cabinets behind the desk was open. A file was lying across the top of the drawer with the cover turned back as if someone was referring to it. She leant over to examine it more closely. Grace Hepple did not see the figure clad totally in black slowly move up behind her. Nor did she see the heavy torch it was carrying. She saw nothing.

It was mid-morning in Singapore by the time Drake had risen from his fitful slumbers, dressed, eaten his breakfast, and completed his emails. He was rather proud of getting all this technology to work. He sent off the last message with a grunt of satisfaction. Tom's apartment, like so many in Singapore, was too small to have a spare bedroom so he had offered the couch in their living room but it was not really Drake-shaped. He needed to get some sleep to counteract the jetlag. This hotel was right in the centre of the city and it would be easy for him to move around independently. In fact the room was so large he could go for a walk without leaving it. He shambled around aimlessly for a while exploring, stretching and yawning in equal quantities. Wanting to see it more clearly he tugged at the floor to ceiling curtains stretched right across one wall. The only result was a slight flapping of the heavy drapes.

He guessed more technology was involved and searched around behind the ends of the curtain for something that might be a button. No luck. He sat on his bed plucking up the courage to call room service and ask them how the hell you opened the curtains here. His hand was poised over the phone on his bedside table and then he saw it. Lurking there all the time on his bedside panel was the single word 'night' separating two outward pointing arrows. A soft whirring sound briefly preceded the brilliant flash of daylight that flooded the room. The whole wall was now a great patch of dazzling white light. 'Day' opened the gauze curtains still covering the windows. The sky was bright blue with a distant vertical cloud loitering in the distance, trying to get enough others to join it in becoming a tropical thunderstorm. With each pace towards the window, more of the city of Singapore below came into view. It was a stunning sight and for a moment he was quite intoxicated by it. He flopped into the armchair placed beside the window and picked up the electronic card that was his room key from the coffee table. He read his room number, 6014; of course he was sixty floors up.

At first the view had been just one great panorama but after a minute or so it began to reveal detail. He could see the buildings alongside Boat Quay where he had sat with his son and daughter. He could trace the line of the river snaking its route from the heart of the island out to the harbour and the sea. Out there he could see more ships than he could shake a stick at, every one obediently pointing out the direction of the tide. They looked like some huge naval parade as they waited their chance to dock. In the far distance, over to his right, he could make out the cranes of the port where they might unload their cargoes.

Drake's eyes panned back down and across the city. Facing him, across perhaps a mile of space, was the busy cluster of towers forming the banking quarter where Tom worked. They made a contrasting but surprisingly appropriate backdrop to the small historic buildings lining the river where the young Jimmy Cheung must have operated. Cynthia and her friends would have talked about an architectural dialogue between the old and the new. Actually Drake thought they weren't so much in conversation as giving each other the cold shoulder. Either way it worked. It was a unique and special place.

His eyes wandered across the intervening landscape and settled on what looked like a large area of grass with a cricket pavilion. Surely not cricket here, he thought but a small group of white clad figures practicing in some nets removed any doubts. He remembered his walk the day before and wondered how it was possible to play cricket in this climate. What was that they said about mad dogs and Englishmen? Rather them than him.

Grace Hepple felt a searing pain in her head, a headache like no other she had ever known. She wondered how it had come on so suddenly. She instinctively put her hand to her head and felt the bandage. A shock travelled the length of her body. Why was she in bed? What time was it? What was that smell? Where was she?

'Are you feeling better, Sergeant Hepple?' said a voice softly. Grace sat up suddenly. Actually she did no such thing. Her brain issued sitting up instructions but nothing happened. A soft light appeared and a figure in a nurse's uniform came into focus, held her shoulder reassuringly and smiled.

'You had a nasty bang on the head,' said the nurse. 'You must rest now.' Grace tried to argue. She knew she had something to do but she could not remember what it was. She smiled weakly back at the nurse and felt a wave of tiredness come over her. Her head throbbed again. She struggled against the sudden weight of her eyelids but the battle was short and she lost it.

The drive to the hospital took an eternity. Every traffic light was red and every pedestrian crossing obstructed by dodderers; didn't they realise he had to get there to see her? Henshaw had immediately terminated his morning interview with Sheng Tian when Denson interrupted with the news that Grace Hepple was in hospital and unconscious. Sheng Tian was being more inscrutable than ever and had obviously spent the night stiffening his resolve to say nothing further no matter what the question. The news about Grace had felt like a stab in the heart to Henshaw. He had no idea what she had been doing in the SEABU building but he felt responsible. They had parted slightly tetchily the previous evening. He wondered if she had gone off to try to prove something to him. He arrived at her room with his professional and personal feelings swirling in a maelstrom of confusion as he was told she had briefly recovered consciousness.

'You do expect a full recovery then?'

'I see no reason why not,' said the young hospital registrar who had now also joined the little throng of people outside Grace Hepple's room. 'It would be best if she is left to rest for a day or so more before you start asking her to remember the events.'

'As I understand it,' said Henshaw, 'she was found by ambulance staff on the floor in one of the rooms in the SEABU building in Deva University at around ten thirty last night?' The manager of the emergency unit nodded agreement. 'You received an anonymous call. Is that right?'

'Yes, Inspector,' she said. 'The emergency call centre should be able to trace it if you want.'

Henshaw nodded. 'I need to establish what she was doing. It looks like she may have disturbed someone. If so, he or she may have panicked once Grace fell unconscious. Later that panic could have turned to concern that she should not die, escalating the crime to murder, hence the anonymous call to the emergency services. If I'm right then tracing the caller may not only give us Grace's assailant but may also lead to important progress on our murder enquiry.'

'OK,' said the emergency unit manager. 'We can probably sort this out immediately if you come to my office.' The group moved away from Grace Hepple's hospital room, leaving the nurse with instructions to call them when Grace woke again. Several turns of corridors and two staircases later, Henshaw had lost track of where he was except that he was drinking a welcome cup of tea while several phone calls were made.

'Bad news I am afraid,' said the unit manager. 'The call centre has logged the call as number unknown. It is almost certainly from a mobile. It may be possible to get the major networks to search their records but this may be a lengthy process.'

'There is no sign of a break in at the building as far as we can see,' said Henshaw. 'This suggests that the assailant may be someone who works there. I'll get a list of the mobile phone numbers of key people we are already interested in.' Henshaw called Sally Brown at Dr. Percival's office and asked her to obtain the numbers of any university provided mobile phones for the SEABU director Hamish McFadden and his deputy, Dr Marcia Elliot. He made it clear to her that under no circumstances must the two of them be alerted to this request. Henshaw's own mobile phone rang. He did not recognise the number on its little screen except that it was from another mobile.

'This is McFadden here from SEABU. They gave me this number at the police station. I rang to complain about our building being closed off this morning. It is just not good enough, Henshaw. We have important visitors arriving today and I have all my staff standing around outside, with your bloody silly blue and white tape across the doorway.'

'I'm sorry but a serious crime was committed in the building last night and it is sealed off until our scene of crime officers have completed their investigations. We will allow you in as soon as we possibly can.'

'Surely you don't need the whole damn building, Henshaw?'

'I'm afraid we do, for the time being at least. We have no way at this stage of knowing where in the building we may find crucial evidence.'

'When will we be able to get into the building then?' demanded McFadden, with an air of resignation about losing the first part of his battle.

'I am coming over there in a few minutes. I will confer with my colleagues and give you an estimate.' It was Henshaw's turn to be angry at McFadden's bombastic approach. On the other hand he now had McFadden's number and he passed it back to the station with a mild rebuke about giving out his own mobile number and instructions to have McFadden's traced back twenty four hours.

Turning a corner from the hotel lift lobby, Drake was hit by the buzz and hustle that is the Singapore shopping-mall experience. At eye-level was a sea of mainly young people doing what young people do in shopping centres. As far as Drake could tell this did not involve going into a shop, choosing the cheapest, making sure you really wanted it and could afford it, paying for it and leaving. Whatever it was they did, there were an awful lot of them and they were doing it very noisily. High up above in the atrium, two circus performers swung on trapezes advertising a new phone network. He watched them idly for a while, trying to make a connection between telephones and trapezes.

Drake had collected a map both of the streets and public transport of Singapore. The Mass Rapid Transit system map clearly showed a station called Bugis and another one was marked right over this very shopping mall. He checked the symbol, a circle with two wavy lines across it. Yes MRT station. He drifted across the mall, finally picking up the signs, down the escalator and onto the station platform. It all looked rather similar to the new London Underground Jubilee Line, with trains whispering into the platforms behind glass doors. He needed the green East-West line, neatly appropriate he thought.

As his train entered Bugis station a few minutes later, a female voice announced their arrival in soft tones and pretty much half the train stood up to escape. Bugis also turned out to be under a shopping mall with yet another hotel rising above. Drake was getting the hang of the place. It seemed to work by having these complexes of malls and hotels all conveniently air-conditioned and connected below ground by the MRT system. Getting around was not going to be quite such hard work as he had expected.

He set off along North Bridge Road and soon began to recognise places he had seen the previous day. Somehow though all the streets had developed a nasty habit of looking the same. After several fairly randomly chosen turns, he saw the AAA shop. The window featured a huge blue and white vase standing on a black wood table in the window. Drake stood as if he was looking at it but in fact he was scanning the interior of the shop itself. Looking beyond the vase, he could see furniture and silk hangings that reminded him of Sheng Tian's office at Deva University. So hard was he concentrating on this that he failed to notice a tall figure approaching him, until the very last moment.

'Good morning, sir,' it said with a polished accent as Drake turned to meet that rarest of experiences for him, a face at his own level. The face was clearly European. 'Please come in and look around. We have many more beautiful things to see.'

'Thank you,' said Drake, 'I would love to.' The tall figure stood aside and with an exaggerated wave of his arm beckoned Drake to enter before him. Once inside, his host held out a hand of greeting.

'Unless I am mistaken, I detect an English voice. I deliberately don't say "accent" because it is everyone else who has an accent.' He sniggered. 'Welcome to Asean Art and Antiques.' Drake accepted the handshake. 'I am Archie Grayson, proprietor along with my beautiful wife to be.'

'Carlton,' said Drake making use of his normally redundant first name. It was time for it to do some hard work and earn its keep.

'Pleased to make your acquaintance, Mr. Carlton,' said Archie Grayson. 'And whereabouts in England are you from?'

'Chester,' said Drake, before he had calculated the consequences of this small deceit.

'How extraordinary!' exclaimed Grayson. 'We were in that fair city only a couple of weeks ago and we shall be back there again next week. We have an important trading partner there who handles all our exports to Europe.' Drake smiled, trying to look as if he was really more interested in examining the artefacts than talking to Grayson.

His study was much more of the man than the shop. Grayson had wispy white hair, thinning and in need of a cut. He wore rimless spectacles covering blue eyes with large bags below giving him a rather weary expression. His nose was long and slightly hooked and his lips thin and wide. Although he was clean shaven there was a hint of white stubble on his face. Although very obviously English, Grayson did not look a stranger to Singapore. He wore a thin, black, Chinese smoking jacket with buttons right up to the high neck with a simple plain white tee shirt underneath. Out of the corner of his eye, Drake noticed a small delicate figure coming down the staircase at the rear of the shop.

'Amanda my dear, come and meet Mr. Carlton. Believe it or not he is from Chester!' The figure reached the bottom of the stairs and came to join them. 'Mr. Carlton this is Amanda Goh. We run this business together but she is also the light of my life.' By now the figure had reached Drake and held out a hand as Grayson rested one of his on her shoulder. She was little more than half Grayson's height and perhaps also his age.'

'Pleased to meet you Mr. Carlton. Welcome to our shop,' she said, bowing even lower so Drake had to stoop to shake her hand. She spoke immaculately. There was no mistaking her oriental accent but from even those few words Drake was sure that she was well educated.

'Charmed but I am not at all sure I could afford all this.' Drake waved an arm expansively around the showroom. 'I came in to look around at your husband's invitation. You have many beautiful things here.'

'Don't worry, old chap,' said Grayson 'We enjoy showing discerning people the art of the ASEAN region. There is no obligation to buy whatsoever. I see you were looking at our little Peranakan display in the window. We have more material down here.' Grayson strode off deep into the shop until he reached a large dining table set out with a complete dinner service in yellows, pinks and greens. Drake had never seen anything like it. It was obviously old and yet daringly modern in its adventurous use of colour. 'We can supply to the UK of course,' continued Grayson. 'Strictly speaking we should not but we have ways of circumventing difficulties.' He touched the side of his nose and gave Drake a very significant stare.

'What are these "difficulties", Mr. Grayson?'

'Oh nothing to worry about. There is a shortage of really good Peranakan pottery in complete undamaged sets and there is a growing collector's market. There is a general agreement that such material should not go outside the Straits Settlements. Nothing more than that but for other reasons we prefer not to have the attention of our export control people.' Again Drake was flashed the knowing smile. He had only the vaguest notion what Grayson was talking about but this last comment was reverberating in his head. Perhaps his digging was getting near to uncovering something interesting after all. Grayson was a delight; his open and almost innocent manner was playing right into Drake's hand.

'It has been interesting to meet you both,' said Drake, feeling he should get better informed before this went any further. 'I am sure I shall want to come back when I have more time. Thank you Mr. Grayson.'

'Archie,' said Grayson, 'please call me Archie.' Drake declined the implicit invitation to invent a first name and turned to leave.

As he headed back towards the front of the shop, he noticed a stack of familiar-looking wooden boxes standing on the floor behind a table. Making a detour around the table, he checked back and could see that Archie Grayson and his partner were now deep in conversation at the back of the shop. He lifted the lid of the top box. It was completely empty and as he tried to fix the catch it slid across the pile and came to rest against the box behind which seemed to offer more resistance. He tried the lid on the second box behind but found it locked. He was certain that these boxes were identical to the one in which Sheng Tian kept his pistol. Drake moved away from the boxes quickly and then sauntered his way out through the front of the shop.

It seemed so incongruous. The MRT train station at Raffles Place tested Drake's maturing architectural sensibility. This highly automated and modern transport system swept him along in air-conditioned comfort while all around him teenagers swapped text messages, hammering their thumbs on phones and giggling to each other. Here was a society dependent on modern technology and celebrating it. This station was expressed above ground as two classical temples facing each other across the green open space of an urban square, giving no clues about the modernity below. Surrounding them were the towers of the central business district obliterating much of the sky. Drake felt dizzy just trying to see the top of them.

He wandered haltingly to the side of the square that is Raffles Place. Partly he was drawn to the shade; partly he was getting a better view of Tom's building looming above but it was not the banks but a museum he was searching for. A sign above his head announced that the passageway before him was called Change Alley. He checked his map and followed signposts to Boat Quay and Empress Place that took him out of the square at the nearest corner. Two turns later, he was walking down the side of the rather grand Fullerton Hotel. Tom had told him the previous evening how it had recently been converted from the old quayside post office into a sufficiently prestigious location to attract the patronage of Bill Clinton.

He came to the Singapore River where the young Jimmy Cheung had worked. Stretching away in a great curve to his left was Boat Quay where he had spent such a pleasant evening with Tom and Lucy. According to his map the museum should be on the opposite bank but first he had to cross a bridge.

The delightful structure was painted white just like the Queen's Bridge at Chester where Jimmy Cheung had been murdered. Both were iron suspension structures and carried only pedestrians. This one however had solid bars replacing the cables of the Chester bridge and it was an altogether lower affair. The clearance underneath was minimal. The bum boats giving their trips, chugged by only just passing beneath it, passengers straining their necks to see the structure above as the audio commentary told them of its history. A sign built into the tower at the end, told him that The Cavenagh Bridge had been prefabricated in Glasgow. When built it must have spoken to the locals of a Victorian industrialised country half a world away.

Standing back on the opposite bank at the end of a footpath was The Asian Civilisations Museum, a white building in a version of colonial classical. Drake was glad to be enveloped by the elegant cool interior. Paying his admission fee, he was soon lost in the magical world created by the exhibits it contained. They told of a myriad of Asian cultures with far longer and more distinguished pasts than those of his Western world. History had not been Drake's strong suit at school. Since then he had little time for reading dusty tomes of boring facts. That was how he saw it anyway. So the extent of his knowledge of ancient oriental cultures was embarrassingly small. He knew that Chinese cultures had been fairly sophisticated for many centuries. He tried to think what else he knew. Right now he couldn't think of anything.

In here were the artefacts, clothing, art and architecture of Malays, Dyaks, and Khmer as well as tribes with names like Batak that Drake had never heard of before. There were objects from

Cambodia, Sumatra, Java, Thailand and Vietnam as well as the Malay peninsular. It was the most exotic collection of peoples, places and objects that Drake had ever encountered and he was soon transported by it all. He wondered why he hadn't got interested in history before. Cynthia would be proud of him. First architecture now history. This was a new Drake indeed!

Then there it was. A section devoted to the Peranakans. They weren't an ancient civilisation at all but a more recent culture created by the intermarrying of local Malay women with Chinese traders travelling along the Silk Road sea routes. A map explained Grayson's reference to the Straits Settlements. These were the cities that grew up along the Straits of Melaka, starting with Singapore and Johor, just across the border in Malaysia, and continuing further north through Melaka itself and on up to Georgetown on the Island of Penang. It was beginning to come together now. That was why the local newspaper was called the Straits Times! He examined his copy of Mallory's oration telling how Jimmy's parents moved from Johor to Singapore. Perhaps Jimmy Cheung had Peranakan blood in him.

Drake learned how the Babas, as Peranakan men were known, rapidly became wealthy and influential. During the Victorian era they enthusiastically embraced modern western technology and were among the first in the region to install electricity in their houses. Their wives, the Nyonyas, governed highly ritualised households and stood as guardians over a strict set of traditions for the marrying of their children designed to preserve and maintain the Peranakan culture. Drake studied all the exhibits of the crafts, furniture and artefacts of Nyonya and Baba life. He was genuinely fascinated by all this but he was also determined to be able to hold a more convincing conversation with Archie Grayson should the need arise. There was a dazzling display of a complete Peranakan dining service with all the plates, bowls, dishes, cups and saucers, tureens, urns, teapots as well as every shape of jug that could be imagined to have a purpose and a few more besides. Drake was so wrapped up in his studies and busy making notes that he did not notice the figure standing alongside him.

'Is there any way I can help you?' Drake spun round to his right, and then his left and finally down to see the tiniest Chinese woman. She wore a high-necked black top held together with loops over buttons down the front. Looking even further down, Drake could see her black skirt reaching almost to the ground. On the end of her nose was a pair of gold-rimmed half spectacles over which she was looking up at him.

'I'm a curator here,' she said in a faint breathless sort of voice full of enthusiasm. 'We run guided tours starting from the lobby but for a student such as yourself I am only too pleased to offer personal assistance. My name is Wu Dao Rui.' Drake made an embarrassing sort of curtsy in order to shake her hand, which completely disappeared inside his own.

'Carlton Drake. Nice to meet you. I had no idea how much there was to learn about this part of the world. I suddenly feel very ignorant.'

'Sadly the West is generally not well educated about eastern cultures and their histories. If we all knew as little about you as you do about us, then the world would be in a terrible mess.' As she spoke her voice rose in pitch until she burst into a giggle that shook her small frame almost into convulsion and she beamed up at Drake. He realised that he had just been rebuked in the politest possible way and smiled back an acknowledgement.

'I see you are interested in the Peranakans,' said Wu Dao Rui, clasping her hands in front of her and half turning to look at the display while still keeping Drake in view. 'They had, still have, the most remarkable and elaborate culture. It involves a great deal of ritual around dressing, eating and marrying. Meals were lengthy and complex affairs in the height of the Peranakan period. Weddings went on for days and involved many of these formal meals. The Nyonyas ran the household often with rods of iron. More recently there has been much intermarrying of Peranakans with other races but many still disapprove of it.

This panel here shows how a daughter would be chosen by a mother for her son. Look how they valued certain facial features and body shapes. Mothers would only allow their sons to marry women who were well trained in the Peranakan ways. I always think it odd that they had such elaborate mechanisms to prevent intermarrying and yet their whole existence depended on that in the first place.' She shrieked with laughter as if the idea had only just occurred to her. 'But it was not always so funny,' she continued very earnestly lowering her voice again. 'There are stories in the old days of girls and even sometimes boys who married without permission being murdered. Terrible. Terrible.'

'Fascinating,' said Drake, 'I'm trying to learn more about the history of Singapore.'

'This place has been called by many names; Temasek, Singapura, Syonan-to, Si Lat Po,' replied his new guide and mentor. 'But Singapore as such has only a very short history. It only came into existence in 1965.'

'I am particularly interested in the early period of trading on the river.'

'That is in another part of our museum. I can show you how to get there. It suddenly seems very popular with you English.' Then as if in a sudden panic and putting her hand to her mouth she added, 'you are English aren't you?'

Drake nodded and smiled.

'Thank goodness. I usually get that right. I give guided tours some days and I so much prefer the English tourists you know. They ask far more sensible questions than the Americans.' This last sentence was whispered in a highly confidential sort of way as if she was giving away some state secret.

'Has someone else been asking about the Singapore River then?'

'Only a couple of weeks ago another English visitor. Very colonial he looked,' she gave another little giggle. 'I could tell he was English straight away. He wore a white crumpled linen suit and carried a big floppy hat. He asked me endless questions and came back to see me twice. He was a history professor too!'

'Really!' said Drake, 'perhaps I know him.'

'Professor Marrolly, was his name. He gave me his card,' she said proudly.

‘I think you must mean Professor Mallory.’

‘Yes, yes, Professor Marrolly.’ In truth she managed to make both consonants sound almost identical. Surely this was research beyond the call of duty for a public orator.

‘You know him then? He has a bad limp, poor man.’

‘Well, I know of him,’ answered Drake, though he was not sure she understood the subtle distinction. ‘What was Mallory interested in?’

Wu Dao Rui described how the Singapore River had worked as a harbour worked by coolies ferrying goods to the old godowns in their bumboats. She explained the Chinese clan structure to Drake and how to tell which clan a bumboat belonged to from the colour around the eye on the prow. Apparently Mallory had also wanted to know about the period of British rule and how the coolies were organised, managed and lodged in Kengs.

‘Singapore is more fascinating than I had expected,’ said Drake.

‘Poor Singapore,’ said Wu Dao Rui, looking wistfully into the distance. It has been buffeted by so many unfortunate events in a very short history. It is a story of so many cultures and the struggle that inevitably results from the mistrust that builds up between them.’

‘Really?’ exclaimed Drake. From what I have seen it seems such a wonderful multi-cultural place where so many peoples co-exist so happily.’

‘On the surface maybe. Today we are prosperous and these problems disappear in good times but go back to more troubled periods and you see nothing but conflict. The Maria Hertogh case could stand as a symbol for this.’ She directed Drake’s attention to a screen. He read the heartbreaking story of the young Dutch girl who became separated from her parents in the Japanese occupation and was then brought up as a Muslim. At the age of 13 in 1950, a law court ruled she should be returned to her original parents. Riots ensued as the Muslim community interpreted this judgement as an attack on their religion.

‘What a mess,’ said Drake, ‘but what ever judgement the courts could have made, would have resulted in trouble.’

'Exactly,' said Wu Dao Rui, in the manner of a schoolteacher pleased to see her pupil understanding a complex lesson. 'When we intervene in the lives of cultures like this we create nothing but agony. But Singapore has moved on. We have been fortunate to have such a progressive government and we have been remarkably lucky in shaking free of the problems that follow colonial rule but you British were nothing like as benevolent as your own history books suggest.'

'What sort of problems did we leave behind then?'

'All sorts of things,' said Wu Dao Rui, putting on a stern expression. 'Mostly it came from a complete ignorance and insensitivity to culture rather than from any malevolence. Take the 1870s riots as an example. Here we had the Chinese fighting each other, all because of a clumsiness on the part of the British. Many people were killed and families were set against each other. It took many years to recover. Perhaps it never did.'

'What did we do wrong?' asked Drake, remembering McFadden's lecture about British administrative incompetence.

'The government awarded the new mail contract to a Hokkien company. Previously the traditional letter writers and carriers had all been Teochews. With a little bit of care, perhaps someone taking a little local advice, all this could have been avoided. Originally the Boat Quay trade that you are so interested in was run mainly by the Teochews but after the Japanese occupation, Hokkiens took over more. The history of Boat Quay is one of clashes and clan societies and protection rackets. It is a story of murder and extortion and of poverty and appalling conditions. It is not as romantic as it looks but the Japanese occupation was surely our most unhappy time.' A sad expression washed across Wu Dao Rui's face as she ushered Drake to a panel about the Second World War. She began again in a hushed voice.

'Singapore was renamed Syonan-to by the Japanese which translates as "Light of the South". What an irony. All light was surely extinguished during that awful time!'

There were examples of the Japanese currency and taped interviews with old folk who lived through the occupation. There were displays of how the Japanese tried to obliterate the Chinese culture insisting on children learning Japanese in school. Drake learned about the earlier Singaporean support for China over its long war with Japan of which he knew almost nothing. Wu Dao Rui showed him a section on the wartime resistance in Singapore and how this was countered by the Japanese. Displays documented the atrocities of the so-called Sook Ching when intellectuals and members of the resistance were sometimes identified by local informers. Those who were betrayed in this way were mostly taken away and shot. So poor were records that the true scale of this operation remained uncertain, with estimates ranging between five and twenty-five thousand killed.

Drake was shocked to hear Wu Dao Rui argue that even these atrocities could be seen as the result of the British simply evacuating and leaving the poor Singaporeans to their fate. A pamphlet for Fort Siloso on Sentosa Island showed him the British gun emplacements pointing out to sea. The Japanese invaded from the north through Thailand and Malaya, rendering the British guns useless. Drake remembered some reference to this in Mallory's oration for Jimmy Cheung's degree. Wu Dao Rui shuddered and then smiled as she told him how the British came back at the end of the war. She pointed out a picture of a tableau of the surrender by General Itagaki to Mountbatten in City Hall in 1945.

'Do you know?' she continued again in her confidential whisper, 'we have had Japanese teenagers in here who have no knowledge at all about the war with China and the occupation of Singapore, Malaysia and Thailand. It is shocking to think that their education system blanks all that out. I have seen some of them here in tears when they discover the atrocities that were committed by their ancestors. It must be difficult for them, I think. At least the British are more able to learn from the past. Professor Marrolly was very interested in this period. Now I am late for a meeting.' She touched Drake on the forearm and stared up into his face as her diminutive frame began to shake with laughter. 'You have been a very attentive student,' with that her laughter rose to a piercing shriek and she scuttled off round the display cabinets.

To: c.drake@aol.com
Subject: Grace
From: m.henshaw@cheshire.pnn.police.uk
Date: Thu, 21 Sep 2000 17:41:21

Grace has been found unconscious in the SEABU building was obviously attacked late last night have no idea why she was there...hope to be able to talk to her soon...doctors think she will make a full recovery but thought you should know.
How are you doing?
Martin Henshaw

To: m.henshaw@cheshire.pnn.police.uk
Subject: re: Grace
From: c.drake@aol.com
Date: Fri, 21 Sep 2000 09:53:23

Oh my goodness, how awful. Do you think the silly girl went there to investigate by herself? Tell me how she is. Give her my love if you can.
AAA are definitely involved in this somehow, I am more sure than ever now. But the amazing news is that Mallory has actually been over here poking around. Can you confirm if he has a limp? Have you hauled him in yet? If so do not tell him I know about his visit here, I want to handle that myself when I get back. I have promised to go and see Lucy perform. I will get a flight back as soon as I can after that.
Drake

In the distance Drake could see the extraordinary roof of the theatre. He remembered Cynthia telling him about how this building had been designed by a British architect and showing him drawings and photographs of models in her journals. She did not live to see it finished. The realisation of this caught him suddenly and he stood, slightly hunched, looking at the building.

Drake had several times debated with Cynthia and her friends. He had argued that detective work is similar to being an architect. The architect has to see the wishes and needs and behaviours of all the people using his building and imagine the various possibilities of form that would somehow fit them all. The detective has to take in all the behaviours and personalities of the characters involved in a crime and his job is to imagine all the possible scenarios that could fit the facts. He sees exactly what everyone else sees, as does the architect but only he can imagine the actual events that fit. He has to invent, to imagine, to create; just like an architect. Cynthia's architect friends had been unconvinced by the analogy. They had an infuriatingly egocentric way with them, architects.

Already the locals had started to name the building. Some said it was an armadillo, others that is was a durian. Drake thought the latter was perhaps some character from a science fiction film until Tom had explained that durian was a local and highly sought after fruit with a heavily armoured skin. As he explored the foyer, Drake could now see that the roof was a sort of inverted kitchen sieve of enormous proportions. Each little cell in the mesh was protected from the sun by a hood; Lucy had explained that every one was unique. The actual auditorium in which Lucy was performing sat inside this great irregular dome. Drake wished Cynthia had been with him to explain it all. To his eyes, the idea of putting up a glass dome in a tropical country and then shading it to avoid solar gain just seemed perverse. He thought that the cool, classical language of the museum had translated more naturally to this climate than this contrived highly technical modernism.

He was enveloped by a sadness that Cynthia was not there. His atheism wavered for a moment as he contemplated the idea of her looking down on them both. Lucy excitedly getting ready in some changing room deep in the bowels of the building, Drake wandering the foyer distractedly, wanting to tell all the other members of the audience that it was his daughter they were coming to see. He was looking for Tom and Jenny who had arranged to meet him here for a drink before curtain up.

More problematic was finding a way to explain to his children that he had just booked his seat on a flight home for the next day. This would mean missing the party they had organised for the end of Lucy's run but he owed it to Grace to get back She would never have been allowed to get into such danger if he had been there, and what the hell was Henshaw doing arresting Sheng Tian? It was all his fault. So here he was again, this time not with Cynthia but with Lucy and Tom and Jenny, making excuses for missing another domestic event because of the demands of a case. He hated himself for it but he knew he had no alternative. The case was accelerating too quickly for him to remain away any longer.

# 10 - Tin

Was she awake or dreaming? She guessed awake but it was hard to be sure. Her surroundings were curiously hazy, generally white and with little discernable detail. A gentle reassuring sort of hum filled her ears but her nose was detecting an unusual smell. Grace felt warm and contentedly detached from the world. She was still in bed but this was not like her bedroom. She was lying on her back but she never slept that way. The comforting looseness of her familiar duvet was replaced by a top sheet drawn tightly over her. Of course she was away from home in Chester but this was not her room there either. A wave of anxiety flooded through her but it passed as quickly as it arrived. Something told her she should feel worried but in fact she was almost euphoric. She must have had some great success but she could not think what it was. The room was coming into focus.

The nurse talking very quietly on a telephone on the far side of the room glanced anxiously at her as she stirred. Grace remembered she had felt very tired and in need of a long sleep but now she felt much better. She pulled her left arm out from under the sheets to wipe her eyes but it felt heavy and strangely slow to respond.

'Take it easy.'

'What's happened?' asked Grace in a whisper. 'Why am I here?'

'You had a bit of an accident, and banged your head. Have a little drink.' The nurse was propping Grace's head up and holding a glass to her mouth. Grace felt the bandage around her head as the nurse held slowly back down. She felt woozy, perhaps she had drunk too much. The room swam back into that white haze.

Grace opened her eyes again to see Martin Henshaw sitting beside her. She could see little but his face and it looked worried; things must have been going badly for him. Her gaze went from his frowning expression down his arm to his right hand. It was holding her left, resting on the bedclothes. Odd that; she could see it but not feel it. She must be dreaming after all. She had several times thought of being in such a position, or something not too dissimilar but this was no fantasy. Henshaw pulled his hand away embarrassed.

Suddenly an awful feeling of panic returned and consumed her. She remembered the combined emotions of fear and elation that she experienced in the SEABU building. The scene started to play through her mind, like watching a film. She concentrated on it for what seemed ages but in reality it was barely a moment. Henshaw saw the look on her face and called the nurse. He patted Grace gently on the forehead to calm her. Now she was alternating wildly between fantasies about Henshaw and recollections of the events at Deva University. The nurse urged rest but Grace was putting things together. She wanted answers and she wanted them now.

'You were found lying on the floor in the SEABU building,' said Henshaw. 'Do you remember?'

'I can remember being there,' said Grace carefully.

'What happened?'

She gave him a quizzical look. 'I guess someone hit me on the head?'

'Did you see who it was?'

'Am I OK?' she demanded. 'You sound worried.'

'You are going to be fine,' said the second nurse, 'but you need to rest.' She was pulling Grace's other arm, feeling her wrist and staring at the watch hanging from her uniform. Grace could feel her own pulse as the blood pumped against the nurse's thumb. It all made her feel like a little girl again, at home off school sick with her mother doting on her. She was calmed and reassured by the memory but with every second that passed, her mind was dealing more in the present.

'I'm in hospital!' Henshaw laughed as much from relief as the comedy of Grace's awakening.

'I was walking past the SEABU building late last night.'

'Actually it wasn't last night,' said Henshaw, 'but carry on.'

'It was dark. Then I saw a light. I went to investigate. The front door just opened automatically. I went looking around inside. I am sure there was someone there, probably with a torch but whoever it was escaped round the other side of the courtyard and ran across the grass into the trees.'

Henshaw looked disappointed and puzzled. 'So how did you get injured then?'

'No idea. Wait, now I remember. There was a room with the door open. It was a desk and a filing cabinet. Someone had opened it and was going through the files. There was an open file.'

'What happened after that?'

'That's it,' said Grace slowly. 'I don't know. I can't remember.'

'Well, you got a very nasty bang on the head. Our pathologist says it was the legendary blunt instrument.' Henshaw was grinning. Grace smiled.

'Glad to know it was a routine assault,' she said.

Henshaw took her hand again. 'You were certainly in a room with a desk and loads of filing cabinets. You were found lying on the floor of the file store but we found no cabinets open and there were no files out.'

'There was a wooden plaque. You know a sort of nameplate, with the files on the desk. It said Asean Art and Antiques and then some letters I can't recall.'

'The missing nameplate from the sponsors' notice board in the entrance,' said Henshaw. 'The letters were probably "Pte", which I think is like saying "Ltd" in Singapore.'

'That might have been it,' said Grace.

'Whoever hit you had the cool to put everything away.'

'Or took them away,' said Grace yawning. Henshaw gave her another pat on the arm. Her mind was working logically again. As the nurse gently ushered him away Grace gave him a smile and looked at him in a way he had never seen before. He walked off down the hospital corridor in a confused daze. Now it was *his* head that was spinning.

'I've set a small office aside for your use, Inspector', said Sheila Wilkins. 'We thought it might be more convenient.'

'We?' asked Henshaw as Mrs. Wilkins ushered him around a corner of the SEABU building.

'Mr. McFadden and I discussed it earlier. We thought that if you were moving around in our open plan area, it could become difficult and you would feel overlooked.' Henshaw deliberately opened the wooden Venetian blinds so that they could see across the corridor into the courtyard.

'That was very thoughtful, Mrs. Wilkins,' said Henshaw. 'Please sit down.'

'Coffee or tea?' asked Mrs. Wilkins putting her hand on the telephone on the desk between them.

'Tea please; milk no sugar.' Henshaw studied Sheila Wilkins as she called for the refreshments. She was dressed in a dark blue suit with short dark brown hair that was carefully styled. Henshaw guessed she was in her early forties and obviously married. Her appearance was a carefully calculated combination of businesslike and attractive. She had an air of confidence and efficiency. He guessed McFadden trusted her and that he might even take her more into his confidence than his deputy, Dr. Marcia Elliot. He wondered if there was more to their relationship. She sat across the desk waiting politely as if ready to take dictation with her notebook open. Henshaw began.

'Detective Sergeant Hepple entered the building late in the evening, we not sure exactly what time, probably around ten. Would you expect anyone to be working here then?'

'Certainly not me and definitely not any of my administrative staff. I can't speak for the academics. They keep irregular hours and there is no accounting for them. I am sure that some of them have worked here that late at times but on that evening we have no record of it.'

'Would you expect to have a record?'

'It depends who it was and what mode the security system was in. Perhaps if I explained the security system you would understand. In my office, just off the main entrance, there is a panel that we use to control the alarms and locks.'

'Who does that?'

'Normally it is just me but Mr. McFadden and Dr. Elliot have security codes too. I can give anyone else a temporary security code that lasts for twenty-four hours. I very rarely do that and I did not do so on Wednesday.'

'What does the security code allow you to do?'

'Once you type it in to the panel you can then give commands to set or release the alarms or to change the pattern of alarm or to change the door lock modes. Normally in the day, we leave the front door on "automatic" as it would have been just now when you came in.'

'So it opens as someone approaches it?'

'Exactly. Mr. McFadden is very insistent that we are an open organisation so the door must welcome any visitors, not make a barrier for them.'

'But at night you change it?'

'Yes normally when I go home I change it to "locked" but open to standard swipe cards. All staff have a swipe card. There are three groups of them. Those held by most staff which are standard, those held by post graduate students and short term visitors which have automatic expiry times on them and those held by senior people such as Mr. McFadden, Dr. Elliot and myself. I can also set the door lock so that it will only open to those very restricted cards and so on.

'So on Wednesday evening you went home and set the door locks as normal?'

'No. On Wednesday, Dr. Elliot had left me a message saying that she was expecting some late visitors and I should leave the door on automatic.'

'Who were these visitors?'

'I have no idea.'

'Does that happen very often; you just leave the door on automatic?'

'Occasionally. We have a lot of visitors from overseas. Often they arrive at very odd times, Inspector. Usually I know about them. In this case I did not and you would have to ask Dr. Elliot who they were. I am afraid she has been away since then.'

'One more thing,' said Henshaw. 'Have you any idea why the name of Asean Art and Antiques Pte has been removed from the sponsors' notice board in the entrance?'

'Yes, I took it down a couple of weeks ago,' answered Mrs. Wilkins without hesitation.

'Why?'

'I had an email from Dr. Elliot instructing me to do it immediately.'

'Didn't you think that was a little odd?'

'Not particularly. I expect it was something to do with a sensitivity of one of our major sponsors. Some of them are very touchy about things at times. They come from different countries and with varying cultures, ethnic backgrounds and religions. I can find the nameplate if you like. Dr. Elliott asked me to put it somewhere where it would be safe but out of sight.' She stopped and laughed. 'I remember putting it inside a biscuit tin in a drawer in my desk.'

Henshaw and Sheila Wilkins walked to her office to see the control panel and then she opened the bottom and largest drawer in her desk to reveal a large black tin covered in a pattern of red Chinese characters. Sheila Wilkins chuckled.

'One of our overseas visitors gave it to us as a token of thanks when he left after staying here for a few days. They are so polite you know, people from the Far East. Most of them are lovely.' She lifted the tin out of her desk drawer and, holding it against her hip, pulled the lid off towards her. Henshaw could see into it before she could. They stood staring at the few biscuit crumbs that were the only contents.

'Good gracious,' said Sheila Wilkins, 'now whoever could have taken that and why? I'll ask the girls in the office if they know.'

'No, I think it might be better not to do that for now,' said Henshaw. 'The mystery of the empty biscuit tin should remain our secret for a little while if you don't mind.'

'You look like you've just seen a ghost, sir,' said Denson as Drake arrived at the Cheshire Police Headquarters building.

'I am too old for long haul flights,' growled Drake. 'Your head just feels as if it doesn't belong on your body. It's like trying to think through concrete. I just cannot get my head around this ridiculous time difference.'

'Never done it meself, sir,' said Denson, 'never had the money like. The Missus always wants to go to Australia but I'd rather go to Llandudno; you don't get no jet lag there I can tell yer.' Denson waddled off back to his office chortling and muttering to himself, while Drake sagged into the chair behind his temporary desk. He wondered how Tom and Jenny's party had gone. He had left for the airport just after the guests had all arrived. He realised Tom was furious but what else could he do? He would have to make it up to Tom some how, even Drake could see it from Tom's point of view, after all Drake had been the big attraction, the famous detective from Scotland Yard now investigating the murder of Jimmy Cheung. Word had got round and Tom and Jenny's apartment was crowded out with curious locals.

Drake dragged himself back to the present as Denson reappeared clutching a sheaf of papers. 'You'll want to see this, sir I dare say.'

'Where is everyone, Denson?'

'Inspector Henshaw's at the University this morning, SEABU I think he said. He's like a man possessed over this attack on Sergeant Hepple. You'd think it was his daughter or sommat. Silly girl should never have gone in there on her own at night. She should have called in for assistance. That's the trouble with these high flyers from London. They think they're so dead clever and all that but they forget the basics you see. Begging your pardon, sir. No offence meant to yerself and all that, sir.'

'In this particular instance you may be right,' groaned Drake yawning. 'Tell Inspector Henshaw to wait for me before he interviews McFadden, will you. When did this lab report come in, Denson?'

'This morning, sir. Inspector Henshaw hasn't seen it yet, sir but I thought as how you would want to see it straight away like.'

'I assume we have released Sheng Tian by now?'

'No sir. Inspector Henshaw don't think he is being very cooperative neither.' Denson hovered while Drake read on.

The lab report was the result of an investigation into the pistol found in Sheng Tian's house. It began with all the customary background and caveats, which he skimmed over. In his experience the first few paragraphs of such documents usually say something along the lines of 'well we might be wrong of course but here is our best guess, and by the way sometimes our guesses aren't very good.' Drake turned the page and was riveted. As these things go it was unequivocal.

The gun showed no signs of having been fired in the recent past. The report accepted that the gun had been extensively used but that there were no deposits to be found anywhere. The conclusion was that either the gun had been fired and very carefully cleaned or it had not been used for many years. The first alternative was then dismissed as highly unlikely. The sort of cleaning that would have been required to leave the gun in this condition would have also left some tell-tale signs. These were not there either. The gun was completely free of lubricant. The author of the report was convinced that the gun would not fire properly without various adjustments. Of course they could test this but then such a test might destroy any other evidence that could be gathered. So it went on. Drake read each short paragraph several times. The conclusion was inescapable. This gun had not been used to kill Jimmy Cheung.

The next set of papers included transcripts of the three interviews that Henshaw had so far conducted with Sheng Tian.

Drake settled down to read them, dismissing Denson with one of his arm-waves. He read the three interviews several times. He could not see any variation in the story or doubts that would support a case for an extended holding of Sheng Tian without charging him, and there was no real case for a charge. Drake was angry with himself. Sheng Tian would never have been arrested if he had not flown off to Singapore. Who knows what damage might have been done by this. Damn that hothead Henshaw! Now he had no alternative but to undermine his authority. He called Denson and gave instructions for Sheng Tian to be released immediately and provided with transport back to his home.

It looked oddly different. The old familiar seemed strange again. Drake stood on the pavement outside Janet's hotel. Singapore had heightened his awareness of his own country. He started to notice things on the buildings in Eastgate that he had never seen before; things like gutters and drainpipes. He must have seen them; the truth was he had not noticed them. Chester was even richer architecturally than he had remembered. When this case was over he must explore Chester, never mind Singapore. Cynthia had often told him that architecture could only be learned through travel. At the time he thought this was a convenient justification for her leaving him yet again but now he could appreciate the argument. It was all a matter of what you took for granted and then stopped seeing. Worryingly, this was exactly the lesson he had always taught Henshaw and Grace Hepple about detective work.

Janet was waiting for him in the same suite in her hotel. She looked composed and dignified as ever and greeted him politely enough but with an air of formality that only just managed to disguise her annoyance at the arrest of her brother. A silver tray with a teapot and two cups was on the low table in front of the sofa that she and Sheng Tian had sat on during their first interview. She poured Drake a cup of tea in the manner of a perfect hostess but as Drake took his first sip, she could not contain herself any longer.

'I have been complaining to Inspector Henshaw about the treatment of my brother. I have several times asked to see you but was told you were unavailable. Sheng Tian could not possibly have killed my father, Chief Inspector. I can assure you of that.'

'We have not charged him. He has simply been helping us with our enquiries, and I have just ordered his release.'

'I am delighted to hear that but why has he been kept all this time, and against his will?'

'Your brother had a motive, he had the opportunity and we found a gun in his possession. In addition he has been less than straightforward with us.'

'I repeat, Chief Inspector, Sheng Tian did not kill his father.' Janet said forcefully.

'It would help me if you could tell me why you know this, Miss Cheung. Do you have another alibi for him perhaps?'

'I was at the ceremony with my father and Sheng Tian was not.'

'We have been over this,' continued Drake slightly wearily. 'You left early and you were not then with Sheng Tian, so how can you be so certain that he did not later meet your father, argue with him and, perhaps in a rage, pull the trigger? Your brother appears to have a terrible temper.'

'This is absurd. Even if he had met my father on the bridge, he would not walk around carrying a gun. He could not have killed his own father. He is not capable of such a thing. It is ridiculous even to suggest it.' Drake had just a slight suspicion from Janet's attitude that perhaps her certainty was based on something more substantial. He wondered if she knew where Sheng Tian had been.

'Janet, can you tell me, was your father a Peranakan?'

'Good gracious, Chief Inspector, what an odd question.'

'Why is it so odd?'

'Few people in the West know about the Peranakans. You have been doing some research.' She smiled and nodded graciously to Drake. 'It is possible but I doubt it. So many people these days claim Peranakan blood. It has become quite fashionable in certain quarters.' She sniffed slightly.

'Did your father never tell you more about the family history?'

'I never discussed that with my father. It was never an issue that would have occurred to me and he certainly never made any claims about it himself. There were however stories that his mother was a Nyonya; that was what Peranakan women were called. The past of our family is shrouded in mystery. It was never talked about. My father always looked forward not back.'

'What about documents and certificates?'

'Few records were kept and my parents moved around leaving little trace of their past. My father was not interested in history and never talked about his family. Frankly I cannot say. My aunt Emily would be a greater authority on all this family background than I am but why do you ask, Chief Inspector?'

'I am trying to establish the range of motives that there could have been for your father's murder.'

'And you think he could have been murdered because he had Peranakan blood? This I do not understand.'

'Well there are stories of Peranakan families killing their own offspring who married in ways that were seen as inappropriate.'

'I am no expert on such things, Chief Inspector but in any case it is many years since my father married.'

'Yes, of course, silly idea. Have you heard of a company called Asean Art and Antiques?' Drake was looking at her as he asked this and he was sure he saw a change of expression.

'Of course. My father organised for them to sponsor the SEABU building. They provided some of the displays in there and I think we had some other small dealings with them. My father may have bought some things from them for himself.'

'Why would they want to sponsor SEABU?'

'They export to the UK and to other European countries so SEABU would have excellent contacts and offer them good networking opportunities.

'Janet, the first time we met I asked you to list all the people who had been at the reception for your father. One of the people you mentioned was Professor Peter Mallory, the public orator. We are anxious to interview him. Have you by any chance seen or heard anything of him since then?'

'No, why should I?'

'You described him as a kind man. I just wondered if perhaps he had made any contact with you since the murder.'

'No, Chief Inspector. I am sorry I cannot help you.'

The air was laden with tension. Henshaw wanted to discuss the release of Sheng Tian further, Drake insisted they move on. He was just beginning to describe his discoveries in Singapore when Hamish McFadden arrived at the office that Henshaw was now using for his interviews in SEABU. Drake waved him to the spare chair.

'Mr. McFadden we are a little curious,' started Drake. 'I wonder if you can tell us why the nameplate for Asean Art and Antiques was taken unscrewed from the sponsors' board in the entrance?'

'What!' exclaimed McFadden. 'I did not know about this. No one told me. When did this happen?'

'Apparently your deputy, Dr. Elliot asked Mrs. Wilkins to remove it,' said Henshaw.

'Perhaps you should ask Dr Elliot then.'

'We would like to,' said Henshaw, 'but Dr. Elliot has been away since then.'

'I'm having a meeting with her today.' McFadden took out his palmtop computer. 'So she should be here now. I would like an explanation of this myself.' He called Sheila Wilkins on an internal phone and the two policemen could hear him getting more irritated as the conversation proceeded. Eventually he angrily slapped the telephone handset down on its base.

'It seems you are right, Drake. Apparently no one has seen or heard from Marcia Elliot since before this incident. We have no idea where she is and she hasn't left me any messages. It's quite out of character. She can be something of a loose cannon at times. She has a short fuse and can be argumentative but she is very well organised. I can't remember her ever failing to turn up for a meeting without sending prior warning.' McFadden was now agitatedly tapping away at his computer. 'I have sent her a stiff message, demanding that she come in straight away.'

'In the meantime,' said Drake, 'perhaps you could tell us a little more about AAA. Who exactly are they and what is their relationship with SEABU?'

'AAA is a typical organisation with whom we have collaborative relationships. They are based in Singapore but deal with art and antiques from all over the Asean region. They sell a great deal in the UK and use this as a base for importing for distribution throughout Europe. They have loaned many of the objects in our display cabinets in the "Hive" and most of the sculptures in our courtyard. We help to find organisations for them to do business with in the UK. We have a joint venture here in Chester which acts as a shop window for them here.'

'Can you then think of any reason why Dr. Elliot should want their nameplate removing? I understand from Sheila Wilkins that she specifically asked for it to be hidden.'

'Frankly I can't, and what's more I would like to have be been consulted about it. I am sure AAA would be most upset.'

Henshaw interjected, 'Mrs. Wilkins suggested to me that it might be because of a sensitivity of one of your visitors. I got the impression this was not particularly unusual.'

'No,' said McFadden firmly and with a distinct air of impatience, 'I think that is highly unlikely. It is certainly true that in the past we have had some sensitivities but I am really not aware of that at the moment and certainly not in relation to AAA.'

'Thank you, Mr. McFadden,' said Drake, struggling to his feet, 'I would be grateful please if you would let us know the moment you have any contact with Dr. Elliot. In the meantime perhaps we could have a look at her office just to see if there is anything there which might help us to establish her whereabouts?'

McFadden set off down the now familiar corridor running around the courtyard. As they walked, Drake addressed another query to McFadden. 'Would you know if Dr. Elliot uses a desktop computer or only a laptop?'

‘Most definitely a laptop. Like me, she travels a great deal. We only use laptops here; we need all our data with us out there on the road.’

‘So I suppose she is likely to have that with her?’

‘Almost certainly. I doubt she ever leaves it behind.’

Drake and Henshaw conducted an initial search of Marcia Elliot’s office, finding nothing of immediate help. They operated independently and largely in silence. Drake was tired and Henshaw was furious about the way Sheng Tian had been released. In fact he was angrier with himself for having been so impetuous but he was still not prepared to admit this to Drake, or even himself, just yet. Drake told Henshaw to call in a small scene-of-crime team to conduct a more thorough search, and they left, asking Sheila Wilkins to keep the office locked.

Drake yawned; his body and brain argued about whether it was night or day. ‘This jetlag business is a darned nuisance; I’m giving up for the day. Let’s catch up with each other tomorrow morning in the office.’

# 11 - Steel

By mid-morning the autumn sun had finally managed to climb over the trees behind the police headquarters building. It announced itself with a burst of enthusiasm through the window of the meeting room. Drake shielded his eyes until Henshaw tilted the Venetian blind; neither spoke. The silence hung around the room in a sulk occasionally interrupted by thumps from the piles of papers Henshaw was shuffling on his desk.

'Look here,' Drake began, 'I had no alternative but to release Sheng Tian, given the forensic report on his pistol.' He held up a hand to stop Henshaw as he started to mouth a response. It was not so much the actual decision that angered Henshaw as the effect on his status with Grace. Drake had read his expression and seen through him. So now he was moping like a silly schoolboy. Damn Drake! Why was he always right?

A crash behind them startled the two men out of their tiff. Grace Hepple stood, or at least propped herself up, in the open doorway. A dramatic bandage around her head topped a pallid complexion; she looked like a pantomime ghost. Henshaw dashed over to help her to a chair. Drake struggled to his feet only to discover Grace was now sat next to where he had been. He sagged back into his chair almost missing it on the way down.

'Sorry, sir,' said Grace, interrupting his fall, 'I thought it was me who had the bang on the head.' Drake looked daggers at her for a moment in mock anger and then all three collapsed in laughter that took obvious delight in breaking the tension and went on just a little too long. Grace wondered why it had become so easy to amuse these two men.

'Good to see you,' said Drake, 'but we can't have an invalid on the front line.'

'I rang the office this morning,' said Grace. 'Denson told me you had arrived back from Singapore. I knew you would want to see me so here I am.'

'Are you really sure you are well enough?' asked Henshaw. His sulks chased away by overly concerned frowns.

'I thought I was but when I got out of the taxi I felt funny and I have been dropping things. I couldn't cope with another day in that hospital anyway. They are all very kind but it all actually makes you feel ill.' Henshaw disappeared, mumbling about Denson and cups of tea. Drake started to tell Grace about his daughter's last night performance in Singapore. The climax of the narrative was interrupted by the chortling Sergeant Denson coming in carrying a tray with mugs of tea.

'Nothing a good cuppa won't cure; leastways so me Missus always claims.' Henshaw passed the mugs around. The tea worked the promised miracles and Drake and Henshaw sat silently listening to every detail of Grace's story. Henshaw occasionally patted her forearm when she showed the slightest sign of distress at the recollection. When Grace had reached the point of the attack, Drake took over.

'Now we can continue the story a little. Whoever hit you on the head also took the AAA nameplate.'

'I interviewed Mrs Sheila Wilkins,' said Henshaw, 'and she unscrewed the nameplate from the wall under instruction from the Deputy Director, Dr. Marcia Elliot.'

'Who has since vanished,' interrupted Drake.'

'That's strange,' said Grace slowly and thoughtfully. 'All this time I have been lying in hospital turning it over and over in my mind but I never imagined my assailant being a woman.'

'Oh goodness!' exclaimed Henshaw in mock horror, 'Dr. Elliot would be very angry at such a demonstrably sexist set of preconceptions.'

'We need to meet up with Dr. Marcia Elliot,' snapped Drake.'

'She can't have gone far.' Henshaw brandished her passport.'

'Even so, put out a call to all emigration authorities, and get a search warrant for her house. I am not waiting around for her to just show up again. This case seems littered with people who choose to go missing.'

'Apparently she has been looking for her own property since arriving here from the United States and so she is renting an apartment on the university campus.'

'Aren't those apartments right next to the SEABU building?' asked Drake.

'Exactly,' replied Henshaw. 'She could very easily have been Grace's assailant.'

'Does she have a motive for murdering Jimmy Cheung?' asked Grace.

'She seemed very alienated when I interviewed her,' answered Henshaw, 'full of how she does all the work and never gets the recognition. Obviously doesn't like McFadden much. She was pretty negative about Jimmy Cheung. She complained about him getting a professorial post when she hasn't got one.'

Drake grunted again. 'It doesn't sound like much of a case. For goodness sake Marrtin, don't go and arrest her just yet.' Grace allowed a momentary grin to slip across her face. 'Anyway why did she demand the doors were left unlocked when she has a code to let her in?' Henshaw had not thought of this last point. Grace thought it best to keep quiet.

The two men were so busy peering at the screen that they failed to notice Drake and Grace coming into the room. Drake looked over their shoulders seeing nothing but apparently meaningless lists of words and numbers.

'Well done Dave,' said Henshaw patting the young lad on the shoulder. The young technician beamed a grin of satisfaction.

'Let us into the secret then,' growled Drake, impatiently.

'The photographs on the camera found round Jimmy Cheung's neck were indeed taken on the day he was murdered.' Henshaw pointed at the computer screen. 'This particular camera names each picture automatically with a code that at first appears meaningless but in fact it uses systematic combinations of letters and numbers.'

'I thought this might have been the case, sir,' said Dave proudly, 'but I couldn't be sure, so I loaded some more batteries and set the camera date to today, took some more pictures and sure enough it used this coding system. Now if we look at the names of the pictures that were originally on the camera, they are all numbered PSC0912, then a set of digits for each picture. So they were all taken on the twelfth day of the ninth month. Tuesday September 12 was the day of the murder.' By now Dave was grinning like the proverbial Cheshire cat.

'That is of course always assuming the camera had the correct date set when it took the pictures,' grunted Drake. The others turned in unison to look at Dave. 'So what date was it set to?' he demanded. The grin had disappeared.

'I don't know. Forensics opened the camera up and took the batteries out. This one loses its date quite quickly without the batteries in.' Drake stared at the computer screen and the others stared at Drake. The silence was probably no longer than ten seconds but to Dave it seemed an age. Drake said nothing. Dave cursed Forensics under his breath. Then he cursed himself for his own stupidity. This should have been his moment of glory in the investigation.

'Unless you set the date it defaults to January 1,' he said weakly. So someone must have set it and they would be unlikely to set it to the wrong day.'

'Unless…' said Grace.

'Exactly,' said Drake. 'Imagine that getting shot down in court. They can easily argue that it was set to a particular day for the purpose of deception,' Drake resumed his silent stare. 'What about the time of day?' asked Drake eventually. 'Can we tell that? That might be very interesting.'

'The code does not tell you that,' admitted Dave dejectedly.

Drake and Henshaw waited outside Marcia Elliot's apartment on the Deva University campus, accompanied by three constables. They had taken Grace back to her lodgings with Drake threatening to return her to the hospital if she as much as put a foot outside again that day. Before setting off, they had called the University Estates Office and Jim Watson had agreed to meet them to open the door. He cut a comical figure. His almost circular face sat straight on a rather short trunk with no neck and he was carrying a roundish paunch in front of him. His hips were definitely the widest part of his body from which thick short legs protruded. Drake was remembering the 'Kelly' that his mother kept in the bottom of her pet budgerigar's cage. The bird would hop between perches and end up on the floor giving the Watson-like toy an irritable peck only for the wretched thing to bounce and knock the poor bird back a pace. It would let out a surprised squawk but it never learned. Watson was carrying a bunch of keys large enough for an operatic jailor. He examined the door to see if it might offer a clue about which key to try first. The lock remained stubbornly mute on the subject so he was reduced to a random search.

'We have records of all the locks and keys but the secretary who keeps that database is away ill today and I couldn't find the file.' Watson was by now sweating profusely and he paused to straighten his back and wipe his brow.

'There is a simple rule with keys like this,' Drake explained and Watson looked up. 'It will be the last one you try. So try it now.' Henshaw's struggle to suppress laughter ended in failure as he spluttered into his hand. Watson had by now lost his place in the bunch of keys and was starting again in a huff. Drake thought he probably had as much of a sense of humour as the budgerigar's Kelly. By some miracle the next key worked and the lock clicked open. Watson entered the apartment with a defiant look of triumph, followed by a small procession of Drake, Henshaw and two constables. A third constable stood on duty outside.

Marcia Elliot's apartment worked hard at concealing her identity and personality. Virtually all of her belongings were stored in cupboards, wardrobes and drawers. There were a few books on the open shelves but no decorations or ornaments. As far as Drake could tell, there were no items of significance visible that were not provided by the university. The interior décor was from the same stable as the Registrar's office and Drake was well accustomed to the style by now. It was 'cheap motel' rather than home.

'It looks as if she has only just moved in. How long has Dr. Elliot lived here?' he asked Watson.

'It is certainly months rather than weeks or years.'

'She has made little attempt to create a home,' grunted Drake. 'Either she expects to be moving very soon or she has a reduced sense of personal identity.'

Henshaw came in from the kitchen. 'Almost no food in the fridge; she must eat out.' He began systematically opening and examining the contents of the drawers in the desk by the window. Drake was examining the bookcase. 'That's very odd,' exclaimed Henshaw. 'I have just found her passport here. We are holding her passport, so at first I thought this must be an old one but look it is actually current.'

'What is more, she has used it this year to travel to Saudi Arabia.' Drake said flicking through the document. 'I think I have the answer to the conundrum,' he added eventually. 'All the stamps come from that same part of the world. She is a citizen of the USA. I bet she has been granted a special passport to avoid immigration problems in certain counties sensitive to stamps from other states.'

'So that means she is still in the UK then,' said Henshaw.

'No laptop computer here either,' grumbled Drake. The desk boasted only a beautifully minimalist white box. A groove running all the way the vertical faces near the top invited you to think it was a lid. This was obviously some cunning piece of industrial design because it would not budge. Drake picked it up and turned it over in his hand. It was about the size of a thick paperback novel, square and completely plain. A cable dangled from the rear. He looked quizzically at Henshaw.

'Looks like her backup disk.' Drake's blank expression blanked some more.

'It's an external hard disk that she probably uses to keep a backup of the contents of the hard disk in her laptop. Marcia Elliot, she seems highly organised so it would be in character to keep a backup in case she loses her laptop or it breaks down.'

'I would never have even known such a thing existed,' grumbled Drake. 'So can we read the information on this without her computer?'

'In theory yes, unless she has encrypted it in some way. I'll get Dave to look at it.'

'Let's get it back to him straight away. I cannot see any reason to stay here. Brief your team to complete the search.' Drake wandered outside to discover the constable on duty at the door deep in conversation with a very animated woman. Seeing Drake, he held up his hand to interrupt her, and he turned and began to make an introduction that was cut short by the woman herself.

'Oh Inspector Drake, sir; you probably don't remember me.'

'Mrs Partridge isn't it? You cleaned Professor Cheung's apartment.' Mrs. Partridge glowed with pride at this recognition.

'And I do for Dr. Elliot, yes, sir.'

'Can you tell us where she is, Mrs. Partridge?'

'No, sir, no idea but I'd say she has bin away for several days. Nothing has moved in the flat like. I can always tell when she is away. She travels a lot you know. All over the world she does. Pr'haps Prof. Mallory would know where she is.'

'Why should Professor Mallory know her whereabouts?'

'Well he's here a lot he is. I see him leaving in the morning when I'm about like. If you know what I mean.' With that Mrs. Partridge looked down at the ground and shuffled her feet, somehow giggling and showing disapproval at the same time. 'Mind you, come to think of it, he's not bin here for a while, least not to my knowledge like.' She stood scratching her head. 'You know I don't think he's bin here since well before the first time I saw you like. No I don't think so; probably not for a month or so.'

'Can you tell me, does Professor Mallory have a limp?'

'Oh yes, sir. Quite bad it is. Perhaps that's what attracts the ladies to him. They say we like them helpless so we can mother them don't they?' She giggled and swayed side to side.

Drake and Henshaw crowded around Dave. He was less than keen about having both his shoulders looked over as he worked but was pleased to be the at the centre of attention again. The computer in front of him gave a resounding ping, announcing with pride and delight that it had found Dr. Elliot's disk. A mass of computer files and folders appeared on the screen.

'What are you looking for?' asked Dave turning round to look over both shoulders in turn. 'There's hundreds of files here.'

'It's amazing what you can keep in a box with no lid,' muttered Drake.

'Perhaps she keeps her diary on there?' suggested Henshaw. 'We are anxious to know where she is.'

After a flurry of mouse activity, furious clicking and windows opening on the screen, Dave gave a grunt of satisfaction. 'Yep, here we are you beauty! The software automatically opens at today and there are two entries.' He sat back waiting for some congratulation. Drake obliged. Dave grinned smugly and then pointed excitedly at the screen again.

'Those two entries for today conflict but she can't be in two places at once.' Drake and Henshaw crowded down over Dave's shoulder again. The entries were undecipherable collections of letters and numbers.

Henshaw groaned. 'It looks almost as if she is trying to conceal her whereabouts by using code.' Dave flicked back through the days. 'Look, there is the appointment with McFadden that she missed. There is no code used for that. Somehow she is very coy about the events of today. I wonder why.'

'No,' Dave was almost shouting in his excitement. 'Got it. They are flight numbers. There are two of them so she might be making a double journey.'

'Darn it,' exclaimed Henshaw, 'looks like she has flown off somewhere and we have just missed her.'

'It's OK,' said Dave, 'we can go on the web and search for the flights.'

A tray and three mugs of tea came in with Grace Hepple. Drake gave her an old fashioned look and she returned it with assurances on her recovery. Drake and Henshaw looked at each other and shrugged their shoulders in defeat. Grace was back on duty. Drake and Henshaw brought her up to date and sipped at the tea while Dave tapped away at his computer keyboard.

'Bingo!' he shouted a few minutes later. 'She is actually coming home not going away. This is a flight from Boston to Manchester via Paris on Air France. It should be landing very early tomorrow morning. The confusion in her diary is because of the time difference between Boston and Paris.'

'I don't want to hear any more about time differences!' groaned Drake.

Dave continued undeterred. 'The first plane actually leaves Boston today but arrives in Paris tomorrow. Looking back through the diary I can also see the corresponding flight that she took out on the 20th.'

'Exactly what do you think you are doing? I am a US citizen travelling perfectly legally and I arrive at Manchester airport this morning to be met be immigration officials accusing me of passport irregularities.' Dr Marcia Elliot was not happy. 'Since then I have been virtually under arrest. I demand to know what this is all about. I am tired and I want to go home to bed.'

'Sit down again, Dr. Elliot,' snapped Drake. 'We asked you to hand in your passport and not leave without consulting us.'

'I'm sorry about what happened to Jimmy Cheung but I have already explained to you that it is nothing to do with me. Life and business have to go on. It is not my fault if you don't know that I hold several passports.'

Drake was examining the US passport she had been using. 'What was the purpose of your trip to Boston?'

'I don't see why you need to know that.'

'Dr. Elliot, I can raise a warrant for your arrest and we can do this formally. Indeed that may well be necessary if I am not happy with your answers. Alternatively, you can assist me in my investigation voluntarily.'

For the first time, Marcia Elliot looked a little alarmed and anxious. Then she spoke quietly, 'I have been over for an interview for a prestigious academic position in Boston. I don't want McFadden to know about all this until it is finalised one way or the other.'

'Why did you not inform us of your movements?'

'I thought you might prevent me from going. I would not be able to tell the university over there why. They would almost certainly take me off the shortlist if they thought I might be involved in some crime over here.'

'Before you left, you emailed instructions to Mrs. Wilkins to leave the security system for SEABU turned off. Why was that?'

Marcia Elliot was by now looking pale and her right hand resting on the desk was shaking almost imperceptibly. 'I can't remember. I think I needed to work late that night.'

'But your own security card will open the doors even when they are locked so why risk the security of the whole building?'

'Yes, that was silly.' Drake sat silently looking at Marcia Elliot for what to her seemed like an age.

'No, it was not silly at all,' he said smiling. Marcia gave a weak smile back.

'I repeat, not silly at all. Quite simply, it is a lie. I do not for one minute believe this is the reason you would email Mrs. Wilkins such an instruction.' Marcia Elliot was now the silent one, shuffling her feet and looking down at her hands. 'So why did you also ask her to remove the AAA plaque from the main sponsors' notice board?'

'OK, OK. I was simply passing on instructions from someone else.'

'And exactly who might that be?'

'I can't tell you that.'

'Why was the plaque to be removed?'

'I cannot tell you that either. If I tell you why, you will realise who it is. These questions are unfair.'

'Dr. Elliot, this is not a game we are playing.'

'I will lose my job if I tell you!' Marcia Elliot was shouting and almost crying at this point.

'I thought you had just got a new job in Boston.'

'I hope so. I really hope so but it is very competitive. I think they want me but whether I will get this post, I doubt. It is a very good university and there are a couple of other better qualified candidates.'

'Let me see if I can help you,' said Drake. 'If telling me who this is threatens your job, then I guess the person must have been Hamish McFadden.'

Marcia Elliot looked up with a startled expression. 'Oh no, Hamish has nothing to do with it. At least I don't think he has. Quite honestly that is part of the problem. I really don't know. I wish I had never come to this wretched place.' Drake waited. Marcia Elliot seemed to have regained her composure and confidence and even her anger. 'Why should I worry?' she said finally. 'It was the Registrar, Dr. Percival. It was his instructions I was passing on. It is not the first time he has made such demands.'

'I see but why did you feel compelled to follow his instructions?'

'Well,' said Marcia Elliot as if preparing herself to deliver a long tale, 'he started by promising me that I would get promoted to a professorship. He seemed to have been very close to Hamish but fell out with him recently. I don't understand all the background but I think it was all something to do with the finances over the building. Hamish won't agree to me being promoted. I think he sees it as some threat to himself, possibly because I have a doctorate and he doesn't. It is all very petty really. Actually I think Hamish is very insecure. That is why he bullies people. That is why he bullies me in particular. When I realised that I would not get promoted I stopped cooperating and then Percival started to threaten me with remarks about my work permit. He has the ultimate power over appointments. So I began looking for posts elsewhere. I have been working so hard setting things up here that my own career has been on hold. My own C.V. doesn't look as good as it should do. I'm in a trap. I'm totally fed up with this situation. Now you want to threaten me as well.' Marcia Elliot gave Drake a defiant stare but there was a hint of dampness in her eyes.

'I am not threatening you. Justice demands we get to the bottom of this. I cannot have politics or personal considerations preventing that.' Marcia Elliot nodded a sort of grudging acceptance of this and the two sat silent for a moment. Then Drake spoke again, still softly but insistently. 'Why do you think Dr. Percival wanted the building left open?'

'Oh I think it is fairly obvious,' said Marcia Elliot as if running a student seminar. 'Hamish had specifically set up the security system so that Percival could not come in and snoop around. Our Registrar was not prepared to accept that. I think he's a bit paranoid really. I assume he was looking for something to pin on Hamish. How those two deserve each other! The trouble is they have me caught in the middle. Hamish is effectively running his own private little empire and Percival is trying to rein him in. Percival obviously sees me as the solution to his problem. I can feed him information that he could use to get rid of Hamish and then I would be a much more compliant director.'

'This all seems very odd to me.' Drake was putting on a puzzled expression. 'Dr. Percival is very proud of SEABU. He has boasted about it to us. I got the impression that he and McFadden were on very good terms.'

'To start with maybe. Hamish would have been quite a catch for a university like this and he has raised the profile and brought in lots of money, so Percival would have loved all that. But more recently they have fallen out, probably around the time I was appointed. Fundamentally I think Percival has got nervous about Hamish's success and perhaps some of his methods.'

'So why do you think he wanted the AAA plaque removed?'

'I suppose he thinks they are involved in some odd dealings with SEABU but why he would want their plaque removed I have no idea.'

Grace Hepple entered the room and whispered in Drake's ear. He made his excuses and left.

Dave was still sitting in front of his beloved computer when Drake entered.

'What have you got for me, Dave?'

'I have managed to get her email files open. Lots of academic chatter, organising conferences, exchanging information with students. Just what you would expect. But then there are these messages to and from an anonymous address.'

'What about them?'

Dave shifted awkwardly in his seat. 'They are what you might call intimate.'

'Well, Dave,' said Drake laughing, 'I'm sure she shouldn't use her university account for such nonsense but I don't think we are snooping on her for that sort of thing right now.'

'You might be interested, sir, when you know the name of the account she is corresponding with.'

'I thought you said it was anonymous.'

'Yes correct but it is the same email address that sent us that warning about SEABU and McFadden not being all they seemed, if you remember, sir.'

'You are right, I am definitely interested.' Dave pointed to the screen where he had displayed a number of the messages.

Drake studied them for a few minutes, grunting occasionally. 'Whoever it is, she certainly knows him pretty well. The interesting thing is that just here and there we can see comments that suggest he is a member of the university. Look here, she makes reference to McFadden and there to some university committee. Well, well, well. Given what Mrs. Partridge has told us, I wonder if this is Professor Mallory.'

'That is why I thought you might want to know about it,' said Dave proudly. Drake turned round to see Henshaw and Grace behind him.

'Salacious stuff eh,' laughed Henshaw. 'These academics are not so boring after all.' Grace giggled.

'Let's see if she knows where Mallory is then,' said Drake. 'Grace, come with me please if you feel up to it. It might get to a point where you could ask the questions better than me.'

'Dr. Elliot,' Drake began, 'I must now ask you about your exact relationship with Professor Mallory.'

Marcia Elliot looked shocked and angry at the same time. The break had allowed her to regain her self-confidence. 'My personal life has nothing whatever to do with this. I will not answer that question.'

'You do not deny you have a relationship with Professor Mallory?'

'I did not say that. You are putting words into my mouth.'

'Perhaps I should tell you that we have more than one piece of evidence that indicates you have a rather intimate relationship with Professor Mallory. I am not interested in the detail of that; as you say it is your personal life. However I am interested in the whereabouts of Professor Mallory. We are particularly anxious to interview him in connection with Jimmy Cheung's murder and I have reason to believe you might know where he is.'

'That is ridiculous. Peter could not possibly be responsible for murdering Cheung.'

'No doubt we'll be able to establish that once we interview him.'

'I have no idea where he is. I have not seen him for a few weeks. He travels a great deal.'

'Surely he would have told you where he was going or you would have had an email from him?'

Marcia Elliot looked at him very hard. There was a lengthy pause and Grace took this to be while she rehearsed in her mind what might be in all those emails. Eventually, Marcia Elliot replied very briefly. 'No.'

'Does he normally tell you where he is going?'

'Usually, yes.'

'So, this is an unusual situation?'

'I suppose it is yes. Look we haven't seen each other for a while.'

'Have you been worried about him?' asked Grace sympathetically.

'I have been away myself. I have been busy.'

'Dr. Elliot,' said Drake, 'we now need to be absolutely precise about your movements. We believe that you flew out to Boston on the 20th is that correct?' Marcia Elliot thought for a moment and nodded.

'Yes, in fact it was the same day that I passed the message on from Percival to Sheila Wilkins. Percival had called me on my mobile when I was having breakfast. The man is so secretive; he behaves like a character in some silly spy novel, never calls me on the university system and never comes to see me in the SEABU building. I was at home just getting ready to go to the airport. Of course I couldn't tell anyone so I emailed Sheila.'

'So what time was your flight out that day?' asked Drake.

'I can't remember exactly but late morning.'

'The flights were on time?'

'More or less, yes. But why is this so important?'

'Dr. Elliot. Are you aware of the events that took place that evening in the SEABU building?'

Marcia Elliot looked up suddenly. 'No, what events?' she demanded. 'Oh hell am I in trouble for leaving the building open now? What happened? Has there been a break in or something?'

'In a way.' Detective Sergeant Hepple was passing by late at night and saw a light on inside. She went to investigate and was attacked by an intruder. She was seriously injured and she has been in hospital since. We are obviously taking the matter very seriously.'

'This is a nightmare!' exclaimed Marcia Elliot, 'and you think it is my fault?'

'Well clearly you were out of the country when it actually happened…' began Drake but he was interrupted by Marcia Elliot.

'You thought I was the one who assaulted her,' said Marcia looking at Grace for a reaction that was not forthcoming.

'That had to be a possibility,' said Drake. 'Have you any idea who might have been responsible?'

'Obviously not,' snapped Marcia Elliot. I was overseas so I have no idea what was going on. We don't have a security guard or night porter because the electronic system is so elaborate. Mind you Hamish's Rottweilers look like they could smash anyone's brains out sometimes.'

Drake raised an eyebrow. 'Hamish's Rottweilers?'

'His two Chinese research students; that's what Sheila and I call them. Very solid looking characters they are; never seem to do any academic work and when they are not travelling they simply hang around looking threatening and not communicating with anyone.'

'We will have a little chat with them in due course.'

'You'll have a job,' laughed Marcia Elliot. 'Neither of them speaks much English. Actually I think they understand a whole lot more than they let on but it just suits them not to.'

'I see,' said Drake thoughtfully. 'Have you ever noticed Hamish McFadden's cufflinks?'

'You mean the Chinese ones,' queried Marcia Elliot laughing. 'How could anyone fail to. He is always showing them off, silly man. It is amazing how easy it is to flatter him.'

'Do you by any chance know what the Chinese characters on them mean?' asked Drake.

'The ones he usually wears are supposed to have his name on them. Some time ago he and Percival were both given them on one of their jaunts to Singapore. They were just standard ones. I think they said "good luck" or "get rich" or something silly. Hamish was so taken with them, the next time he went they made these ones especially for him. He was like a kid with a new toy.'

Drake and Grace left the room as Henshaw was coming along the corridor carrying a very small slip of paper.

'Another success, sir,' he said breathlessly. 'The mobile phone company has tracked the emergency call that led to us finding Grace. You will never guess who made it.' Drake looked at Grace and waved his arm indicating she should answer Henshaw's riddle.

'Dr. James Percival, University Registrar,' she said pompously doffing an imaginary academic cap at Henshaw. The latter looked totally deflated while Drake explained.

'Marcia Elliot has just opened up a whole can of worms for us.'

'Well I would never have guessed that!' exclaimed Henshaw. Grace felt the back of her head ruefully.

'Nor would I,' she said to the amusement of the other two. Henshaw gave her a paternal hug.

'Glad to see you have recovered your sense of humour, Grace.'

'Right,' said Drake. 'Time to stop messing about, you two. What's even more interesting is that we now know that both McFadden and Percival were given cufflinks like the one found at the scene of the crime. We need another chat with the University Registrar, our friend Dr. Percival.'

'Somehow I don't think he is going to be quite so pompous this time.' Henshaw was grinning broadly. 'I guess you want him in, sir?'

'Oh, yes I think so. I'll let you have the pleasure of going to collect him, Martin but go carefully, for now at least. I don't want even Sally Brown knowing what this is about so give him a chance to maintain appearances.'

'I guess you know why you are here?' demanded Drake, short-circuiting any introductions. Dr. Percival swallowed hard, shook his head and looked generally rather nervous. 'We have reason to believe you were in the SEABU building on the night of 20th September and that you assaulted Detective Sergeant Grace Hepple.' Percival's head bowed and disappeared into his hands, his elbows propped up on the small table in front of him.

'I am most dreadfully sorry. I panicked. I hit her on the head with my torch. I was trapped and I had no idea she was a policeman, er… woman. In the dark I assumed she was one of McFadden's gangsters. I didn't realise I'd hit her that hard but she just collapsed in a heap on the floor.' He turned around to see Grace Hepple standing at the back of the room impassively. 'It was nothing personal, I was just trying to protect university property. I do hope you have recovered?' Grace Hepple made no response. 'I have been worried sick about it,' continued Percival. 'As soon as I could I called an ambulance.'

'You said something just now about McFadden's gangsters,' said Drake. 'Who are they?'

'It is probably an exaggeration to call them gangsters,' admitted Percival, 'but there are a couple of burly and threatening looking Chinese characters that hang around sometimes. I don't like the look of them at all and when I challenged one of them he seemed not to speak any English. I think they work for a place down in Bridge Street that handles imports from various Chinese countries. They deal mainly in furniture and pottery apparently but I have an uncomfortable feeling about them. McFadden has them registered as doctoral students but I have serious doubts about that.'

'I think it is time you told us all about this. You have both me and the local police force dancing around here trying to sort out the murder of Jimmy Cheung but it is clear that from the beginning you have not been entirely straight with us.'

'I assure you, Chief Inspector,' said Percival, 'I had absolutely nothing to do with Jimmy Cheung's murder. I do hope you accept that. I know this does not look good and I can only apologise for my actions. All my anniversary celebrations are in a total shambles now. Once this comes out I am sure the Vice chancellor will want me to leave my position here and I cannot see another university taking me on. But I repeat I have nothing to do with any murder. I have simply been trying to do my best to create a reputation for this university.'

'It will have a reputation now,' said Henshaw, 'you can be sure of that.' Drake gave him a stare of disapproval. Percival seemed almost in tears.

'Dr. Percival,' said Drake, 'I think you should tell us the whole story from the start. But this time I want nothing left out. I should warn you that we know more than you might think. We are aware of the pressure you have been putting on Dr. Elliot for example.' Percival looked at him blankly, nodded and gulped as if to gather enough air for a long speech.

'It goes back to when I appointed Hamish McFadden. The Vice chancellor was not entirely happy about that from the start but he backed my judgment. Hamish approached us with the whole idea of SEABU. He said he could give it both a local and an international flavour and it seemed an ideal way of gaining some prestige early in the life of the university. You have no idea how difficult it is for a new university to break onto the international scene these days. I gave Hamish a fairly free hand and it was not long before he was raising colossal sums of money. He paid pretty much for the whole of the building for example. I went with him on a number of trips to the Far East and we were wined and dined by people in the highest circles of society. I had no worries at all. However later things went wrong in a number of ways. The main contractor for the building was appointed rather than selected by competition because Hamish said most British firms would not be able to find the right craftsmen. I do not know how Hamish persuaded Watson, Director of Facilities, to use such an irregular form of contract but he did. I should never have agreed to that, and there is probably a grey area as to whether it was all appropriately done within our financial framework. The Director of Finance and I had huge arguments about it. More recently, various rumours have circulated about some of the company that Hamish keeps and some of the business ethics of the businesses acting as sponsors for SEABU.'

'For example, Asean Art and Antiques Plc perhaps?' interjected Drake.

'You have been busy, Chief Inspector. They are certainly one of the more shady organisations. I am not necessary accusing any of them of acting illegally but they may be involved in practices that would seriously harm the University's reputation if they were to become widely known. I have just been trying to keep a lid on things. When I did confront Hamish, he became abusive and threatened to reveal my role in the building procurement process. It was blackmail really. I tried to keep on top of things by reading as much correspondence as I could, mainly in the evening after they had all gone home but Hamish found out and changed my security rating so I could not get into the building. It was then I started using Dr. Elliot as a way in. I knew she was not entirely happy with Hamish herself and it would be mutually beneficial.'

'I am not sure that she would see it that way but carry on.'

'That night I had given her instructions to leave the building unlocked so I could do some more delving. To be perfectly honest, Chief Inspector I was worried that your investigations would unearth something I did not know about.'

'Was that why you asked for the AAA plaque to be removed?'

'Yes, stupid really. I was trying to make sure they did not come to your notice. I seem to have achieved exactly the opposite effect. I am not really very good at this sort of thing, am I?' He sagged into a helpless looking heap again and Henshaw brought him a glass of water.

'What about Jimmy Cheung?' asked Drake.

'Hamish had recommended that we appoint Jimmy. Initially I had no problems with that. Jimmy had entertained us all in Singapore. He was obviously very well connected and enormously wealthy. It was the Vice chancellor's idea that we should give him an honorary degree and then I thought of linking it to the university anniversary celebrations. It was rather neat really.' For a brief moment Percival regained his old pomposity and nearly bristled with pride.

'Yes. Well. It has all backfired pretty spectacularly hasn't it,' he groaned. 'Professor Mallory came to see me one day in quite a state. He said he had been preparing the oration that he would give at Jimmy Cheung's degree ceremony and wanted to talk it over with me. It seems he had been in Singapore for a conference and done some research there. He was not at all happy with Jimmy Cheung's background. He said there was plenty of circumstantial evidence that Jimmy's fortune was based on some shady practice. He tried to persuade me that we should withdraw the offer to Jimmy. I refused, of course. What else could I do at that point? It was already public and we were committed. I decided we would go ahead and then simply not involve Jimmy Cheung further.'

'Did Professor Mallory agree with this?'

'Oh no. He wasn't at all happy. He even threatened to read out an exposé of Jimmy Cheung at the degree congregation. I had to offer him all sorts of things for his department to bring him onside. He is a curious fellow, Mallory. He's a loner and a very principled man at times, and there are stories of him being quite a one with the ladies. But he does have a terrible temper and is quite unpredictable. He threatened all sorts of things if we did not expose Jimmy Cheung after the degree congregation. To be perfectly honest, Chief Inspector, it has crossed my mind that he might have killed Jimmy. I'm sure he wouldn't kill in cold blood but I could easily imagine him confronting Jimmy and doing something stupid. I should have told you all this before but it really was only a faint possibility in my mind. They say that Mallory has disappeared which lends some weight to the theory. Now I really don't know what to think.'

'He did send us an anonymous email raising questions about McFadden and SEABU,' said Drake.

'I'm not surprised. I was never very confident I could control him. This is a terrible mess. I suppose it does all have to come out?'

'That is not our concern at this stage,' snapped Drake.

'No, of course. Quite right. To be honest it is a tremendous relief to tell you all about it. The tension and pressure have been intolerable, especially after the incident with poor Sergeant Hepple.' He turned and smiled weakly at her but got a steely stare in return.

'Obviously we cannot charge you with trespass in your own building,' said Drake, 'but we could charge you with assault of a police officer. One more thing: I understand you have a pair of cufflinks that you were given in Singapore. Apparently they have Chinese characters on them.' Percival nodded again this time with a puzzled expression. 'I would like to see them if that is possible.'

'I haven't seen them for ages,' said Percival, 'but I think they are in a box in one of my bedroom drawers. Surely they are not valuable are they?'

'I doubt it but perhaps we can arrange to collect them just to be sure.' Percival nodded again still looking puzzled.

Drake left the room beckoning Henshaw and Grace Hepple to follow.

'You certainly put the frighteners on him,' said Henshaw.

'Just a little back for banging my sergeant on the head,' said Drake. 'It is interesting that he thought he was being followed by one of McFadden's thugs. I suspect he was, and Grace simply complicated the situation. That was who Grace must have seen leaving the building. Percival was inside all the time.'

'I just assumed I was only following one person,' said Grace. 'How stupid of me!'

'It's an easy mistake to make,' said Henshaw reassuringly.

'The questions about the cufflinks seemed to confuse rather than frighten him,' said Drake. 'I don't think the one we found belongs to him but it could still be McFadden's. However that can wait. We really must find Mallory now.'

'There has been no activity at his home in the Wirral and his brother in Manchester hasn't heard from him for ages,' said Henshaw. 'We have circulated details and pictures to all forces. There have been a number of possible sightings, which our boys are following up. A couple in London, both several days ago, and there were some calls made to taxi firms in Berkshire around the same time. The phone has gone silent since then. We have a watch on all the ports and airports and we are pretty confident he has not left the country.'

'It's almost as if he knows we are chasing him,' said Drake.

# 12 - Linen

The citizens of Chester were out taking advantage of what could easily be the last warm and sunny Sunday of the year. Many were gently strolling up and down the Groves, while some of the more active were on the River Dee itself. Even more energetic souls played football or cricket in the park just up from the bridge. The café was doing a brisk trade in ice cream and soft drinks. The fresh air and sounds of laughing children began to lift the gloom that had descended on Grace Hepple. For the last couple of days she had felt totally exhausted and drained. The Jimmy Cheung case kept gate-crashing her attempts to think calm and relaxing thoughts. Trying to repossess her mind, she had strolled down Bridge Street and then inevitably along the riverbank. Reaching the Groves she felt a wave of exhaustion wash over her and flopped onto one of the seats behind the bandstand. This had turned out to be pretty silly. Now she was sitting pretending to read the Sunday newspaper while confronted by the scene-of-crime. The latter inevitably won the contest for her attention, reducing her to alternately scanning headlines and staring at the soaring structure overhead.

The bridge was alive with children throwing bread to the swans below. Next to her a child threw a tantrum because the ice-cream stall appeared not to have its favourite flavour. Grace's brain stubbornly refused to relax and yet it wouldn't do anything useful either. Instead it just worried. She segued between her relationship with Martin Henshaw, whether she was cut out for motherhood, the scene-of-crime, and trivia such as the flavours of ice creams. A stiffening breeze first fluttered her newspaper and then excited it into uncontrollable flapping.

She was due to meet Martin Henshaw for lunch at a café in Bridge Street. He had been so attentive and caring during her stay in hospital and she was more drawn to him than ever, and yet they often seemed to be at loggerheads over the case. Quite how the relationship could develop and if so where it could go was not at all clear but she couldn't stop turning the possibilities over in her mind. She struggled up from her seat and began a slow but steady progress back along the path downstream towards the main road bridge. Climbing the steps up to the road took all her available energy. Her body seemed to be doing its best to offer an early glimpse of old age. Her heart was trying to break out of her chest and she felt dizzy and out of breath.

Martin Henshaw was already in the café on the upper level of the Rows by the time she arrived. In fact he was so keen to see her again without Drake around that he had arrived indecently early. He had a choice of tables and this one in the window offered a great view down over Bridge Street.

'I am so sorry,' gulped Grace, as she collapsed into the chair opposite Henshaw. 'I lost track of time.'

'Don't worry,' said Henshaw putting his hand over hers on the table. 'It takes longer to get over these things than you realise. You must take it easy; we need you fit.' Grace flashed him a weak smile. The waitress arrived and they ordered salads. The place had a Victorian look with a pervasive odour of freshly ground coffee and a background hum of polite conversation. There were old-fashioned cake stands on some of the tables. It was hardly the sort of place she imagined that Martin Henshaw would normally be seen in.

'My mother used to bring me in here when I was a boy,' laughed Henshaw. 'I thought it might amuse you. The speciality of the house is a swan, except this one is made out of meringue and clotted cream. Mum used to promise me one if I had been good. Of course it kept me quiet while she chatted to her friends.'

The salads arrived and the conversation tailed away while they ate. Neither seemed quite sure how to move the situation on so they ended up gossiping about the passers-by down in the street. Henshaw lectured Grace on the techniques that Drake had taught him for remembering the appearance of people.

'You have to come up with a name of a character that reminds you of the height, body build, clothes, and walk, and you are allowed to use several names,' he explained. 'It takes quite a lot of practice but once you get going it really helps.' They competed for a while to make the most compact descriptions of people on the pavement across the street.

'It's so difficult,' complained Grace, 'people have gone past before I have thought of even one name.'

'Don't try to be too clever at first, just look at people who are standing or moving slowly. Look at that young couple, they look like real fifties throwbacks, they could be John Travolta and Olivia Newton John in Grease.'

Grace giggled. 'They look more like Popeye and Olive Oil to me. He seems to have bulging biceps.'

'Well there you have the problem,' laughed Henshaw, 'I was ogling her legs but you saw his muscles.'

Grace blushed. 'Drake would be horrified at us. Look at that woman. She looks just like the Queen, short straight pastel coloured coat, handbag over her arm and a fluffy hairstyle. She even looks as if she is doing a royal walkabout, and the guy with her walks with his hands behind his back just like the Duke of Edinburgh.'

'That's very good,' said Henshaw. 'You'll be able to impress old Drake in no time.' The waitress brought a menu of sweets and they broke off to study it.

'I think the swan has too much cholesterol for me,' said Grace. 'To say nothing of the calories.' They ordered two sorbets and resumed their pastime.

'Hey' said Grace, 'this guy coming up the street should be named after our friend Professor Mallory. Look he has quite a pronounced limp.'

Henshaw's initial laughter tailed away as he stared silently and intently. 'You don't think it really is him, do you? Look at that pale crumpled linen suit, just like the picture from his office.' The man below was hobbling along, stopping and looking up at the buildings. He crossed the street towards Grace and Martin and looked straight up the window they were sitting in.

'It could be him, you know,' said Grace. 'If it is, we'll look total idiots if we let him slip through our hands.'

'I wish I had that picture with me' said Henshaw. 'You know I probably ought to check this out. Hang on here. I'll go down and get a better look, just in case.' He disappeared to the back of the café to find the staircase down to the ground level while Grace craned her neck to see if she could follow the man below. He was crossing back to the other side of the street and walking more quickly towards the Cross in the centre of town. His limp was less noticeable as he speeded up. Henshaw appeared on the pavement below and looked back up at Grace in the window, holding his hands out in a questioning shrug. Grace pointed up the street and Henshaw set off. Grace tried to attract the attention of a waitress to pay the bill but by now the café was full and they were all busy serving.

By the time she left five minutes later the street below seemed much more crowded than it had appeared from higher up in the restaurant window. She could see neither Henshaw nor Mallory, if indeed it was Mallory. She dialled Martin on her mobile phone.

'Hello,' said a breathless voice.

'Have you got him?'

'I thought I saw him briefly but no sign at all now. We're probably wasting our time; it's not really likely to be him.'

'I thought it definitely looked like him when I got a better view after you left. He seemed to set off more quickly up into the town centre.'

'OK. Look I'll run right up the street and then work back; you come up more slowly.' The phone went dead.

Grace walked deliberately along Bridge Street. If it was Mallory what could he be doing? Most of the buildings were shops catering for the tourist trade or selling fashion items. A sign in an upper floor window caught her attention. It was not what it said that caught her attention because she had no idea what that was. The sign was in Chinese calligraphy: black characters on a red background. Grace wondered what to do. She could carry on up the street or she could investigate this building or she could simply wait here. Normally she would be more decisive than this. She called Henshaw again but his phone flipped through to voicemail. Instinctively she checked her watch. 2.05 p.m.

A flight of stairs between two buildings led up to the first floor. She climbed slowly. At the top was a half-glazed door with another smaller version of the Chinese sign in the bottom left corner of the window. She prodded the door; it swung open. The room was dark with piles of books and stacks of paper reaching nearly to the ceiling. The sun was streaming in from the windows opening onto the street to her left but the whole room was so full that little light was reaching her at the back of the room. Dust motes filled the air and running her finger across a shelf next to the door, she easily wiped it clean. There was a high desk; the sort you would stand up to rather than sit down at, and she could imagine some clerk writing in a ledger with a quill pen. Dickens could have set a story in here.

There were two doors to her right, both half-glazed just like the one she had come through. She carefully tried the first door. The floor creaked as she moved across to it causing her to stop. The door was locked. The second door opened to reveal a staircase. She was in a sort of internal courtyard. High above her she could see a lantern roof light covered in rubbish and bird droppings. About half the panes of glass were either missing or broken. She looked down to see bird droppings on the steps below her. The space was roughly square in plan and the staircase went down turning through right angles on small quarter landings at each corner of the space.

Grace stopped and listened. Silence, save for a faint rumble of distant traffic. She leaned to look over the balustrade to see where the staircase went below. A sharp bang startled her. In her state of heightened anticipation it seemed like a gunshot, then a slapping noise raised her anxiety even higher She was like a taut string ready to snap. The slapping was repeated. It was definitely overhead. Looking up her eyes were dazzled by bright flickering sunlight.

The pigeon landed on one of the glazing bars in the roof over her head. It peered at her in triumph and their mutual stare was held for several seconds before the bird nonchalantly edged along its perch looking for more mischief. Its mate, greyer and more mottled, joined it with even more flapping. The two exchanged some brief pleasantries, reached agreement about their next action and flew off together into the bright blue afternoon sky.

Grace felt her heart pumping and remembered her adventure in the SEABU building. She should call Henshaw again but it would make too much noise. She stood and listened. Was that a footstep? No. Slowly, step-by-step, she descended the staircase to the next level below. She must now be back at ground level but she could not see a doorway to the front, only one to the rear. It was locked. The stairs went on one more level and she could now see a door ajar down there. She stopped and silently sent a text message to Henshaw's phone. No one would accuse her of the same mistake again. She would leave a trace just in case.

Henshaw had reached the old Cross at the junction between the four main streets right in the centre of Chester. A character dressed up in a medieval town crier's red frock coat was drawing a laughing crowd as he rang his hand bell, bellowing out news of local events. Cameras were clicking incessantly as tourists took photographs of members of their families standing in front of him. A queue of small children had formed to take the handbill and ring it, each one trying to outdo their predecessor. The crowd applauded every effort, and proud parents congratulated their children as they returned from their moment in the spotlight.

Henshaw could not see any sign of the man they had spotted from the café window. He twisted around again wondering which way to go. He could take the little turn right and left and go on further up Northgate towards the town hall and the cathedral: he could turn right down Eastgate towards the hotel where Jimmy Cheung had stayed or he could turn left down the narrower Watergate. He tried looking a short way down each street but it was hopeless. Perhaps he had overtaken the slower limping man. The best bet would be to retrace his steps back down Bridge Street. He called Grace on his mobile. Infuriatingly there was no answer.

He set off slowly back down Bridge Street, scanning left and right trying not to miss a single person in the crowd. A few paces later his mobile phone rang and his heart leapt but it was not Grace, just a text message alert. He never used text messaging but his phone company, determined to get him to see the error of his ways, was always sending cheerful messages of encouragement. Henshaw had learned to ignore the irritating bleep they made. He put the phone back in his pocket. He wondered whether to call Drake but what could he say? He and Grace were both wandering up and down Bridge Street looking for a man in a crowd who happened to be limping. He rehearsed the conversation silently and decided it sounded too silly for words.

Slowly Grace descended to the next level. This was as far as the stairs went and there was only the one doorway. It appeared to be a security door with steel panels and a huge keyhole. There was no knob but a large curved grab handle. The door opened outwards towards her. She held it and pulled the door wide open. There was a faint glimmer of light coming from somewhere high up and right across the room. She listened again. Silence, or was that a muffled groan? Probably more birds. She ran her hand across the wall next to the door hoping to find a light switch but no luck. She backed out again wondering what to do. Then she saw what she had been looking for. There was an old-fashioned round brass switch on the wall outside the door. She pulled it and the rocker flipped down with a resounding clunk. Fluorescent light strips across the ceiling pinged on and off creating stabs of light flashing around the room. Gradually they settled down leaving the room bright enough to see clearly.

It was much bigger space than she had expected and, as she had guessed, a basement. It appeared to be used as a store and was full of plain buff cardboard boxes and stacks of crates that obscured the view. The air was musty and noticeably colder. The light she had seen earlier was from glass blocks that she guessed were in the pavement in the street above. The basement must project out under the street. She moved towards it between the piles of boxes.

It was then that she heard the first footstep. She froze. It was followed by another and then another. These were not so much purposeful as stumbling steps. She swung around only to see more piles of cardboard boxes. The footsteps stopped. She remained motionless for what seemed like an age. The footsteps started again and she counted them; they came in pairs. Four, five, a slight gap, six, seven. It must be Mallory with his limp. The footsteps seemed to be going away. There was that muffled groan again. Instinctively she shouted, though even as she was doing so, she wondered if this was the right course of action. 'Professor Mallory, stop! This is the police.'

Clunk. The sound rushed round the room meeting its echo on the far side. Instantly she understood. The lights went out. Another bang echoed around the room, followed by a muffled clang. The last vestige of the daylight from the doorway had gone. She listened. She could no longer hear the footsteps. Her eyes were slowly adapting to the dark and she began to retrace her steps. Just as she feared the door was closed. She pushed but it would not budge. She felt all around systematically. She could not find a handle or even any protrusion on the inside of the door. She was locked inside a large secure room.

She was furious with herself. She was never going to be allowed to forget this. Thank goodness she had her mobile phone. She pulled it out and the little screen briefly glowed so brightly it almost dazzled her. Then it faded a little. She dialled Henshaw and held the phone to her ear, removing the earring she was wearing as she did so. There was no answer except a long bleep.

She looked back at the phone screen. Her heart sank. The reception indicator was showing no signal.

Perhaps she would get reception under the windows in the pavement. She crossed the room again taking a different route between the piles of boxes to get nearer to the brightest light. She walked slowly and carefully around the last pile of boxes and turned towards the light. Her foot caught something and she tripped, clutching at the pile of crates to her left. Her heart raced and she calmed herself down again. Looking to her left she saw what tripped her. It was a shoe, a man's shoe. She leaned forward tentatively. The shoe was attached to a leg. The leg was attached to the rest of a body. Even in the dark the outline was unmistakable. Someone was lying on the floor right behind a huge stack of crates. Perhaps this was the source of the groans she thought she had heard.

'Are you alright?' she said 'Who are you?' There was no response. She felt the leg. There was no movement even as she ran her hand up towards the torso. It was warm. She felt a momentary sense of relief that this was not a dead body. She was not awfully good at dealing with those. Then her hand hit something hard and she felt wetness. The knife was plunged deep into the body right up to the hilt. Grace felt her head float uncomfortably. She went alternately hot and cold in rapid succession. The room began to spin.

The sun streaming through the window warmed Drake's back as he sat in his hotel room going through all his notes from Singapore. He was grateful for some solitude together with a full English breakfast, the Sunday Times and time. Singapore was fascinating and he must go back and learn more but England was his home. It was where he felt at ease and where he could think. He flipped through notes about the Singapore River, his conversation with Wu Dao Rui at the museum, the meetings with Archie Grayson and his wife at the AAA shop. He tried to remember her name in vain. It seemed that he had not made a note. He was losing his grip. He needed the younger Grace with him on trips in future. His mood darkened as he reflected on the process of aging and how he had been cruelly deprived of Cynthia's company just when he needed it most. He realised that such an emotion was purely selfish. The real cruelty was dealt to poor Cynthia. This only served to make his mood blacker still. What would he do after this case was finished? Should he retire properly and be done with it, or was there life in him still?

All this was pretty irrelevant right now, he thought. The Jimmy Cheung case was far from solved. Could Mallory really have killed Jimmy in a rage on the bridge? Was it even possible that Percival had seen murder as the way out of his mess? Marcia Elliot did not seem to be a very likely suspect but Drake wished he could make up his mind about McFadden and just who were these Chinese thugs of his that Percival had been worried about? What about Sheng Tian? There was another man with a terrible temper but surely not? Just what was the role of AAA in all this? Drake was in one of those infuriatingly circular mental traps, going round over the same material again and again without making any progress.

There was a niggling suspicion in the back of his mind that he was missing something. He could not quite put his finger on it but he recognised the feeling. It was just like being blocked on a crossword clue. It called for a walk. Somehow, time after time, this technique allowed him to come up on a problem from behind, take it by surprise and find some really obvious solution that had been pretending not to be there all along.

Grace was resolutely determined not to pass out. Breathing deeply she moved her hand across the body, carefully avoiding the knife, up to the shoulder and down an arm. She thought she could hear breathing but there was absolutely no movement. She could feel a man's jacket sleeve and she pulled the cuff back slightly and took the wrist to feel for a pulse. Nothing. The hand certainly did not feel cold. She listened again for the sound of breathing, and heard it once more but it was her own unnaturally shallow and in rapid gulps. She was certain there was no life and yet the body was warm.

She must have arrived just after the murder. Why would Mallory, if indeed it was Mallory, have killed this man? She wondered who it was that she had in front of her. Could it be Sheng Tian? She felt the hair and thought it was softer than she imagined his to be and anyway surely too long? Unfortunately he was face down and her training told her not to disturb the body until the SOC team got here. She resumed her journey back to the light; perhaps Henshaw would call her.

A succession of faint and ghostly shadows drifted across the wall across the room. Her heart thumped against her chest again. She had assumed she was alone save for the dead body. She stopped and crept forward on tiptoe. Then she had the pavement lights in her direct line of vision. The shadows were nothing more than the movement of people passing by above the glass block pavement. The phone was showing a single bar on the reception indicator. Grace crammed herself up against the wall under the pavement lights and tried to send a text message but it failed to go through. To add to her horror the battery was now showing low. She slumped down to the floor and desperately kept transmitting the same message in the hope that at least one attempt would coincide with a moment of signal availability. A cocktail of fear, frustration and anger overwhelmed her and she lay back against the wall taking long slow breaths.

Henshaw arrived back at the café in Bridge Street that he and Grace had sat in not half an hour previously. He had seen no sign of Mallory and, more worryingly, none of Grace either. He felt helpless. He had to assume that Grace would not have simply left the scene. Perhaps her phone battery had run out but knowing how efficient she was that seemed unlikely. The only other alternative that he could think of was that Grace had seen and chased after Mallory and was now in some trouble. There was nothing else for it he would have to call in and ask for backup. Much to his surprise Drake was only a few minutes away on what he called his "Sunday Constitutional." Henshaw miandered back up Bridge Street partly in the hope of seeing some clue as to Grace's whereabouts and partly to intercept Drake.

Perhaps it was the less purposeful walk that allowed him to see it, or maybe it was that he was no longer watching people. Either way Henshaw was simultaneously worried and embarrassed by the obvious Chinese sign in the upper floor window that he was now walking past for the third time. He pulled out his phone to call Drake. Another irritating text alert sounded as he did so and seeing Grace's number against the message set his heart thumping.

basement of building Chinese sign in upper floor window

There was now a second message.

Locked in with dead body. Mallory got away

He called Grace. No answer. He summoned scene-of-crime officers to join the backup team that he could already hear arriving with loud sirens.

Even at the top of Bridge Street, Drake could tell where the incident was from the crowd that had gathered and was being slowly pushed back by uniformed officers. He had a minor altercation with a middle aged woman who accused him of 'pushing to the front when he ought to know better and let small children stand in there to get a view'. She was still shouting at him as he ducked under the tape and stumbled forward, showing his ID to a constable.

The cleared area of pavement was occupied only by a couple of pigeons running around in delight at having such rich and uninterrupted pickings as they pecked at all the scraps left behind by the recent passers-by. They compulsively argued over every crumb in turn, screeching, hopping and wing flapping in their anger. Two officers in riot control kit were just going up the stairs with gear to open the door to Grace's prison. Henshaw was dashing around aimlessly, holding his mobile phone to his ear.

'Grace Hepple is locked in the basement, sir. She texted me to say there is a dead body there. I will just feel happier when we get her out,' he said. 'I think her phone battery is going. We were following Mallory, at least we think it was Mallory.'

'And he locked her in the basement?' demanded Drake incredulously.

'We think so. I just need to get her out.'

'OK, I am sure it's all under control now. She will soon be in good hands.'

Henshaw recounted all the events in the café and afterwards. Drake raised first one eyebrow then the other but listened in silence until he was finished.

'So you think Mallory has got away then?' he asked finally.

'I've set up an outer cordon and requested an alert on ports and airports. We're circulating his details nationwide. But Grace is in there with a dead body.'

'Haven't you noticed? asked Drake dismissively. 'Dead bodies are our business.'

Grace was more grateful than she was prepared to admit when she heard the work beginning outside her temporary prison. She made her way back to sit by the door which gave way rather more easily than the officers outside had expected and light flooded the room followed by two constables stumbling with the ram they had been using and three more from the support team walking behind.

'Where are you, Grace?' It was Henshaw's voice.

'I'm here. The body is over there on the floor.' She tried to stop her voice trembling. 'I think he has a jacket on so perhaps there will be some identity in one of the pockets.' Henshaw led the way across the room and round the boxes. Drake arrived puffing and helped Grace to her feet, put an arm around her shoulder and passed her over to the paramedic who had just arrived on the scene.

'Well I never!' exclaimed Henshaw. The little recovery party escorting Grace to safety stopped its tracks. 'Are you still there, Grace?'

'Yes.'

'I thought you said Mallory escaped? Far from it, he's here. We have finally found him.'

'Surely he hasn't been hiding in here with me all the time?'

'He couldn't hide. He's dead. This is the man we were following. He is certainly wearing that linen suit we saw, and what I can see of his face looks like the picture we have of Professor Peter Mallory.' Drake beckoned the paramedic to take Grace away, and joined Henshaw by the body.

'He looks very dead indeed,' confirmed Drake, 'Thank goodness it was dark and Grace never saw the expression on his face.' Henshaw nodded grimly. The two men stood back in silence and let the scene-of-crime team take over. Climbing back up the stairs, Drake tried the door off the landing at ground level. It was locked but the dust on the door handle had been disturbed.

'It looks as if someone has recently gone through here,' he said to Henshaw. 'Get the lads to check it out.'

First thing on Monday morning Drake met with the whole team in the meetings room at the police headquarters building. Grace seemed to have recovered all her spirits and was inevitably treated to a variety of jokes about getting stuck in places and having to be rescued. Henshaw promised not to let her out of his sight for the foreseeable future. A number of looks were exchanged and eyebrows raised around the room. There was some more giggling and smirking. Grace looked at her feet and felt her face flush with embarrassment. Henshaw busied himself with his notebook. Drake called everyone to attention.

'One thing about this case is now clear,' he began. 'We are not going to be able to interview Professor Mallory.'

A faint ripple of laughter.

'However, we now have several more questions to answer. Who killed Mallory and why? What, if anything was Mallory's role in the Jimmy Cheung case? What is the connection between the Jimmy Cheung case and the building in Bridge Street that Grace has so spectacularly introduced to us? Thank you Grace.' There was a more raucous wave of laughter around the room and Drake held up his hand to quieten everybody down. 'And what the hell was Mallory doing there anyway? That will do to start with but several more questions may occur to me in due course. Henshaw, what can you report so far?'

'The building in Bridge Street is undergoing some renovation and there is a planning application in for a major retail development there. The building is listed so the approval is far from a foregone conclusion but if successful the site will become even more valuable. It is owned by a holding company registered in London but we have not been able to trace them fully yet. The shop on the ground floor appears to have been leased separately and the upper floors and basement are apparently unused, though they are connected by the light well to the rear. The shop on the ground floor is known as "The Orient" and sells crafts, ornaments and the like, mainly of a Chinese flavour. We also found a door at ground level that led straight to a small yard at the rear. We are examining that area. It may well be that the murderer could have escaped that way, maybe locking the door behind him, and perhaps having a vehicle in the yard behind.'

'What about Mallory?' asked Drake.

'The initial pathologist's report confirms that the time of death was within an hour of our arrival. The cause of death is obvious but there were also signs of a scuffle and detailed examinations may reveal tissue under the fingernails and there may or may not be blood other than the victim's at the scene. Work is going on today to investigate the scene thoroughly. We are looking for fingerprints now but we already know that there are only Mallory's on the knife.'

Drake grunted and everybody waited to hear his thoughts. 'Is it possible that Mallory began the conflict and ended up coming off second best?'

'A possibility, certainly,' said Henshaw, 'but what makes you suggest this?'

'Your descriptions of Mallory before the event was that he was looking around, apparently searching for the building,' said Drake. 'This suggests that he was going to a prearranged meeting. We know he had a very volatile temper. This meeting could have been an ambush but it also could have been an argument that simply got out of hand.' Drake looked round at Grace. 'Have you got any ideas? You were there.'

'I am still wondering why I was so convinced that the person I heard leaving and who kindly locked me up.'

More laughter.

'…was actually Mallory himself. I keep replaying it in my mind. It definitely sounded to me as if the person I heard leave was limping, just as we had seen Mallory doing.'

'Yes we must add that limp into our calculations,' said Drake. 'One reason for the limp might have been that murderer may have been injured in a struggle with Mallory. Another might be that he was carrying something heavy.'

'If the latter was the case,' said Henshaw, 'then perhaps the meeting was to exchange something. Given the location, perhaps something illegal.'

'And heavy, or at least bulky,' added Grace. 'Mallory was certainly not carrying anything when we saw him in the street.'

'Let's be careful about all this,' said Drake, 'we need to keep an open mind here. Mallory has been bugging me. Everywhere I go he seems to have been there before. Clearly he knew more about Jimmy Cheung and was very busy finding out about him. We know that from Percival, the Registrar. This meeting could have been about that.'

'You mean Mallory was blackmailing someone?' asked Grace.

'Maybe. It is possible that Mallory knew something about Jimmy Cheung which would have led him to suspect the murderer and that he has now paid the price for that. I think we should immediately check out all the main players to see if they can help us. Let's begin with Percival and McFadden, and even Marcia Elliot. Perhaps one of them has been seen limping. I want as much information as you can get with the help of your team, on the whereabouts of Percival, McFadden and Marica Elliot at the time of Mallory's murder. Grace, I want you to stay here and co-ordinate any incoming information.

Denson appeared and whispered in Henshaw's ear. Henshaw held his hand up for attention.

'We have some news that might be quite important I think,' he announced. 'Scene-of -crime have found a couple of bloodstains in the yard to the rear, and one in the corridor inside at the back. They have closed off the street behind and are conducting a fingertip search but so far cannot offer us any more.'

**ANOTHER VARSITY MURDER**

An astonishing scene developed yesterday afternoon when police swooped on The Orient shop in Bridge Street. A man had been found stabbed to death in the basement by an off-duty police officer investigating suspicious behaviour. The victim is believed to be another professor at the university leading to concerns that this may be related to the recent murder of a visiting professor on the Queen's Bridge. University officials were remaining tight-lipped however today. The police are asking members of the public who were in Bridge Street yesterday afternoon to come forward. Chief Inspector Drake has also asked anyone who has noticed unusual behaviour of any kind since Sunday lunchtime to contact the police. "The murderer may have had to clean or dispose of clothes with blood on them", he said. Meanwhile the proprietors of The Orient say they hope to reopen the shop again tomorrow.

The weather had taken a more seasonal turn and there was a persistent drizzle in the air. It was nearly midday by the time Drake was walking along the Rows in Bridge Street, reading the report of his press conference in the paper. Drake wanted to experience these historic galleries for himself and they conveniently offered perfect shelter from the rain. The Rows, by contrast with the shophouses he had seen in Singapore, were continuous galleries a storey up in the air. According to the history books the exact reason for this entirely civilised but unique form of construction was not without some mystery. In places they could be dated back as far as the thirteenth century although authoritative records of their construction had never been found.

The most popular theory, which Drake rather liked, was that the high level timber framed walkways were initially built over the ruins of the previous buildings including Roman barracks that had been destroyed by a huge fire. Traders built shops and houses off and above the walkways and only years later was the rubble below excavated and buildings inserted as the city prospered and land became more valuable, with more traders wanting to ply their trade as close as possible to the city centre. Drake could not help but wonder why architects had not taken up these ideas and developed a modern version of the Rows or for that matter the Singaporean five foot way system. Both seemed to offer shelter from their respective climates and yet not seal their customers off from the outside world.

In the modern Chester, many shops were at both levels and it was possible to move between levels inside such shops. At various points along the walkway there were also steps down to ground level. Drake reflected that the whole scene with its black and white timbered buildings must have seemed magical to a foreigner such as Jimmy Cheung. By now he could see The Orient across the street. It was on the ground floor level only with the shop lot at the upper walkway level empty. There was a woman constable on duty outside the shop door and the usual blue and white police tape across the steps to the side leading up to the door Grace had pushed open. The sign over the shop simply read “The Orient”, and in very small letters below, “Proprietors D and F. Watson”. Drake acknowledged the WPC standing next to the door which she opened to allow him into the shop.

Just inside the low doorway Drake found himself on a small landing with a spindly wooden balustrade in front of him. To his immediate left was a pair of steps down to the main floor that was slightly lower than street level. The air inside the shop was heavy with the combined scents of soap and Chinese incense. The place was empty of people but full of objects. Every available horizontal surface contained some object considered desirable by the shopkeepers, though from what Drake could see most were hardly essential items. Every object was individually labelled by hand with small folded stand up labels onto which the shopkeepers had written the price and, in many cases, some little message of exhortation about how to use the apparently useless objects. Standing behind a counter chatting to Police Constable Katie Lamb, were two almost identical rather short rotund women with white fluffy hair. They had red faces and were wearing aprons tied at the back over floor length flowery skirts. There was nothing even remotely oriental about them, thought Drake.

‘Hello Ladies,’ he began. ‘I am Chief Inspector Drake. I am sorry we have had to ask you to close your shop this morning but I hope we shall be able to allow you to open very soon. The two ladies replied in perfect unison.

‘Oh thank you, Chief Inspector,’ they chimed, looking at each other and nodding as if to confirm they had said the right thing. The one on the left made the introductions.

‘I am Doris,’ she said, ‘and this is my sister Florence.’

‘I am pleased to meet you both,’ said Drake shaking two podgy hands in turn, ‘would I be right in guessing that you are twins?’

There was much giggling and nodding from Doris and Florence so Drake assumed he was right.

'This is awful,' said Doris.

'…awful,' said Florence nodding vigorously.

'To think that yesterday there was a dead body just below us,' said Doris.

'…just below us,' said Florence.

'Well don't worry, ladies, it is all cleared away now. My officers are conducting a more detailed examination of your basement.'

'Oh no,' said Doris, 'it isn't our basement. We only rent the ground floor shop.'

'…ground floor shop,' nodded Florence.

'We moved here only six months ago, you see. Our last shop was knocked down for redevelopment and we were homeless.'

'…homeless.'

'Our new landlord was very kind. He said we could use this shop rent-free until he had to close the whole building next year. It is going to be a wonderful new shopping centre and we shall have a stall in it,' said Doris. Drake waited for the echo from Florence but she only nodded. 'Our landlord said he would be using the rest of the building but we don't think he does really, do we Florence.'

'No, we don't think he does.'

'But this is quite enough for us,' said Doris. 'It's lovely and much better than our old place off Werburgh Street. We get much more passing trade here.'

'…much more.'

'Who is your landlord?' asked Drake.

'We have never met the boss, have we Florence but the Company is called Cheung Enterprises UK. They are part of a much bigger Chinese company. They have supplied us with incense for many years. Every now and then, Mr. Grayson calls in to see us when he is in England.'

'…in England.'

'Is that by any chance Mr. Archie Grayson?' asked Drake.

'Yes, yes,' they said in unison, 'do you know him?'

'I have met him,' said Drake, 'but that was in Singapore.'

'Oh yes,' said Doris, 'Singapore. That's in China isn't it?'

'Not exactly,' said Drake, 'but near enough.'

'We are expecting him to come in sometime this week, aren't we Florence?'

'...sometime this week.'

# 13 - Lace

The luxury of a night in his own bed at home in Berkshire was an unexpected pleasure for Drake. Now he was on his way across the Home Counties to north London where Grace had arranged a meeting for him. The train journey into Paddington was comfortingly familiar. He knew every curve and bump in the track and each stretch of scenery on both sides of the train. The journey was like an adult nursery rhyme - many twists and turns but ultimately predictable and with an assured ending. He always used this journey to muse over his cases and he was glad to be back into the old routine, even if only for one day.

Fergus Marshall, his boss at the Met, wanted a progress report and Drake could 'kill two birds with one stone'. It was going to be a difficult conversation with Fergus. Things were not getting any clearer and he was going to have to admit that the murder of Peter Mallory was almost certainly linked to the Jimmy Cheung case. He knew his friend Fergus was going to look long and hard at him over those half-glasses of his and then ask if everything was really under control. Drake would, of course, give assurances and Fergus would receive the news calmly but they would both know that things could be better and that Fergus' patience was finite.

As the train rumbled on, Drake sat worrying about whether going to Singapore had been wise. He ran through everything as he had countless times before. There was the characteristic smell of smoke and soot that was Royal Oak station, time to get his bag down off the rack. He'd probably done the right things on the whole. He always liked to have things more or less resolved by Royal Oak. London Underground trains were too frantic for considered reflection.

In the taxi across north London, Drake nursed his expected bruises. Fergus had been tougher than expected. The Foreign Office was getting very anxious and relations with Singapore were tricky. They not only wanted the crime cleared up but also were anxious that the subsequent court case, if there were to be one, would not cause embarrassment. Poor Fergus had tried to explain this assurance was not in his gift. He was obviously feeling the heat and now so was Drake.

The doorbell sounded oriental, a sort of tinkling that was slightly edgy. Drake pulled out his warrant card and stood back from the door to wait. Almost immediately patches of brilliant colour swirled around, distorted by the reeded glass of the door. It was like a dynamic abstract painting, a Jackson Pollock or more likely one of his many imitators. The composition of lime green and pink swirled around getting steadily larger until it covered virtually the whole of the glass panel. It came almost into focus as the door opened to reveal an elderly woman, striking in almost every aspect of her appearance. This was no cautious old lady hiding behind her door latched by a security chain to arrest the progress of unwanted visitors. The door opened to its full width immediately.

'Chief Inspector Drake?' she asked.

'Yes, of course,' said Drake, bowing slightly and extending his hand in greeting while holding up his identification in the other. 'Miss Emily Cheung, I presume.'

'Perfectly correctly young man. I have tea ready for you.' She made a sweeping gesture of welcome. Emily Cheung was obviously oriental but unusually tall. She was undeniably old and yet with an ageless appearance and a certain style and poise. Her greying hair was smoothed back and clipped behind her head. She wore the most amazing costume that Drake had ever seen and yet it also seemed familiar. The colours were now even more brilliant than their performance through the door. She wore an ankle length sarong, folded at the front, in a brilliant pinkish sort of red with gold thread stitched into it coming into florid detail at the edges and forming triangular geometric patterns stretching around to the back. There was a glittering silver belt above and beaded slippers below. Above all this she wore a silk camisole under the most delicate lace, semi-transparent top fitted to her still-slim waist and flaring out into pointed triangular shapes hanging down over the skirt. This lace top was the pièce-de résistance of the whole ensemble being elaborately detailed in the finest material and embroidered with flying birds and flowers.

'You like my Kebaya? I have put it on especially for you. I may be into my seventies now but I am still allowed to dress for a gentleman caller, especially when he is a Chief Inspector.' Drake was speechless. This septuagenarian Chinese woman was a complete stranger and yet she was definitely flirting with him and teasing him. Drake could do no more than smile and bow as courteously as he knew how. Emily laughed and Drake joined her. The moment of tension was broken.

'What is a Kebaya?' asked Drake eventually.

'This is my very best Kebaya.' Emily wafted a hand across her body from the neck down to her waist. 'Of course they would disapprove of a woman of my circumstance wearing one quite like this. The well prepared Nonya has many Kebayas, each suitable for only one particular kind of occasion but I do not believe there is one just for receiving senior policemen.' She sat inviting Drake to join her. 'I understand that you are interested in the history of our family.'

'I am investigating the tragic murder of your brother.'

'Of course,' said Emily, the pitch of her voice rising, 'but you think I should be in mourning, and not wearing such clothes?'

'Of course it is for you to dress entirely as you wish and I do appreciate the gesture. Your appearance is extraordinarily elegant.'

Emily nodded graciously, looked momentarily to the ceiling and began. 'Jimmy and I were not close. He was not kind to me when we were children. We have hardly seen each other in recent years. We had little in common. He was in any case old. He would have died soon I think. Does that sound cold-blooded? Perhaps it is. Even though I hardly saw Jimmy, I do feel more alone now. I am the last one left of our generation. Of course I regret his passing. I too am old, Inspector but I have no intention of acting my age.' She poured Chinese tea from the smallest teapot Drake had ever seen into two miniature cups. Emily lifted her cup with a balletic grace. Drake struggled even to grip his.

'My family history is interesting,' continued Emily enthusiastically. 'Our grandmother was a Nonya.'

'So you are Peranakan then?' asked Drake. Emily bowed slightly and drew herself up.

'I am impressed at your research, Inspector. Yes we have Peranakan blood. But the last two generations have rather been in denial about this. Being Peranakan in Singapore just after the Second World War was difficult. Some Chinese had become suspicious of them during the Japanese occupation. Mostly they did not speak Chinese and were less persecuted by the Japanese. Thankfully things have changed; there has been a revival of interest in Peranakan culture and, as you can see, I celebrate it now. Jimmy of course was never interested in such things. Always one for the short term, he lived for now and did not want to know the lessons of the past.' She tutted and frowned. 'My mother however spoke Mandarin and, of course, English as well as Malay. We children were brought up speaking English and Chinese. We never spoke Malay. When I was older and more interested in these things my mother would talk to me about our heritage. I think by then she regretted that they had neglected our culture. Jimmy was embarrassed when I wore these clothes; that simply encouraged me.' She chuckled to herself and wore a glazed expression as she recalled past events.

'My parents lived in a world completely different from the one we occupy. It all seems so long ago now. I think history is accelerating. My mother would not have been able survive modern London or Singapore. She would not have understood them. My parents moved from Johor in Malaysia so my father could get work in the port in Singapore. They left behind all their roots. It distressed my grandmother and she died not longer after. My mother never got over that but she would only talk about it to me. My father would not look back. Jimmy has inherited that attitude from him.'

'Did you have more brothers and sisters?' asked Drake.

Emily paused for a moment and dabbed her left eye. 'Yes we had another older brother but he was lost to us many years ago,' she answered enigmatically. Drake waited and eventually, Emily continued. 'He went missing during the Japanese occupation of Singapore in the Second World War. Many men went missing in those times.'

'You mean he was taken prisoner?'

'The Japanese did not take many prisoners. This was how Jimmy came to look after Janet who is in reality his niece but we do not normally tell people that.' Emily tapped Drake's knee confidentially.

'Yes, so I understand,' said Drake.

'You already know this?' said Emily, startled at the revelation.

'Sheng Tian told me.'

'Did he indeed.' Emily wrinkled her nose in disapproval. 'This does surprise me. It has been the custom in the family not to talk about it for Janet's sake. My family has many secrets, some darker than others.' She shrieked with laughter as if to lighten her own words. 'All families have secrets and rumours and stories I think,' Drake smiled his understanding and she continued.

'About a week after Janet's father went missing, the Japanese soldiers came for her mother in the middle of the night. They told her that she could visit her husband and that he had been complaining about the night-time cold and she could bring a blanket for him. She of course went willingly but they had deceived her. They took her to the YMCA building, which they were using as a sort of headquarters and removed all her clothes and possessions save for the blanket. She was kept in a large room with many other women. They were given little food and only a bucket in the corner of the room. She was interrogated most days and I think this must have been very cruel; always promising she could save her husband or even see him. I have long suspected he was already dead.' Emily dabbed her eyes with a lace napkin and drew a deep breath. She turned her head away from Drake and gazed out of the window.

'I have not spoken of this for nearly fifty years,' she said sadly, 'but it is no less painful now than it was then.' She turned back to Drake and smiled.

'Janet's mother was eventually released. By then she was out of her mind with grief. She never recovered. She could not remember what she had said and what she had kept secret. Whenever another man went missing from the locality, she would convince herself that somehow she must have betrayed him. She became gloomy and withdrawn. I was the only one who talked to her. Probably today she would have been given psychiatric treatment but in Singapore at that time such things were hidden from society. Eventually she died. I think she simply no longer wanted to live. She had a broken heart and by then a deeply disturbed mind.' Emily tailed off lost in painful memories.

Drake thought it best to change the subject. 'Can you tell me about the day of the degree ceremony?'

'Jimmy was in high spirits.' Emily laughed. 'He relished the whole business. He loved to be the centre of attention and he was in fine form. To begin with, he was pleased to see me and we talked about our childhood and family over lunch.' Her expression changed. 'Later he got more argumentative with me. He could not tolerate any criticism of the government in Singapore. Of course I do not believe everything the government does is bad any more than it is all good. But Jimmy would not even contemplate the possibility that anything could be improved. He used to have huge rows with Sheng Tian about this. Sheng Tian, thank goodness, is a free thinker; he will do well in a university here. This is why Sheng Tian would not come to the ceremony. Jimmy was furious and called him ungrateful. He told me at lunchtime that they argued that morning and that he regretted it but he could never admit this to Sheng Tian. It was their tragedy never really to know each other.' She paused and lowered her voice. 'Now they never will.'

'Did you talk to Jimmy again later in the day?'

'No he wanted the attention of the university people. I was not important enough for him,' she sniffed.

'I was told that you left early and did not go to the reception,' said Drake.

'Jimmy had made it clear over the lunch that he would be busy. He said he didn't want the reception to go on too long as he had another meeting so I said I was tired and came back to London. Anyway I prefer to sleep in my own bed.'

'Do you know who this meeting was with?'

'I remember only some reference to someone he called A.G. I assumed it was some deal he wanted to strike. Jimmy loved doing deals; that was his life.' She chuckled and stared into the empty space in front of her.

'Who exactly is A.G.,' asked Drake.

'I have no idea, I am afraid, except that I think he must have known him for some time. I have heard him refer to A.G. before.'

'Do you know where this meeting was or what time it was?' asked Drake.

'No Inspector, I am afraid I can't help you further. You know all I can tell you. I had even forgotten this myself until you asked about it. Oh dear, I should have told someone this before. Do you think this A.G. killed my brother?'

'That has to be a possibility we must consider,' said Drake grimly.

Emily looked hard at Drake and then she spoke very softly. 'Chief Inspector, unless I am very much mistaken, I think you know who this A.G. is.'

'Possibly,' growled Drake, 'possibly.'

By the time Drake had returned to Chester, Martin Henshaw had already visited "The Orient", established that Archie Grayson and his partner were checked into a hotel in town and put a watch on his movements. He had also checked with Sheila Wilkins at SEABU and discovered that, while there was no meeting scheduled, Archie Grayson had certainly been a visitor in the past. She thought that Hamish McFadden had also had meetings with him both in Singapore and in China.

'We have a new phantom in this case,' said Drake. 'First it was Mallory, now it is Grayson. Except that in this case, I have already met the man. He is in for quite a surprise when he sees me this time.'

Denson came in to announce the arrival of Archie Grayson, and the three detectives processed down the corridor to interview him. Drake gave Henshaw instructions to start the proceedings.

'Mr. Archie Grayson?' asked Henshaw, as he entered the room. Grayson nodded.

'I am Detective Inspector Martin Henshaw and I have two colleagues with me. We want to talk to you about your meetings with Mr. Jimmy Cheung recently here in Chester.' Archie looked puzzled.

'I had no meeting with him as such. My only contact with him was at the University. There was a formal ceremony that we attended.'

'We?' queried Henshaw.

'My partner and I,' said Grayson. 'We were invited and we were over here in the UK anyway. I live mainly in Singapore now.' Drake thought Grayson seemed pretty confident and not worried by Henshaw's line of attack.

'Mr. Grayson,' continued Henshaw firmly, 'we have evidence that you met Mr. Cheung again after the reception which followed the degree congregation.'

Grayson frowned. 'No, I am afraid you are wrong about that. We were not invited to the reception. I remember shaking Jimmy's hand at the end of the degree ceremony and then we left. We both had business in town. I needed to see our two wonderful ladies who run the shop in Bridge Street that we supply. That was the last time I saw poor old Jimmy. Dreadful, simply dreadful business.'

Drake moved forward. 'Hello again, Mr Grayson. I am Chief Inspector Drake. We met recently in your shop in Singapore.'

Grayson looked puzzled for a moment and then appeared suddenly to recognise Drake. 'Oh yes, sorry. I had forgotten your name but I never forget a face. You came in and looked at our little Peranakan display. What an extraordinary coincidence.'

'Not entirely,' grunted Drake.

Grayson's eyes opened as wide as his aging face would allow. 'You mean you were investigating Jimmy's murder when you visited our shop?'

'I was in Singapore for a number of reasons, Mr. Grayson. We have reason to believe you may not be telling us the whole truth here. I should warn you that this is a very serious investigation. I would like you to reconsider your answer of a few minutes ago. Did you have a meeting with Jimmy Cheung after the degree ceremony?'

'No. My memory is not what it was these days but I am sure I would have remembered that.'

'I have specific evidence that you had an appointment with him. Did you perhaps cancel it then?'

'No. I did not have an appointment with him. In fact, he had been to see us not long ago in Singapore. What is this evidence that you have?' Henshaw and Grace looked at Drake to see if he would declare his hand.

'We know that Jimmy Cheung had an appointment later that day with someone called A.G.'

Archie Grayson gave a staccato laugh and replied. 'Ah, A.G.' he said. 'That is not me.'

'Who is it then?'

'I have no idea,' said Archie Grayson abruptly. 'But I have never been known as A.G. Everyone calls me Archie.'

'I see,' said Drake. 'Very well. I would like you to give us a written statement detailing your movements that day. It was the $12^{th}$ of September. Please be as accurate and detailed as you can.' Henshaw and Grace left the room following Drake. The three of them wandered slowly down the corridor reviewing the situation.

'He is not being entirely honest with us. What do you both think?' asked Drake.

'I think he is telling the truth' said Grace. 'He seemed genuinely surprised and not thrown at all when Inspector Henshaw put it to him. Your line of questioning did not seem to perturb him either.'

'I agree with Grace,' said Henshaw. 'Either he is telling the truth or has put on a pretty good show.'

'Maybe you are both right,' said Drake, 'but the way he answered about A.G. had an odd ring to it. It's hard to pin it down but I think there is something else to dig out there. Let's leave him for a while to stew and write out his statement and then I might just have another go at him.'

As they sat drinking cups of tea, Denson appeared to tell them that Grayson was now asking to see Drake again and that he had something new to say. When they arrived back in the interview room, Grayson was pacing up and down anxiously. Drake beckoned him to resume his seat at the small table under a high level window.

'I understand that you would like to make a new statement to me,' said Drake, sitting down opposite Archie Grayson.

'I was not telling you the truth earlier,' said Grayson blurting out his words urgently. 'I did arrange to see Jimmy Cheung that evening.'

'And the meeting took place?'

'I met him in the park and we walked to the bridge.'

'What was the purpose of your meeting?'

Grayson had been sitting on the edge of his seat and now leaned back. 'We had been arguing over a new deal. My company, Asean Art and Antiques has an arrangement to import material for one of Jimmy Cheung's companies. He had been driving a very hard bargain. It would have seriously damaged my business. I asked to see him to discuss it one more time.'

'I imagine then, Mr. Grayson, that the discussion did not go well?'

'He wouldn't budge. You need to understand that Jimmy has almost total control over AAA now. Unknown to us, he had bought the building that we rent in Singapore. That land is now astronomically expensive and is effectively a conservation area. Unless we are going to move to a more out of town location we will have to pay whatever rent he chooses to charge. If I did not agree to his deal, he threatened to put up the rent. I think he was trying to drive AAA into bankruptcy so he could take it over at very little cost. I guess you are aware he has a record of such behaviour?'

'I have been told that his business practice was rather aggressive at times.'

Archie Grayson laughed almost hysterically. 'That is a nice piece of British understatement, if I may say so.'

'So what happened when you failed to reach agreement?'

'We had walked across the bridge when Jimmy stopped and turned round. He said the conversation was over and he was going back to his hotel. I walked back halfway across the bridge with him still trying to get him to see sense. He stopped at the middle to watch the boats on the river. I lost my senses and shot him there.'

'So you left his body on the bridge?'

'Yes, he was already leaning over the railing. There was no one on the bridge and if anyone looked up they would have just thought we were talking.'

'So you planned all this in advance?'

'Oh no, I just lost it, I'm afraid. I had meant to threaten him if necessary but when it came to it, I just saw red and shot him. It was so easy to do there. Anywhere else it would have been difficult.'

'So, do you normally carry a gun around with you, Mr.Grayson?'

'Of course not, I have never used one before. We sell old Japanese army guns that we managed to get a substantial stock of some years ago. I brought one of those with me to threaten him.'

'Mr Grayson,' said Drake, standing up. 'You must appreciate the seriousness of this situation. I'm going to give you a few minutes to consider your position. There will be a constable on duty immediately outside the door.' Drake beckoned Henshaw and

Grace Hepple to follow him, which they did in silence until reaching their meeting room.

'What are we doing?' demanded Henshaw finally. 'You had him on the run there; why back off now?'

'I just don't feel that this is convincing,' said Drake. 'There is something wrong with it but I can't pin it down. I wanted to see what you two thought.'

'It seems OK to me, sir,' said Grace. 'I have to admit though that it is strange, how one minute a case can look unbelievably confused and complicated and the next it all just falls into place,' said Grace.

'Actually it is not strange at all,' said Drake. 'You will learn it often happens like that.'

'Surely we have a result here?' said Henshaw.

'It is all too pat. He has been sitting there working this story out,' said Drake. Henshaw was looking back at his notes furiously and suddenly snorted.

'Yes, of course,' he said, startling the others. 'iI's obvious. He never mentioned the camera.'

'Well done, good yes,' said Drake. 'He talked about propping Jimmy up against the railing didn't he? But he didn't say anything about tying him there with the camera. Surely he would have mentioned that?'

'Maybe not though,' said Grace. 'I think we need to see if he actually knows about the camera or not. After all, you did keep asking him more questions, sir. He might just not have got a chance to mention it or perhaps not thought it important.'

'We need to test him on it,' said Drake. 'I'll go back and ask him again with Henshaw. I would like another pair of eyes and ears with me.'

Drake and Henshaw re-entered the interview room. Archie Grayson was sat in a calmly composed manner drinking a cup of tea as if at a café table.

Drake began. 'One matter of detail I would just like to check out with you, Mr. Grayson. You said that after you shot him, you propped Jimmy Cheung's body up against the balustrade I think.

Exactly how did you do that? Surely he would have just fallen over?'

'No,' said Grayson thoughtfully as if looking back at a picture of the scene. 'He was not a tall man, and somehow that was not a problem.'

'I see. Did he have anything around his neck by any chance?'

'Around his neck?' Grayson sounded surprised. 'No I didn't strangle him, I shot him.'

'When he was found, there was a camera around his neck,' said Drake.

'Oh yes, the camera!' said Grayson. 'Of course, I see what you mean. Yes he had a camera and when I left him it was dangling over the handrail.'

Drake grunted. 'I see. Then why did you not mention this before?'

'I didn't think it was important.'

'I wonder Mr. Grayson. Have you by any chance lost a cufflink recently?'

'I hardly think so,' replied Grayson. 'I never wear such things, far too much trouble and beside these days my hands shake too much to fix them.'

'Well he did know about the camera after all,' said Drake to Grace. 'But I had the distinct feeling he was treating the whole thing like a sort of memory test, almost as if he was sitting an examination. It was the way he said "Oh yes the camera". It was as if someone had told him about it but he had forgotten that detail until I reminded him, then out came the answer pat. He didn't actually say that he had wedged the camera into the handrail as the girls said they found it.' Henshaw raised his eyebrows and shrugged at Grace.

'Then there is the matter of the cufflink,' said Drake puffing himself up. 'Surely if he was the owner, he would have guessed why I was asking and given us even more convincing evidence of his guilt. In fact he did the opposite.' Drake stood up, stretched and began pacing around the room. 'There is some more digging still to do here,' he said addressing no one in particular. 'We will keep him in and perhaps tomorrow I will see if I can come up with something more concrete. I can sense that you two think I am inventing a problem.'

'I have never found your judgement to be wrong before, sir,' said Henshaw hurriedly, 'but on this occasion I cannot see what the problem is. I think we have our man.'

'You thought that about Sheng Tian,' grunted Drake, 'I am going out for a walk to think.' With that he was gone, leaving Henshaw and Grace Hepple feeling slightly foolish, standing in the middle of the corridor.

Drake arrived back at the police headquarters still contemplating the puzzle he had been turning over in his mind. If he was honest with himself, it was getting more tangled and confused rather than clearer. There were too many loose ends and possible directions to go in. He wandered around looking for Henshaw and, failing to find him, called Sergeant Denson.

'Not in, sir,' Denson's voice bellowed down the phone line as if he was not convinced in the capabilities of the electronics, 'went out in a car to see Dr. Percival at his home.' Denson described how Henshaw had phoned Sally Brown to arrange to see Percival, only to discover that he had called in to tell her he was working from home. The reason given was that he had been playing squash over the weekend and had pulled a muscle in his leg and was finding it difficult to walk and drive.

# 14 - Ivory

The morning sun was glinting down the length of Eastgate as Drake made his now familiar way to the Grosvenor Hotel to see Janet Cheung. It caught the gilt work on the clock tower over the Eastgate, which responded by chiming cheerfully as the hands ticked round to ten. Clearly visible in the bright light were the letters VR above and the date 1897 below the clock face, proudly announcing its construction with the confidence and sense of permanence of that era. There were a couple of tourists standing on the bridge under the clock tower itself taking photographs of the street. Janet was her usual elegant and calm self, as ever offering Chinese tea and some biscuits that Drake accepted very readily.

'Yesterday someone confessed to the murder of your father,' said Drake after his first sip of tea.

Janet looked up, her eyes widening. 'Really? That is good news. Am I allowed to know who this is?'

'Of course but at this stage it is not to go any further please. It is Archie Grayson, the director of Asean Art and Antiques.'

'Astonishing!' said Janet, so quietly Drake could hardly hear her.

'You know him of course?'

'Yes we have met many times. He is…was a business partner of my father as I have already told you. I would not say I know him well. Why did he kill my father?'

'He says that your father was trying to renegotiate some deal or other in a way that would put him out of business.' Janet sat silently staring at the tray of teacups on the table in front of her. 'You are aware also Janet, that we had another murder yesterday?'

'I heard there was some disturbance in the centre of town but I took no interest I'm afraid.'

'I believe it may be related to the murder of your father. I'm afraid it was Professor Peter Mallory who was found dead yesterday.'

'No!' Janet began to shake and Drake could see tears beginning to form in her eyes. He placed a comforting arm around her shoulder and they sat silently for a few minutes.

'This whole business is getting out of hand,' said Janet eventually.

'Is there anything you know that might help us to understand this?' asked Drake.

Janet simply sobbed and shook her head. 'He was such a nice, kind man.'

'Janet,' I must ask you this,' said Drake. 'Was he more than that?'

She looked at him wide-eyed. 'You know don't you? Yes I was seeing him. He was so interested in the early history of Singapore. He helped me so much over the arrangements for my father's ceremony. It just happened.'

'When was the last time you saw him?'

'Oh I haven't seen him since then.'

'Sorry,' said Drake, 'I am afraid I don't understand that. When was that?'

'I can't remember exactly but it was some time before the degree congregation. He said he was in another relationship and wanted to sort that out. He has not called me since. I thought he would. Now he never will. Poor Peter.' She began searching in a small bag for her handkerchief, and then dabbed her eyes.

'One possibility that we are considering,' continued Drake, 'is that he had discovered something about your father or that he knew who killed your father.' Janet made no response so Drake probed again. 'Have you any ideas about that, Janet?'

'He made a great number of enquiries about my father in order to prepare the oration he gave at the degree congregation. That is all I know.'

'Janet, I must ask you what you know about your father's business arrangements. Was he involved in any business of a kind that was dangerous or perhaps illegal?'

'Of course not,' Janet replied indignantly and then after a brief pause. 'Well I don't know the details. I looked after his personal diary. I did not really get involved in all his business deals. He kept that very much to himself but I am certainly not aware of anything illegal in his business.'

Archie Grayson somehow looked much older than he had the day before. Drake guessed he had probably got very little sleep. He offered only a weak smile when Drake greeted him and beckoned him to take the seat across the small table by the window.

'Mr. Grayson,' Drake began, 'I want to return to the question of the camera round Jimmy Cheung's neck,' Grayson nodded. 'Was it your camera or his?'

'It was not my camera. I assumed it was his,' answered Grayson.

'Was he wearing the camera when you met him that day?'

'Yes I think so. I think he had it round his neck, a bit like a tourist really.'

'Did you see him take any pictures with the camera?' Grayson paused.

'I don't think so,' he answered eventually.

'Thank you, Mr. Grayson,' said Drake standing up.

'Is that all?' asked Grayson.

'Yes, for now.'

'What happens to me now?' demanded Grayson.

'You will return into custody,' said Drake. 'I imagine you need to get used to that. You are going to be there for a long time. I suspect from your age, that it is your future.' Drake waited to allow this remark to take effect on the old man. It did not take long. He slumped forward, his forehead coming to rest on the table.

'One more thing,' said Drake, now halfway across the room. 'Exactly when did you arrange to meet with Jimmy Cheung?'

'I cannot remember precisely. I think it was 6:30.'

'No,' said Drake. 'That was not my question. I did not want to know what time you met him but when you actually made the arrangement.'

'Oh, I see. I think it was after the degree congregation,' said Grayson. 'He said that he had to go to a reception for an hour or so but would see me afterwards.'

'Thank you, Mr. Grayson,' said Drake opening the door of the interview room and speaking to the constable on duty outside in the corridor. 'Please take Mr. Grayson down again and lock him up.'

As Drake left the room he literally bumped into Henshaw coming down the corridor at speed. As they walked together Henshaw confirmed that his visit to Dr. Percival's home proved that he was indeed limping badly and was claiming an alibi for the whole weekend including a game of squash. So those features of Percival's story that could be checked were standing up. On this occasion his wife at least corroborated her husband's account and apparently the squash opponent was prepared to vouch for both the game and the injury. It seemed that Percival lost the game of squash and was in a thoroughly bad mood about losing to an opponent he expected to beat. Throughout the whole interview Percival was very jittery but Henshaw could not tell if that was because he was still concerned about the charges that might be brought against him for his assault on Grace Hepple. Henshaw reported that he had tried to get hold of Hamish McFadden to check out his alibi for the time that Mallory was murdered at The Orient. Apparently his secretary, Sheila Wilkins had no entries in the diary for him and he had not appeared at the office. She also reported that he was not answering his phone. Henshaw was about to send a couple of constables to his home. Henshaw asked if Drake had made any progress with Archie Grayson.

'I've just left him,' began Drake slowly, reflecting again on his interview. 'I'm trying hard to be severe with him. I want him to understand what he is taking on by admitting to this murder. There are signs he has begun to think about it.'

'So you still don't believe he did it then?' asked Henshaw.

'Things do not add up,' answered Drake, 'Emily said that Jimmy had told her at lunch about his evening meeting with A.G. and that she did not talk to him again. Grayson maintains that he made the arrangement to see Jimmy after the congregation in the afternoon.'

'So perhaps Archie did meet Jimmy and kill him and Emily is wrong about the timing,' suggested Henshaw.

'Or, he had another meeting,' added Drake, 'or Archie for some reason has made up the whole story about his involvement.'

'But why would he do that?'

'Maybe he is protecting someone else,' mused Drake. 'You know Henshaw, I think that might be exactly the explanation I am looking for. Well done!' With that Drake strode off down the corridor leaving Henshaw wondering exactly what he had said that was so clever. He was interrupted by Grace Hepple appearing excitedly.

'Come and see what the scenes of crime crowd have found down at The Orient,' she gulped. 'Apparently one of those cardboard boxes in the basement was not empty. They have left it in-situ in case we want to see it undisturbed but they have brought photographs. Look here in the office.'

'It looks like lots of rods,' said an unimpressed Henshaw, looking at a photograph of an open box.

'Exactly,' said Grace, 'remember the Hanko we found on Jimmy Cheung? I went and fetched it out. Here it is.' She pulled out the little case, opened it up and took out the cylindrical ivory stamp.

'Good grief, yes!' exclaimed Henshaw, 'well done. You're dead right, this looks like a box of blanks, as it were, all ready to have the end carved into a sign for a customer.'

Grace nodded. 'That was exactly what I thought,' she said. 'So The Orient is a front for more undercover trading.'

'You mean ivory trading?' asked Henshaw.

'I hardly think they would set up a big operation like that just for one box of Hankos,' said Grace.

The two were just thinking that they should tell Drake about this discovery when he walked in wearing his serious face. Grace explained the findings about the Hanko and the potential for this to be the tip of a rather larger ivory trading business.

'It all looks as if it might come together here,' said Drake.

'But you still think Archie Grayson is innocent?' asked Henshaw.

'Well it was certainly not him who met Jimmy Cheung that evening,' said Drake.

'Has he withdrawn his statement then?' queried Grace.

'No,' said Drake, 'but I am certain of it from his reaction. One possible explanation was that he is protecting someone else. That someone would have to be a person he cares about a great deal. I believe that person is his partner, Amanda Goh. I asked him if she was here with him, and she is. I have just put it to him that she is A.G. and he simply clammed up completely. The poor chap looks a broken man. I could tell when I met them in Singapore that he absolutely doted on her. She is obviously younger and had apparently promised to marry him. Grace, the usual procedure with airports immediately, please. Henshaw, see if you can track her down. Let's hope she is still in the UK. Perhaps Grace you would also check out Marcia Elliot again. At the very least I think we ought to inform her of Mallory's demise but do it in person and see what reaction you can get.'

Later that day Drake was holding one of his 'rounding up' meetings of the case team in the meetings room at Cheshire Police Headquarters. Henshaw reported that Amanda Goh had been tracked down at her hotel and was on her way in a police car.

Grace had managed to arrange to see Marcia Elliot at her apartment on the university campus. Grace was evidently rather pleased with what she had uncovered.

Apparently Professor Peter Mallory had turned up at Marcia Elliot's apartment on Saturday evening, she said unexpectedly. He told her that he thought he was finally going to nail Jimmy Cheung down and that McFadden was implicated. He said he had a strong suspicion that they were both involved in a major ivory trading enterprise that contravened the laws of Singapore and was in breach of international agreements.

Mallory had been to The Orient and bought a Hanko, initially a bamboo one but when he enquired about ivory versions he was shown one of those too. He had then enquired about more substantial ivory items and was told to come back to their upstairs office when someone else would be there to arrange a viewing. He got the impression that anything could be obtained. He told Marcia Elliot that he was going on Sunday morning. He showed her a small Chinese sign that he said they would put in the window if the meeting was on. She claimed to have told him that we were looking for him and asked him to contact us immediately but he had sworn her to secrecy at least until he had conclusive proof. It seems this whole thing had become an obsession with him. He had tried to tell Percival who earlier on was keen to investigate anything that might ruin McFadden but was by now terrified and wanted to keep out of it. Marcia Elliot had apparently warned Mallory that it might be dangerous and given him her little derringer pistol for safety. She was in a frantic state, saying that if she had called us and told us he was there then he would still be alive. Unfortunately she really had no idea who it was Mallory was actually going to meet on Sunday morning. Drake decided that some further watch on McFadden was necessary.

'Somehow though,' said Drake, 'even if he is involved, I just cannot see McFadden coming to a meeting for the actual sale of ivory. He would have front people to do it for him.'

'Agreed,' said Grace 'Probably the so-called Rottweilers.'

'Maybe,' interjected Drake, 'but almost certainly from what we know about their frequent travelling, they are more likely to be couriers than salesmen, especially if their English is so limited.'

'If Marcia's story is completely accurate then our two dear white haired old ladies must at least be in on it; what were their names?' Henshaw addressed the question to nobody in particular and did not seem to really want an answer. 'But they may have little understanding of the whole operation. My guess would be that they are deliberately kept that way to avoid them gossiping.'

'Good thinking, Henshaw, said Drake, 'so what about Archie Grayson and Amanda Goh? In fact now I remember my conversation with Archie in Singapore makes more sense. He made some obscure references to wanting not to alert the authorities to the nature of their trading.'

'But given their infrequent visits to Chester, they surely cannot be the main handlers here,' suggested Henshaw.

'So perhaps there are other people involved that we don't know about at the moment,' mused Drake. 'We need to find out who the person was who was scheduled to meet Mallory. Presumably the two ladies of The Orient must know this person but would we get the information we need by asking them and would that alert them?'

'We could try staging another expression of interest in ivory,' suggested Henshaw.

'Too soon,' said Drake, 'they must be very wary of that right now and they are likely to have gone to ground for a while.'

Grace was sitting with her case open, fumbling through her pile of sheets of paper. 'Their names are Doris and Florence,' she said finally. 'Good gracious, now I wonder if that really is just a coincidence.'

'Is what a coincidence, Grace? You have me confused,' complained Drake.

'Could I just have a few minutes before I answer that, sir?' said Grace as she left the room. Drake and Henshaw idly looked through Grace's pile of tattered pieces of paper. She returned and went bright red with embarrassment.

'It's just a technique I have been trying,' she said, hurriedly scrambling the papers into a rough pile and stuffing them back in her case. 'I think it might just have paid off. Do you remember telling us about your interview with Doris and Florence at The Orient, sir? You picked up very quickly that they are twins.'

'Yes,' said Drake, 'they look the same, dress the same and echo each others' words.'

'Well I think they might be triplets!' announced Grace very dramatically.

'How come?' asked a puzzled Henshaw.

'Well they are small and round and called Watson,' said Grace knowingly. Henshaw looked puzzled, Drake came as close as he ever had to leaping to his feet.

'Good gracious, yes!' he exclaimed, 'but surely it is just a coincidence?'

'What coincidence?' shouted Henshaw, 'will one of you explain this coincidence to me?'

'I think Grace means Jim Watson, the university Director of Facilities,' said Drake. Grace nodded vigorously. 'He is short and round too.'

'Not only that,' said Grace, 'but I have called his office to make an appointment with him. He has been off sick since the weekend.'

'Remember also,' said Drake, warming to the theory, 'that Percival expressed some concern about how McFadden had persuaded Watson to use what he called an irregular form of contract for the SEABU building. It could be that either they already were in business together or McFadden bribed Watson with some profitable involvement.'

Drake and Henshaw stood outside the house of Jim Watson. It was remarkable for being so ordinary. The front garden was well maintained but unimaginative. The wooden frames of the windows and the roof eaves were painted white and contrasted with the standard red brickwork. The street was full of similar houses and everything about the place suggested conventionality and anonymity. The door opened slowly to reveal a small round white haired woman wearing an apron. It was Doris Watson. At least Drake thought it was Doris but it could easily have been Florence.

'Oh my goodness!' said the indeterminate twin.

'Who is it, Doris?' enquired a voice from within.

'We knew you would come eventually,' said Doris, 'it was just a matter of time.'

'....a matter of time,' said the other head appearing in the doorway.

'I suppose you want to see our brother?' asked Doris, half opening the door.

'Is he here?' asked Henshaw.

'Of course,' said Doris throwing the door wide open.

Jim Watson sat in a large high backed chair with a pull-out footrest. The chair was facing the French window overlooking the neat but conventional back garden. Just outside the window was a small crazy paved terrace leading to a closely cropped lawn surrounded by herbaceous borders. At the edge of the terrace were a small sundial and a rather taller bird table. A couple of sparrows were tetchily arguing over this territory. As Drake and Henshaw entered the room, Watson's ruddy-faced countenance appeared round the wing of the chair.

'Ah, Drake,' he said.

'We knew they would come, didn't we Jimmy,' said Doris. Jim Watson ignored this and beckoned the two policemen to pull up smaller chairs from beside the window.

'Forgive me if I don't get up, Chief Inspector,' said Watson.

'Come on Florence,' said Doris, 'we'll make a pot of tea.' Two dresses and their aprons rustled off into the kitchen.

'You worked it out then, Drake,' squeaked Watson.

'Mr. Watson,' said Henshaw, 'I think you should tell us what you know about the murder of Professor Peter Mallory but I must warn you that....'

'Yes, yes, yes,' interrupted Watson, 'I know the drill. I've seen the police programmes on television.' By this time the policemen could clearly see the bandage around Watson's right leg showing under the plaid dressing gown that fell away over the footstool.

'Doris and Florence made an appointment for me on Sunday morning. It turned out to be Mallory. Of course he recognised me straight away and got angry and shouted. Called me all sorts of names and said that I had brought the university into disrepute. It all got very nasty but there was no real harm in it. He was not really threatening me, just shouting a lot. I tried to explain the situation to him but he was not interested. Boon Lay was with me, and I guess he couldn't understand what Mallory was shouting and thought there was some danger, so he came forward and pulled out his knife. I didn't even know he carried that. Mallory went absolutely berserk and said he was going to call the police.

I think Boon Lay understood "police" and waved his knife at Mallory and backed him up against the wall. Before I knew what was happening, Mallory had a pistol in his hand and he pointed it at Boon Lay. I panicked and tried to separate them, the gun went off and I felt a tearing feeling in my leg. By the time I had examined it and looked up again, Mallory was on the floor with Boon Lay's knife in his chest.'

'Boon Lay,' said Drake. 'Is he one of Hamish McFadden's Chinese research students?' Watson laughed. It was the first time Drake had seen any sign of amusement on the man's face.

'Well that's what they call him.'

'Then what happened?' demanded Henshaw.

'We were just trying to work out what to do. It is hard to communicate quickly with Boon Lay in English. He went to get the car up to the back door. I simply wasn't thinking straight and he took over. I tried to walk but fell over. Then suddenly the lights went out. A few seconds later Boon Lay was back with me with his forefinger to his mouth. He had heard some steps on the stairs above, put the lights off and dashed back. We waited and we could hear steps and the lights came on again. Someone came into the room and we could hear steps going across to the front. Boon

Lay pulled me up and we hobbled out of the room; Boon Lay had me half over his shoulder and I hopped. A woman's voice shouted Mallory's name and something about police. We got outside and Boon Lay closed the door and put the lights off. He got me to the car, took me to a local Chinese doctor who dressed my wounds, and brought me home. Here I am. I have not been hiding Inspector.'

'Where is Boon Lay now?' asked Drake.

'I have no idea,' said Watson, 'but my guess would be China, or well on the way. Those two have plenty of friends who seem to be able to arrange anything.'

'Can we go back to the beginning, Mr. Watson,' said Drake quietly. 'Exactly why was Mallory meeting you that morning?'

'He had bought a small ivory Japanese Hanko; they are a kind of stamp,' explained Watson. He had made enquiries about rather more ambitious and precious ivory carvings, and we were going to discuss that.'

'So, Mr. Watson, am I right in assuming that you run an import business for such items, and that this business is in partnership with Archie Grayson and Amanda Goh?' Watson, looked down and his sweating palms clutched at his dressing gown.

'More or less,' he said, 'I had no choice. My sisters had lost their premises and their business was in danger of collapse. That would have killed them. It is their life. It was at the time we were building SEABU. I stupidly told McFadden about it one day and he said that he could arrange new premises for them, rent-free. It seemed to be too good to be true. It was. First I had to agree to a special form of contract to enable his friends to get sub-contracts for SEABU, then he wanted more.' Watson mopped his brow and adjusted his leg on the stool.

'Once the building was up he blackmailed me and said that unless I fronted up the ivory trade for him, he would let Percival know that my hand had been in the till. What could I do? It didn't seem to be harming anyone but recently all sorts of unpleasant characters have got involved. Boon Lay is no research student. He is in reality McFadden's minder. He made sure I did what

McFadden wanted. It was a trap I could not escape from. I know I have been very stupid. I suppose I am in a bit of a mess.'

'Indeed,' said Drake, slowly rising to his full and very impressive height, dominating the small round melting bundle that was Watson. Watson's eyes followed Drake's vertical progress. 'Mr. Watson, you can perhaps help yourself by co-operating with us fully now.' Watson nodded almost enthusiastically. 'Can you tell me what connection all this has with the murder of Jimmy Cheung?'

'I have been thinking about that,' said Watson. 'I have no real evidence about this but I would not be surprised if in some way Hamish McFadden was behind it. That man is evil. He has a way of orchestrating people around him and yet remaining detached. Somehow he always seems to get away with it. We should never have appointed him. I have told the Registrar that but he won't hear anything against McFadden.'

'Why would McFadden want to see Jimmy Cheung dead?' asked Drake.

'That I don't know. He is always doing some sort of deal and mostly they sail pretty close to the wind. My sisters' shop is actually rented by McFadden from one of Jimmy Cheung's companies. I don't think Professor Cheung was exactly whiter than white himself but all this sort of stuff is beyond me I am afraid. I should never have got mixed up in it. I wouldn't be surprised if Cheung and McFadden had fallen out or perhaps Cheung was blackmailing McFadden. I am sure he knew enough to totally ruin the man if he wanted to. That is my best guess.' Watson winced and clutched at his leg.

'But I will tell you one thing, Inspector. I would bet anything that McFadden did not actually kill Jimmy Cheung himself. Oh no! He would have got someone to do it for him. It could even be Boon Lay or his friend.' Watson paused and wiped his sweating brow with a podgy hand. It was as if the significance of his situation had suddenly dawned on him.

Amanda Goh seemed the most unlikely murderer. She was every bit as small and delicate as Drake had remembered. She was beautifully dressed in a black trouser suit with a small ring of pearls around her neck. She carried a black leather portfolio briefcase. Before any of the assembled police could start, she began to interrogate Drake.

'I believe you have my business partner, Mr. Grayson here?' she said. 'I have been in London for a couple of days. I understand you are holding him for questioning in connection with the murder that happened at The Orient over the weekend? I am sure you must be mistaken.' She sat down as Drake gestured to her.

'We do have Mr. Grayson here, Miss Goh,' said Drake but I am also investigating the murder of Jimmy Cheung. I would like you to tell me your movements on the day he died. It was the Twelfth of September. I understand you attended his honorary degree congregation that day?'

'Yes but we left to do some business in town after the ceremony. I never saw him again. We returned to Singapore the next day.'

'I must warn you, Miss Goh,' continued Drake, 'that I have evidence that you met Jimmy Cheung again after the reception which followed the ceremony.'

'No, I think you must be mistaken.'

'We know that Jimmy Cheung had arranged to meet someone called A.G. and Archie Grayson has admitted being that person and to the murder of Jimmy Cheung.' Amanda Goh looked startled. For the first time her inscrutable countenance broke.

'Why would he do that?' she asked. 'You must let me see him.'

'He is under arrest,' said Drake. 'It is not possible for you to see him now. We shall be charging him with murder later today. That is unless you were the A.G. that Jimmy Cheung was due to meet and not Archie at all.' Drake paused. Amanda Goh looked angrily at him and drummed the table with her fingers several times. She suddenly raised her eyes as if she had just reached a conclusion.

'Yes,' said Amanda Goh, 'you are right. It was me. What on earth is Archie doing admitting to murder,. the silly man?'

'So you killed Jimmy Cheung?' pressed Drake.

'Of course not! Do I look like a murderer?'

'Then why did you deny you had met him?' demanded Drake.

'Surely that is obvious,' replied Amanda, 'I guess I was the last person to see him alive, other than the murderer that is. Since you clearly do not know who the murderer is I would be under tremendous suspicion. Archie would know immediately that A.G. was me. It is how I am known in business circles in Singapore. He, like you, has assumed that I killed Jimmy and, bless him, is trying to protect me by admitting to the murder himself.'

'So why did you arrange to meet Jimmy Cheung in such an unusual way and without Archie?' asked Drake.

'Jimmy and I were doing a deal that Archie did not know about.'

'Did that deal concern ivory?' asked Drake quietly.

'There is nothing illegal about this you understand,' replied Amanda, 'but Archie would not have approved, and Jimmy did not want his son or daughter to know about it, so we arranged to meet privately. Jimmy suggested we meet on the bridge. It was a very brief discussion and I left him to walk back to his hotel.' Drake nodded to Henshaw to take over the questioning.

'Miss Goh,' said Henshaw, 'I don't think you are telling us the whole truth here.' Amanda turned and stared at him in a manner that Drake thought to be quite expressionless. 'I put it to you that Jimmy Cheung was driving a hard bargain, that you argued and in the heat of the moment you shot him, there on the bridge.'

'No,' said Amanda Goh firmly, 'that is not true. At least it is not true that I shot him. Certainly he was driving a hard bargain. That was what Jimmy did. I expected it. This was normal.'

'We believe that Jimmy Cheung was shot with a gun that came from your shop,' said Drake. 'I saw boxes of them when I visited you in Singapore.'

‘Really?!’ exclaimed Amanda, ‘you mean the Nambu pistols?’ Drake nodded.

‘Who would have one of those pistols apart from yourself?’

‘Lots of people. They have been very popular,’ replied Amanda. ‘As it happens Jimmy had several himself. I am sure that he was selling them on at a higher price. I could not prove it of course but that would be typical of Jimmy. Rich as hell but can’t resist making even a small profit like that. If you have the gun I may be able to identify it from our records. They all have unique numbers and I think we made a note of which were sold to which customers.’

‘Would you know if Hamish McFadden was one of those customers?’ asked Henshaw.

‘Certainly. I think he collects pistols,’ replied Amanda. ‘His may even be on display at the university.’

‘We are aware that Sheng Tian also had one of those pistols,’ said Henshaw. ‘I assume he also got his from you?’

‘He had two pistols,’ replied Amanda Goh. ‘I gave him a pair as a present many years ago.’

‘A present?’ queried Drake.

‘Yes. At the time Sheng Tian and I were very close. I decorated his office in the university for him. I thought the pistols might look good there but he didn’t like them. He said they were inappropriate. Sheng Tian disapproved of the way our trade with his father developed and this led to an argument between us. I am afraid Sheng Tian has always had a terrible temper. He is a clever man but he can be difficult to get along with, so we broke up.’ She paused to think.

‘In fact, now I remember that Jimmy told me that he and Sheng Tian had argued that morning. He thought perhaps I was still in touch with Sheng Tian and could help to smooth things over. He was quite surprised when I told him I had not seen Sheng Tian for some time. He said he was hoping to see him that evening to try to patch things up.’

‘You mean Jimmy Cheung told you he was going to see Sheng Tian after he left you?’ asked Henshaw.

'I am not sure when, I think he just said that evening.'

'I need the numbers of the two pistols that you gave to Sheng Tian,' said Drake. 'Can you get that for me please?

'Probably,' replied Amanda Goh, 'but the records are in Singapore, it might take me a few days. Actually I am rather surprised that he had kept the pistols. I thought he disliked such things. I think that was Janet's influence.'

'I imagine Janet would not like guns,' said Drake.

'Well particularly Japanese guns,' agreed Amanda. 'She believes her real father was killed by the Japanese in the war. She has an irrational but understandable dislike of anything Japanese.'

'Do you know who did kill Jimmy?' asked Drake.

'No, Chief Inspector, I do not.' Amanda Goh sat thinking for a moment and then reached inside the small case she had been carrying. She produced a piece of paper with Chinese characters printed on it. 'This is the contract that Jimmy and I agreed on the bridge,' she said. 'You will see his Hanko stamp on it alongside mine. We liked to use this traditional way of recording our agreements. Perhaps if you have found his Hanko then you can verify this. There would be no point in my getting Jimmy's signature, which is what the stamp means, if I was going to kill him,' she said.

'But having killed him, you could have used his stamp yourself,' pointed out Henshaw. Amanda Goh gave Henshaw a look of utter horror and astonishment.

'We do not behave that way.'

'One more personal question,' said Drake. 'I am trying to find some cufflinks that have Chinese characters on them. Would you sell such a thing?'

'Definitely not,' snapped Amanda Goh. 'We are not in the trinket business. We sell only genuine artefacts.'

'Thank you,' said Drake. 'You must remain in residence please at your hotel or consult with us if you wish to change address. Otherwise you and Archie are free to leave.'

# 15 - Crystal

Henshaw let out a mock groan. 'Dave thinks he has made another important computer discovery.' He winked at Drake. Dave was wearing a broad self-satisfied grin on his face.

'Oh good,' Drake said. 'So you've proved the camera date was set correctly.'

'No, sir but I have managed to get the times the photographs were taken. I downloaded the camera manufacturer's own software from the Internet. If you load the pictures onto the computer in that software it reveals information on the time of day the pictures were taken.'

'Hmmm, some progress,' muttered Drake.

Dave pointed to his computer screen. 'We can now see the ones of the bridge were all taken within about a five minute period at about 4:15 in the afternoon.'

'Well that's good to know but I'm not sure it gets us anywhere,' grunted Henshaw.

'Nonsense,' snapped Drake. 'It tells us a great deal. Assuming the date and time were set correctly, Jimmy Cheung was getting his honorary degree right then and so he could not have taken the pictures himself.'

'And nor could anyone else who was at the ceremony,' added Grace entering the room.

'It has always seemed a little odd that there were no pictures of the ceremony or the reception on the camera. It's not odd at all because, if this is correct, the camera was not there' added Drake.

'It suggests that if Jimmy did not take the pictures, someone else did, and that person could well be the murderer,' Grace speculated.

'In which case the murderer was not at the degree congregation either,' continued Drake. The three stood looking at each other wondering who would state the obvious conclusion first. It was

Drake. 'Sheng Tian was not at the degree ceremony,' he said very quietly. The three stared into the void between them contemplating this new angle. It was Drake who broke the silence again.

'What is your analysis of all this?' The question was not directed at anyone in particular and Henshaw and Grace looked at each other to see who would answer. Grace waved her hand in deference to her superior.

'I think we need to speak to Sheng Tian again, sir,' Henshaw said. 'I know you thought I pulled him in too quickly last time but the evidence just keeps mounting. We now know he had two guns and so far we have only found one of them. He is the only one of all our known suspects who could have taken the photographs on the camera. It even seems likely that Jimmy Cheung arranged to meet him after seeing Amanda Goh.'

'I agree,' added Grace.

'Assuming that we can believe all that Amanda Goh has told us,' snapped Drake. Of course you are right but I still feel I am missing something. Perhaps questioning Sheng Tian will tell me. OK, go get him.'

Drake paced around his office. He had always thought his brain was in some mysterious way linked to his legs. He could not imagine the precise biological reason but walking always seemed to help him to think. Perhaps there was some very primitive survival mechanism at work here. This time though it was not working. He sat down at his desk and turned on his computer. Perhaps he might follow Grace's idea and look back through all his notes. The computer cheerfully pinged to announce that it was alive and well. Drake thought that the ping had a slightly assertive tone as if to reprimand him for keeping it turned off for so long.

He read through the documents in his Singapore folder. He looked at notes of the meetings with Philip Lim at the Singapore Policy Authority, his jottings about visiting AAA, descriptions of Archie Grayson and Amanda Goh. Then there were his notes from the Asian Civilisations museum. What a wonderful place that was, and dear little Wu Dao Rui, the curator who had so enthusiastically described all the artefacts in her care and the history of Singapore.

He opened his email system and flicked through all the messages he had sent and received while he was out there and then he saw there was a new message. How silly, he had not thought to check his email again since coming back. It was from his son, Tom. It somehow communicated that Tom was still cross about Drake leaving his party so abruptly but the main drift of the message was that Jenny had more accurately translated the Chinese obituary for Jimmy Cheung that he had found in the newspaper. It did not seem to amount to much. Apparently it said "Jimmy Cheung the shining light of the south has finally been extinguished." Drake looked at the notes he had made in the museum again. He wondered if this obituary could possibly tell them anything new. It seemed an odd phrase to use about Jimmy Cheung but it had a strangely familiar ring to it.

Sheng Tian was angry. Every question prompted an irritable response. No, he did not see his father again on the evening of the murder. He had answered these questions before. Yes, they had argued that morning but no, he did not kill his father. He had never fired the gun they found in his house. It was purely an ornament. Sheng Tian was annoyed but under control. Drake sensed that it was time to put some pressure on. He nodded to Henshaw to take over.

'You claimed an alibi for the evening of the murder. We now know that to be false. Why did you do that if you are innocent?' demanded Henshaw. Sheng Tian's expression changed from one of anger to a more anxious look. His response was now far less aggressive.

'The porter said he saw me that evening at the University,' he replied feebly.

'But we know that the porter was not even there that day,' said Henshaw. 'He left early due to ill health.' Sheng Tian's expression changed again to one of astonishment and then puzzlement.

'I don't understand,' he stuttered.

'I put it to you, Dr. Cheung,' said Henshaw in his best formal and accusatorial voice, 'that you bribed the porter to obtain an alibi, and that he did not see you at all.' Sheng Tian looked completely crestfallen.

'Stupid man,' he muttered quietly. 'I was worried that I had no alibi and that you seemed convinced that I had killed my father. I did not kill my father.' Henshaw leaned forward.

'Investigations we have completed on the camera found around your father's neck, have revealed some interesting facts,' he said firmly to Sheng Tian, who looked up hearing this news. 'Are you aware of what pictures were on the camera?'

'No,' said Sheng Tian, 'how could I be?'

'There were pictures of Chester, of the bridge and some taken from the bridge of the river,' said Henshaw, pausing and looking very directly at Sheng Tian.

'Why is this important?'

'The camera records the time that pictures are taken. Those pictures were taken at about 4:15 which is the same time as the degree congregation was taking place at the University, so your father could not have taken them.' Henshaw sat back. 'You were not at the degree ceremony.' A look of sheer panic washed across Sheng Tian's face, as Henshaw continued. 'I put it you, that you took those pictures and, after shooting your father, and then you put the camera around his neck.'

'No!'

Sergeant Denson entered the room and passed a note to Drake. Drake read it, raised an eyebrow and came forward to Sheng Tian who was deep in thought.

'Sheng Tian, we have just completed a further search of your house. We have found a second box like the one you keep your pistol in. The one you got from Amanda Goh. That second box is empty. Where is the second gun?' Sheng Tian looked blankly at Drake for a few seconds, put his head in his hands and shook as if sobbing. Drake demanded an answer.

'I want to see my lawyer.'

'Of course, just answer my question,' said Drake.

‘I….I gave the second pistol away.’

‘Who did you give the pistol to?’

‘I want to see my lawyer.’ Sheng Tian, collapsed in a heap on the table in front of him.

‘Of course I will get someone to make arrangements for you to see a legal representative.’ It was clear that he was not going to be any more forthcoming, for a while at least, so Drake called Henshaw and Grace Hepple to review the position in their base room.

‘Opinions please,’ demanded Drake abruptly.

Henshaw thought Sheng Tian was guilty. He pointed out that his responses were weak and offered no real way out for him. Grace Hepple thought that the McFadden line of enquiry needed to be followed up more but was at a loss to suggest what they could do until at least Boon Lay or McFadden himself could be traced. She suggested that a warrant be raised to search McFadden’s house. Henshaw pointed out that Boon Lay stayed at a post-graduate room on the campus and that could easily be opened and searched. All agreed that Watson’s account seemed genuine although Drake recommended some caution. Drake speculated further for a while about the situation with Amanda Goh. All three agreed she had the opportunity and a possible motive and that she was cool enough to have pulled it off. They all thought that Archie Grayson was out of the frame.

‘We might try going to see Janet again,’ said Drake suddenly, ‘on the pretext of a courtesy call to tell her about her brother being under arrest again. If Sheng Tian is guilty it’s hard to believe that she has not by now worked it out. Perhaps she will give something away. Grace, I would like you to come with me on that visit. Henshaw, perhaps you will set all the searches in place. It remains a pretty complicated mess of possibilities. Usually that means we are missing something. I am going for a walk to think. Grace, meet me at the Janet’s hotel in say an hour and a half. Perhaps you would give the hotel a call just to let her know we are coming and make sure she is there.’

This was the second time something had told Drake to go back to the bridge. By now there were no signs at all of the murder and life was entirely back to normal. Some schoolgirls were crossing the bridge just as Becky and Deborah had. Two parents were trying to persuade their small son that the bridge was safe and that he would not fall in the river. The father was growing impatient with the boy and the mother getting cross with the father. The band was playing down in the Groves and the river cruiser passed by going upstream. A few tiny clouds marked an otherwise clear blue sky punctuated only by swooping gulls.

Now he was here, Drake could not think for the life of him why he had come but it was pleasant enough so he leant against the handrail where Jimmy Cheung had been found dead only a month earlier. He looked around wondering where he would get inspiration. He looked upstream and downstream. He looked at the trees in the park with their tops swaying gently in the autumnal breeze. He panned around and focused on the houses high up on the bank upstream. The band finished playing and a ripple of applause reached Drake on the bridge.

He crossed back to the downstream side of the bridge and looked down at the octagonal bandstand. The players were sitting chatting, some emptying their brass instruments of spittle and others idling turning the sheet music on their stand. The conductor stood arms by his side, giving his players a few minutes rest.

Just as he began to look away Drake's eyes focussed on the bandstand itself. It was as if the whole structure leapt off its foundations and hit him in the face! Of course, the man who had been watching him the very first time he stood on the bridge! The sun had reflected off his binoculars into Drake's eyes. That was what was wrong. Why had he not seen it before? How stupid he had been. He pulled out the prints he had in his pocket of the pictures from Jimmy Cheung's camera to check. This might throw the whole pack of cards up in the air again. As if to announce Drake's changed perspective, the band struck up again playing a

Sousa march. He needed to think it through. He wanted silence, not that wretched insistent military rhythm.

He strode back across the bridge towards the town and up into the park. For a few minutes he wandered along the paths between the trees and bushes until he emerged into the open space beyond. A series of park benches lined the path and he sat on one under a shady spreading lime tree. A group of teenage boys were playing football across the open grass space in front of him. One side had taken their shirts off and laid them down in piles as makeshift goalposts. Drake idly watched the game for a few minutes. It looked as if 'skins' had just scored a goal against 'shirts' and the ball rolled and bounced along the turf towards Drake. The reluctant goalkeeper obviously expected Drake to leap up and return the ball while behind him the lack of a referee was leading to disputes over whether the ball had actually gone in the goal or missed it. Drake did not see the ball or the rest of the argument; he stared into the empty space beyond, trying to understand what it all meant. Still clutched in his hand was one of the photographs taken from the bridge.

Drake looked at his watch and cursed under his breath. All this modern computer technology had been the source of the problem. He was already convinced he would have seen all this far sooner if it had not been for Dave and his computer. Not of course that it was Dave's fault, Drake thought more charitably. In fact the lad definitely deserved that university sponsorship he was hankering after.

Grace Hepple arrived at the hotel in Eastgate early for her meeting with Drake and Janet. She went and sat in the library with a coffee and shuffled all her notes around on her lap. Drake arrived breathless and unable to speak clearly. She had not seen him in such a condition before; his favourite indigo shirt showing signs of sweat. She sat him down in some concern only to realise he was grinning.

'You had me worried for a moment there, sir,' she said.

'Sorry, Grace,' gulped Drake, 'I forgot the time and it is further from the park than I remembered. I am not as young as I was! Maybe that is why the old brain is slowing down but it still gets there in the end.' His grin was even broader now.

'I think you've had one of those breakthrough moments you talk about, sir,' said Grace.

'Maybe, maybe.' Drake nodded his head and puffed some more.

'Are you going to tell me about it, sir; or do I have to guess?' Drake raised his eyebrows quizzically.

'Let us go and meet Janet first and then perhaps you will see. Get reception to call her room and announce our arrival.' Grace left Drake making a call to Mr. Watson about something he said 'needed checking.' It was only a few minutes later when she returned looking concerned.

Drake saw the expression on her face. 'Don't tell me she has checked out and gone,' he groaned.

'There is no answer from the suite. Reception says that no one has seen her go out but it seems she does tend to slip out without leaving her key. Apparently my earlier telephone message was passed on to her by someone.'

'Damn!' I hope we are not too late.'

'Do you think she is in danger?' asked Grace.

'Get the manager to open her room immediately,' said Drake grimly.

The small party stood outside the suite that Janet Cheung had initially occupied with her father and, since his death, by herself. The hotel manager insisted on knocking on the door and waiting before he unlocked the door with her master key. He was prattling on about the sophistication of their security system and about how well their guests were looked after and how nothing like this had ever been necessary before. Drake did not hear him. There was no answer, and after two more knocks and the manager calling to Janet, Drake insisted that he open the door.

The suite was exactly as Drake had seen it many times. There was the same sense of quiet order partly imposed by the presence of Janet Cheung and partly by the traditional elegance of the décor. The dining chairs were all carefully placed at the table. The perfect flower arrangement in the middle of the table looked as immaculate as ever. The curtains were pulled back from the windows in swags and neatly clipped into position in their brass rings. The doors to the bedroom and bathroom were shut. The small search party stopped inside the door. There was not a sound. Not a thing seemed out of place. Grace went to look in the bedroom. Drake wandered around the great chesterfield sofa facing the fireplace. The hotel manager remained by the door fretting.

'Mr. Montcrief,' said Drake. 'call a doctor urgently. Grace, call Henshaw for backup. We have found Janet Cheung.'

Drake, Grace and Henshaw were sat at the dining table in Janet Cheung's suite. All round them the scene-of crime-officers were moving about methodically performing their duties. Constable Katie Lamb stood on duty outside the door of the suite, which was firmly shut. Montcrief was back in his office fretting even more. The body of Janet Cheung lay on its front with her head twisted unnaturally to the side. Her left arm was underneath her and her right was out to the side bent at the elbow. In her right hand, held only loosely, was a second world war Japanese Nambu pistol. Blood had run down across her face from the gunshot wound in her right temple. Her body was curled around the crystal cut glass decanter that Deva University had presented to Jimmy Cheung at his degree ceremony.

'It has all the signs of being suicide,' announced the police pathologist who had been making a preliminary inspection of the body. 'The shot from a right hand held pistol position to the right forehead is exactly what you very often see in such a situation. Consciousness was probably lost instantaneously: death effectively following almost immediately. Probably not more than a couple of hours ago. The body would have collapsed as we see it. There are no immediate signs of it being moved. I think it likely that she was sitting on the floor leaning on her left hand rather than standing. The pistol is partly dislodged from the grip by the short fall. It is possible that it could have been placed there by someone else but unlikely. I cannot be sure about all that until I make a full examination.'

'I should have thought this through better,' said Drake dismally.

'I think you are miles ahead of Grace and me,' said Henshaw finally. 'We have no idea how you knew Janet Cheung was going to commit suicide.'

'I didn't,' said Drake, 'I thought she might make some sort of run for it, though the alternative of suicide was obvious if I had been more focussed.'

'Why should she run for it?' asked Grace.

'Because, unless I am very much mistaken, Janet realised we were close to working it out.'

'Were we? That's news to me!' admitted Henshaw.

'When Grace called to say we were coming to see her, she must have thought that,' groaned Drake. Henshaw and Grace looked at each other in blank puzzlement.

'I think you need to explain please, sir,' said Grace.

'Just too late,' said Drake, 'this case seems crystal clear. The whole thing has turned out to be about time difference, in years as well as hours. Some anniversaries are associated with good memories and some not so good. Remember Jimmy Cheung was here to celebrate the foundation of Deva University. In his oration, Professor Mallory drew a parallel with the anniversary of the forming of Singapore. There is another anniversary that has been lurking around all the time, and it is a rather older one. It is the liberation of Singapore from the Japanese occupation at the end of Second World War in September 1945. After the horrendous nuclear bombing of Hiroshima and Nagasaki, the Japanese surrendered to the Allies in August 1945. This news reached Singapore in early September and the occupying forces were allowed to quietly withdraw to an encampment in the south west of the island. The Allies arrived on British warships and on 12th of September 1945 the Japanese occupying General Itagaki formally surrendered to the British Lord Louis Mountbatten.'

'That is a fascinating history lesson, sir,' said Henshaw, 'but I still don't understand the connection. What am I missing?'

'Jimmy Cheung was murdered on 12th September,' said Drake. Henshaw and Grace sat, only half understanding the significance of this point. 'I should have seen the connection earlier but once I did, then a possibility was that this was some form of ceremonial murder. We have heard repeatedly that Jimmy Cheung began to establish his fortune during the Japanese occupation. Professor Mallory's spoof oration all but accused Jimmy of being a collaborator. Inspector Philip Lim in Singapore hinted at something similar but it seems likely that Mallory thought that he had more solid proof.'

'So Mallory was our murderer after all,' said Henshaw. 'Janet was more attached to him than we realised. It has all got too much for her and this is the result.'

'No,' said Drake. 'Mallory did not kill Jimmy, though if I am right he certainly caused his death.'

The others waited in silence while Drake looked into the distance.

'The Japanese renamed Singapore "Syonan-to". Apparently that means something like "Light of the South", and they intended to make Singapore the southern capital of their extended empire after the war. Modern Singaporeans must be extremely grateful that this never happened.'

Drake pulled the email he had printed off earlier. 'My son, Tom found a short anonymous announcement of Jimmy Cheung's death in a Chinese newspaper, which translated as "The Shining Light of the South has finally been extinguished". Taking it at face value, this seemed a brief but rather flowery tribute. However in reality it was a carefully coded message of vengeance. Jimmy Cheung was murdered because of rumours about what he did in the Second World War. I believe that message in the newspaper was sent by Janet.'

'And she was not really his natural daughter,' said Grace. 'He was her uncle and adopted her.'

'Exactly,' said Drake. 'Her father went missing and was never seen again during the Japanese occupation. Almost certainly he was killed in what was known as the Sook Ching. The Japanese screened all Chinese males, and many of those who were working against the occupying forces were betrayed by collaborators wearing hoods to protect their anonymity. The coded suspicion has always been that at worst Janet's father was actually betrayed by his brother, Jimmy Cheung. Whether or not this is true, at least there remained the suspicion that Jimmy benefited by collaborating. Those men who were killed were often summarily shot on beaches around Singapore.

I suspect we will find that Janet's Nambu pistol was the gun that killed Jimmy. I also suspect we will find that it was Sheng Tian's second pistol. When we interviewed him he remembered that he had given it to his sister. He simply could not think what else to say and called for his solicitor.'

'Now I remember how upset Janet was about the Japanese Hanko being found on Jimmy's body,' said Henshaw.

'I think probably not so much upset as angry that she had left it behind,' said Drake. 'She would have preferred to destroy it.'

'So Jimmy Cheung adopted Janet out of guilt?' asked Grace.

'We can only speculate on that,' answered Drake. 'Emily, his sister, suggested that it would have been expected by the family and he had little choice.'

'But Janet has always seemed to us to be devoted to her father…sorry Jimmy,' said Henshaw.

'I suspect she was until her liaison with Professor Mallory sowed seeds of doubt in her mind as he discovered more about Jimmy's past,' said Drake. 'She must have wondered for most of her life how her father really died.'

'So what made you so sure of all this and so suddenly?' asked Henshaw.

'Time difference,' said Drake. 'Remember Dave's discovery about the timing of photographs. In particular, the effect that this had on Sheng Tian set me thinking. He understood immediately what it took me far too long to work out. Even then it was not until I was standing on the Queen's Suspension Bridge in the late afternoon that I saw it. The camera was of course set to Singapore time. You would expect that. People do not normally bother to reset such things when they travel. Singapore is seven hours ahead of us. Those pictures were not taken in the late afternoon but in the early morning. If I had not been deflected by the technical stuff of getting the times from the computer I would have realised earlier that the angle of the sun on the pictures does not match the reality in the late afternoon. Once you look carefully at the octagonal bandstand from the bridge it becomes blindingly obvious. I have been very stupid.'

'We all have,' agreed Henshaw. 'We assumed that Sheng Tian had taken the pictures because everyone else was in the degree congregation but actually anyone could have taken them. So it is highly likely that Jimmy took them himself as we assumed all along!'

'Not quite,' smiled Drake, 'think again. At that time we know that Jimmy and Sheng Tian were overheard and seen by Mrs. Partridge the cleaner having a blazing argument at the apartment in the university. In fact neither of them could have taken the pictures. Janet took them. Presumably she had planned the murder by then. I think she was clever enough to work out the way of using the camera to hold the body leaning over the railing. It was probably her camera anyway. She took the pictures to give added weight to the idea that Jimmy was spending time there innocently.'

'She must have waited for Amanda Goh to leave,' said Grace, 'and then joined Jimmy on the Bridge and shot him. That is so calculating and cold blooded.'

'She has always shown enormous self control,' said Drake. 'The whole thing, the date, the place and the method are intensely meaningful. She even selected the apartment for Jimmy to use at the University. It was number 4. In Mandarin "four" sounds like death. Number 8, which is the luckiest to Chinese was available but I checked with Watson just now, and he remembers that she specifically requested number 4. There is a ghastly elegance to this symbolic act of vengeance. This was not a murder. It was an execution. I doubt Jimmy had any forewarning and so there would have been no scuffle or commotion. This kind of pistol makes very little noise and playing of the band would have obscured it down in the Groves. After shooting him, she walked back to the hotel, went up to her room and called the police to say her father had not turned up. We have recently heard she frequently went in and out without leaving her key or letting them know at reception. My guess is that she has been using the fire escape.'

'But what about the cufflink we found under Jimmy's body?' asked Grace.

'Good question, Grace.' Drake stood up as if to deliver a lecture. 'Janet fed us several negative comments about McFadden. I don't think she liked him at all, her brother certainly doesn't, and I guess Jimmy must have shared his growing doubts with her. Janet would have had easy access to such cufflinks. I think she planted it there to give us a gentle lead towards McFadden. Remember how Janet told me that Jimmy was known for not wearing cufflinks. She knew that she would have the opportunity to say that at some point when we questioned her. If I am right it was subtle and clever, except that she missed the lack of fingerprints, which has worried me all along. This also at last answers the question we both asked right at the very beginning of this mystery, Henshaw. Janet needed to find a place to commit her murder where she would stand some chance of establishing an alibi. The hotel and the university were both problematic for her. Her only chance was a public place. The bridge was as public as you could get and yet paradoxically she could be alone with him there.'

There was a sudden commotion outside the door of the hotel suite and Henshaw went to investigate. As the door opened, they could all hear a Chinese voice shouting. Drake rose as Emily Cheung pressed past Katie Lamb on duty at the door and the stunned Henshaw.

'They will not allow me in,' shouted Emily Cheung at Drake. 'I want to see Janet. I want to see her now.' Drake took her by the arm and led her to a chair by the table.

'I am afraid that is not possible, Emily,' he said gently.

'Something dreadful has happened. I know it has, and it's all my fault,' sobbed Emily.

'How could it be your fault, Emily?' asked Drake.

'Something has happened then?'

'I am sorry to have to tell you that Janet is dead.'

'I knew it. I knew it. I should never have told her.'

'Told her what?' asked Drake.

'It was last night,' gulped Emily. 'She called me on the phone very late. She was so dismissive about Jimmy. I know I had many disagreements with Jimmy and but he was my brother and she said some terrible things about him. All about the war and how she believed Jimmy had betrayed his brother. There have always been rumours but I am certain that Jimmy never betrayed anyone. She said Professor Mallory had found evidence. I have no idea what he thought he had found but I am certain he was wrong. Janet seemed besotted with him and she said he too had now been killed.' Emily dabbed her eyes.

'She started to go back over all the years and list all the bad things Jimmy had done. She said he was even still involved in trading with the Japanese now. She had become convinced that he had simply exploited her devotion to him. I told her Jimmy had never betrayed his brother all those years ago, at least not in the way she thought. She wouldn't listen to sense. So I told her. I knew afterwards it was the wrong thing to do.'

'You told her what?' asked Drake again.

'I told her the truth of course, that Jimmy really was her natural father.' Drake, Grace and Henshaw sat staring at Emily open-mouthed at this revelation waiting for her to explain. Emily sat quietly as she recalled the long past events. 'He was a devil in those days, he fancied his brother's girlfriends; always did, anything in a skirt. Janet's mother told me that Jimmy was the father of Janet, not Zhao Meng.'

'Zhao Meng?' queried Drake.

'Our brother,' whispered Emily. 'I have not used his name for fifty years.' She sobbed briefly, dabbed her eyes and continued. 'Of course I was sworn to secrecy. It would have been a tremendous scandal if it had ever come out. We agreed it was better for Janet not to know. It would have left her unable to discuss it with her mother, who sadly soon became mentally ill and died not long after. She had always loved her mother and we thought the news would be just too difficult for her to take.'

'This changes everything,' said Drake. 'But why are you here, Emily?'

'I knew she was upset. I shouldn't have told her, least of all like that over the phone.' Emily started to sob again. 'All I could do was come up today and try to help her with it. I wanted to explain to her and help her to understand. I had a dreadful foreboding on the way here. When I saw the policeman at the door my heart told me. I just knew it. I suppose she has committed suicide?'

'We think so, yes,' said Drake. 'Grace, would you please ask Montcrief if Emily could have a room of her own. I think she probably needs some quiet and may want to stay overnight rather than travel back to London now.' Grace nodded and helped Emily into the arms of a WPC.

'It's just as well she doesn't yet realise that Janet actually killed Jimmy,' observed Henshaw.

'Yes,' agreed Grace, 'imagine how she will feel then. She effectively told Janet last night that she had mistakenly killed her own father.'

'So our call to Janet was probably only the final trigger for her suicide,' grunted Drake. 'She has spent the whole night trying to come to terms with what she has done, and she just couldn't live with it. She probably felt unable to keep up the pretence with us any longer. She simply could not live through another interview and carry on her deceit with any conviction. She must have sat looking at that crystal glass decanter thinking that it really was her natural father's name around the neck. She has chosen to die hugging it. I think her actions speak more loudly than any written suicide note could.'

'How are you going to tell Emily?' asked Henshaw.

'Tell her what, Henshaw?'

'That Janet killed Jimmy,' replied Henshaw.

'What possible evidence have you got for saying that, Henshaw?' demanded Drake. Henshaw spluttered and looked nonplussed.

Grace first looked startled, then grinned and patted Henshaw on the shoulder comfortingly. 'That's not going to do your clear-up rates much good,' she said. Drake gave one of those expressive waves of his arm clearly indicating that such matters were no longer of concern to him. Constable Katie Lamb entered the room and passed a note to Henshaw.

'Poor Jimmy,' said Drake reflectively. 'It seems pretty likely that he was getting suspicious of Hamish McFadden who must have got wind of this and sent his minder Boon Lay to follow him. Almost certainly Boon Lay was responsible for breaking into Jimmy's university apartment after his death in case there were any incriminating documents there; of course he found nothing. I am sure it was Boon Lay who followed us around on the first day I was here.

In all probability Jimmy was an entirely innocent party in all this. He may have driven the odd hard bargain or two in his life but he never conspired with McFadden or his collaborators in the major ivory scams. He may have had an affair with his brother's wife but these things happen. Later he took his responsibilities to his illegitimate daughter entirely seriously. I am sure Emily would know if he had betrayed their brother to the Japanese. Perhaps it is just that suspicions tend to grow around successful and high profile people. Sadly for Jimmy, if his vanity had not persuaded him to accept this honorary degree, Janet would never have met Mallory, and Jimmy would almost certainly be alive. It is a case of a degree of death!'

'What really bugs me about this case,' snapped Grace. 'Three people are dead. Percival and Watson have ended up with criminal records and even if they don't go to prison will probably lose their jobs. Poor Doris and Florence have probably lost their shop. Sheng Tian has been arrested twice and lost his father and sister. But there is one person who is at the source of all these problems and he is getting away with it all.'

'Not quite, Grace,' interrupted Henshaw. 'This is a fax from Inspector Philip Lim to say that his boys have intercepted Hamish McFadden entering Singapore with a fake passport. They are holding him on some pretext or other, and want to know what we would like them to do with him.'

'I am sure we can reach some agreement over that,' said Drake. 'In fact I might even fly over there myself and sort it out. I have rather taken to the place and there is so much more to see. I want to explore some of the buildings Cynthia used to tell me about, and that museum deserves a much longer and more relaxed visit. Besides I need to make my peace with my son, Tom. Can you hold the reins at the Diplomatic Unit, Grace? A couple of weeks should do it.'

'I am sure Inspector Henshaw and I can clear everything up here on this case, sir,' replied Grace Hepple.

'Yes, sir,' added Henshaw enthusiastically. 'You get off, Grace can help me tidy up all the loose ends.' Grace smiled at him.

'I get the distinct impression you two are trying to get rid of me,' grunted Drake in mock irritation, and then he smiled as he struggled out of his chair. He rose slowly to his feet, eventually reaching as near to his full height as his characteristic stoop would allow. Grace Hepple and Martin Henshaw watched Chief Inspector Drake's back as he lumbered his way across the capacious hotel suite. As he disappeared through the doorway he turned slightly towards them and Grace thought she saw a knowing wink flutter across his face.

Printed in Great Britain
by Amazon

31323188R00150